"*Echoes of a Silent Song* is bot

Amanda Wen has woven a beautiful story of how God can take the least harmonious parts of our lives and create a symphony of praise."

—Erica Vetsch, author of the Of Cloaks & Daggers series

"In *Echoes of a Silent Song*, Amanda Wen has crafted an ode to the creative process, masterfully weaving a narrative where music becomes an instrument of reconciliation and healing. Fans of Susie Finkbeiner will appreciate the Americana essence and be drawn back to the Vietnam War era, a time that both horrified and defined our nation. The storytelling is rich, evocative, and deeply resonant. Through its lyrical prose and profound themes, *Echoes of a Silent Song* stands as a testament to the enduring power of art and the human spirit."

—Allison Pittman, coauthor of *Something Borrowed*

"This love letter to music and creativity is passionately executed and brimming with secrets and romance. The profound language of music speaks not only into the characters' intertwining histories but also into our own. Readers of Susan Meissner and Patti Callahan Henry will marvel at the expert and seamless way Amanda Wen moves us from past to present. *Echoes of a Silent Song* is reverently and lovingly told by a talented author at the top of her game."

—Rachel McMillan, best-selling author of *The Mozart Code* and
The Liberty Scarf

"With a seamlessly structured split timeline, *Echoes of a Silent Song* by Amanda Wen hits all the right notes. The sweeping prose, tender romance, and immersive plot flow rhythmically together, creating a beautiful reading experience. I was mesmerized from the first page. I highly recommend!"

—Rachel McDaniel, award-winning author of *The Dreams We Knew*

SEDGWICK COUNTY CHRONICLES

Roots of Wood and Stone
The Songs That Could Have Been
The Rhythm of Fractured Grace

MELODIES AND MEMORIES

Echoes of a Silent Song

MELODIES
AND
MEMORIES

Echoes of a Silent Song

A NOVEL

AMANDA WEN

KREGEL
PUBLICATIONS

Library of Congress Cataloging-in-Publication Data
Names: Wen, Amanda, 1979– author
Title: Echoes of a silent song : a novel / Amanda Wen.
Description: Grand Rapids, MI : Kregel Publications, 2025. | Series: Melodies and memories
Identifiers: LCCN 2025019080 (print) | LCCN 2025019081 (ebook)
Subjects: LCGFT: Fiction | Romance fiction | Christian fiction | Novels
Classification: LCC PS3623.E524 E34 2025 (print) | LCC PS3623.E524 (ebook) | DDC 813/.6—dc23/eng/20250521
LC record available at https://lccn.loc.gov/2025019080
LC ebook record available at https://lccn.loc.gov/2025019081

ISBN 978-0-8254-4981-9, print
ISBN 978-0-8254-4983-3, epub
ISBN 978-0-8254-4982-6, Kindle

Printed in the United States of America
25 26 27 28 29 30 31 32 33 34 / 5 4 3 2 1

To the glory of God in memory of Lori Hoppock—

singer, pianist, educator, mentor, friend, daughter of God,

and the reason I am an accompanist today.

CHAPTER ONE

$\mathcal{B}$LAIR EMERSON couldn't recall ever praying for patience.

She must have, though. Once upon a time she must've flung a plea heavenward for that particular virtue, because it took a special kind of patience to adjust to a sixth boss in six years.

It hadn't always been this way. When Vic Nelson was choral director, top ratings at contest and packed-house concerts were the norm. During his nearly four decades at the helm, the Peterson High choral program had been synonymous with excellence. Blair counted herself fortunate to have had him as both her teacher in high school and her boss as an adult. In fact, after receiving two degrees in piano, she'd turned down other job offers and eagerly returned to her alma mater to work with Vic for the last two years of his tenure. And sad though she'd been when he retired, she'd been confident that a new director could fill his sizable shoes and maintain the program's stellar reputation.

But since his retirement, directors had been in and out on an annual basis, with the predictable damage to enrollment, morale, and music making. The latest hire hadn't even lasted long enough to start the year. He'd gotten a better offer two weeks ago and had done an abrupt about-face. Vic had pulled a few strings and made the most of his connections, and now Blair had a new name to learn: Callum Knight.

Leaning into the crook of the choir room's ebony Steinway grand, Blair pulled her phone from her pocket and resumed social-media stalking her newest colleague. His degree in music education was standard, but dual master of music degrees in composition and choral conducting? Those weren't. Nor were the slick, high-quality website, the list of published works and commissions, or the baton-wielding professional headshot. With a sigh and a roll of her eyes, Blair set the phone down on the piano. That shiny website might as well have had "Teaching Is My Fallback Plan" scrolling across it in giant red letters.

The door burst open with its typical click-squeak-bang, and a haggard-looking figure stumbled in. Espresso-colored hair, wild and wavy and so far past needing a trim that hedge clippers might be required to subdue it. A square jaw and cleft chin shadowed in what must have been a week and a half of stubble. Rumpled dress shirt, the top three buttons undone, and a blue-striped tie draped haphazardly around his neck. An enormous travel mug clenched in a white-knuckled grip. All of it a far cry from the dangerously handsome tuxedo-clad man whose headshot had just filled her phone screen.

Blair tilted her head and studied her new colleague. Was he hungover? No . . . that wasn't the vibe. More like barely awake.

At just past noon.

On the first day of staff meetings.

Way to make a first impression.

"Morning," he said, more grunt than greeting.

"*Afternoon*," Blair replied with a pointed glance at the digital clock hanging above the whiteboard. "You've already missed half a day's worth of meetings."

The new director set his travel mug on a table near the board. "If they were anything like every other meeting in the world, I missed nothing of consequence. But if I did miss anything, you seem like the type who took good enough notes to catch me up."

Blair stiffened. She had taken notes. She always took notes. How this just-rolled-out-of-bed champion of condescension could possibly know that, though, was anyone's guess.

"Hmmph." She jammed her phone back into her pocket.

He finished buttoning his shirt, then applied a manufactured smile to stubble-shrouded lips and extended his right hand. "Callum Knight. Pleasure to meet you."

"Blair Emerson." She returned his handshake but not his pleasantry.

The evaluation his piercing green eyes gave her was thorough and penetrating but unreadable beyond that. Oh well. She'd learn to read his expressions well enough in time. It was part of her job, after all.

"Ah, yes. The accompanist."

"Collaborative pianist" came her automatic reply. Normally Blair found the two terms interchangeable and had no preference. But the latter, though more verbally unwieldy, carried the weight of an equal musical partnership, something she suspected she'd have to fight to receive from this arrogant creature.

"Of course. Apologies." His tone conveyed much—mild exasperation, a hint of amusement, perhaps even curt dismissal—but not a hint of apology. "It's all the same, really. I wave my arms, you follow me, and it'll all be peaches and sunshine."

Blair drew herself to her full, hopefully intimidating height. "You don't need to tell me my responsibilities, Mr. Knight. Especially since I'm confident I have considerably more experience working with high schoolers than you do."

Straightening his still-untied tie, he gave a lopsided smirk. "So you've researched me, then."

"Of course I have. And I certainly hope you paid attention during your ed degree, because I am not in the mood to handhold. I'm proud of this program and ready to see it return to its former glory, and I'm prepared to do whatever it takes to achieve that goal."

"Well, currently," he drawled, weaving his tie into a quick knot, "that involves putting up with me for this school year and then giving that rousing pep talk to my replacement."

Wow. So it had come to this. Directors who announced their days were numbered before the students even darkened the doors.

Her hands found her hips. "You're not even giving this a chance. Wonderful."

"Look, let's be up-front with each other." He tightened his tie. "Composition is my passion. It was enough to keep a roof over my head for a few blessed years, but now, for a variety of reasons too long and boring to explain, I find myself in need of a steady paycheck. Since I have no dependents and since cost of living here is low, this year's salary should be enough to keep me afloat until . . . well, until I . . ."

For the first time, Callum faltered. Gave some indication that his blustering, blowhard act was, in fact, just that. An act.

"Until you . . ." She made a keep-going gesture, her voice intentionally crisp.

He pinched the bridge of his nose. "Until I've finished the year. With any luck at all, then I can return to composing on the East Coast, and you can find someone more suitable for"—he took in the choral room, then indicated its space with a wave of his hand—"this."

"Fine. But right now you have a job to do. One at which—up until this point, anyway—you've failed miserably. We're due in the auditorium for another meeting in five minutes. I expect to see you there."

Without waiting for a reply, she brushed past Callum and banged through the door. Since Vic's departure, she'd learned to temper her natural optimism. But even her most tamped-down dreams were a moon shot compared to the disaster unfolding before her. A summer's worth of prayers for a director who'd invest, who'd care, who'd *stay*, seemed to have been answered with a resounding no.

Okay then, God. Guess I'll just muddle through as best I can with this . . . special, special human being you've brought into my life and start praying for lucky number seven to be the one to repair the damage.

And in the meantime . . . I could really use some patience.

The coffee at the bottom of Callum Knight's travel mug was stone-cold. So much for the lofty promises from the mug's manufacturer to keep it tongue-searing hot through the longest of days. Well, despite clocking in past noon, this had indeed been the longest of days thanks to an afternoon of lame icebreaker games with a passel of overly enthusiastic new coworkers.

Best bite the bullet and buy a new mug before next week, then. Because next week, for the first time in almost a decade, he'd have to clock in obscenely early and be responsible for teenagers seven hours a day.

God help them. God help them all.

With great reluctance, he switched on the obnoxious fluorescent light in his new office, a concrete reminder of his unpleasant new reality. His previous time in the trenches of the educational system was a distant, hazy memory after several years of successful full-time composing and the creation of his own hand-selected professional choir. But then came the pandemic, and among the casualties had been that choir, his fiancée, and his creative muse. A stack of unfulfilled commissions and missed deadlines had caught up with him, and now—unthinkably—here he stood in a high school choir office, the dull ache at the base of his skull a physical manifestation of having fallen back into his fallback plan.

The office was nothing to write home about. Not that he had much of a home to write to, of course. Tiny. Dimly lit. Squeaky, fake-leather chair with a rip in the back—the result of some sophomoric shenanigan, no doubt. A moderately sized coffee-stained desk with a strip of Formica dangling from the front. A few framed photo collages of past choirs mugging for the camera in front of the Washington Monument and the Empire State Building. The upright piano near the door with chipped keys and a cluster of circular stains on top, where a parade of idiots—or perhaps the same overly consistent idiot—had stashed their drinks. Everything was covered in a layer of dust, with only past glories to cling to.

He could relate.

Callum set his mug on the desk with a heavy thunk and dropped into the office chair, which gave an unholy shriek at being disturbed. Gritting his teeth, he tried and failed to restick the strip of Formica, then gave up and yanked it off, revealing the cheap particle board beneath. With a sigh, he tossed the strip into the trash can beside his desk. A fitting metaphor for the turn his career, his life, had taken.

At least he had a plan to fall back on. That was his mother's attempt at forcing him to find the silver lining. "You're keeping a roof over your head, Callum," she'd said when he'd reluctantly told her the news. "You're staying connected with the choral world. Who knows? Maybe those kids will give you the inspiration you need to get back to composing. Remember, God's in control."

God. Control. Two words that always rankled when appearing together. If God were truly in control, then why did Callum's life feel like utter chaos?

However, his mother was right on one point. This job would keep him financially afloat. He should be grateful. No way would he even be here if not for his friend and mentor, Vic Nelson, who'd clued him in to the last-minute opening and—he suspected—gone to bat for him with administration.

The buzz of his phone against the desk set his teeth on edge, but his ire lessened with a glance at the screen. A text from Vic himself.

> Settling in?

Ha. That was one way to put it.

Callum tapped out a reply. *As much as can be, yes. Icebreaker games today.* This he punctuated with a sarcastic confetti-horn emoji.

> Icebreaker games? Then you've doubtless met your right-hand woman, Blair.

His jaw tightened. That uptight redhead certainly hadn't seemed impressed with him on first meeting. Though she'd refrained from judging him out loud, he'd heard her just as clearly as if she had. One glance into those golden-brown eyes had been enough. She'd thought he was hungover.

If only.

Instead he'd done what he did every night for the past two years: tinker at his piano into the wee hours, trying and failing and trying again and failing again and failing and failing and failing some more before falling asleep to late-night sports talk shows on the cheap hand-me-down futon his younger sister had given him.

Hungover would be a dream compared to his current misery.

I have, was all he typed in reply.

> And how'd that go?

> Fine.

> Liar. I can hear it in your voice.

Callum frowned.

> But this is a text.

> I stand by my statement.

Callum sat with the phone in his hands, leg bouncing up and down beneath the dilapidated desk. Before long, another text vibrated its arrival.

> A bit of advice, if I may? Blair is the key to winning over those kids.

The kids. Gah. He'd been trying not to think about the kids. Four choirs' worth. *Four.* Plus a music theory class, a piano class, and something called Extended Learning Time. Winning them over was the last thing on his agenda. He didn't care about winning them over. He cared only about recapturing his muse, so he could resign this job as quickly as he'd taken it, return to Boston, and get his life back. Irritation surging, he started to type a reply to that effect, but the little animated ellipsis stopped him. Another incoming text from Vic.

I'm under no illusion that this job is permanent for you. But this school year will be what you make it, Callum.

Callum leaned back in the chair and studied the little gray speech bubble. Based on what he'd seen today, this year would land somewhere between Moderately Terrible and Complete Dumpster Fire. Thanks to his prickly pianist, his puppylike colleagues, and this tiny, dusty office, Actually Good was out of the question.

But he could grit his teeth and do what he could to move the needle as close to Moderately Terrible as he could.

He texted back, the letters appearing slowly beneath his thumbs.

I'll do my best.

That was all anyone—including himself—could ask.

CHAPTER TWO

*M*ORNING, SUNSHINE!"

At the cheerful greeting, Blair scanned the auditorium for her best friend. Joy Westinghouse's purple-streaked platinum-blond pixie cut and crimson butterfly glasses weren't hard to spot, and her voice—perpetually loud thanks to seven years directing orchestra at Peterson High—wasn't hard to place. Sure enough, there she sat, five rows back, clad in one of her music-themed vintage-style dresses and clutching her trademark royal-blue *It's a sharp, not a hashtag* tumbler.

Blair slid through the row of plush black chairs and took a seat beside Joy, whose ice cubes clanked in the tumbler. Joy always drank iced coffee, even when it was fourteen degrees outside, and thanks to the auditorium's enthusiastic air-conditioning, it didn't feel much warmer than that.

Blair tugged her cardigan around herself—normally not necessary at the tail end of an Illinois summer—and glanced at Joy. "I'll never know how you do that."

"Hot coffee is for weirdos." Joy lifted the tumbler to her lips but paused before she could take a sip, theatrically lowering her glasses and staring at something just beyond Blair's left shoulder.

Blair frowned. "What?"

"Who. Is. That?"

"Who is *who*?" Blair followed Joy's gaze to none other than Callum, who'd just entered on the opposite side of the auditorium, clutching the same stainless steel travel mug as yesterday and wearing a dusty-looking tweed sport coat complete with elbow patches, as though he'd based his wardrobe entirely on cinematic university professor stereotypes. His hair, both facial and otherwise, was still less than kempt, but at least he'd bothered to show up this time.

"*That* is the latest in our revolving door of choir directors and the current bane of my existence," she said.

"You figured that out on the first day?"

Blair met her friend's level gaze with one of her own. "Did you see him here yesterday morning?"

"If *that* guy had been here yesterday morning?" Joy pushed her glasses back up and resumed ogling Callum. "I'd have definitely noticed."

Blair swatted Joy's upper arm. "Stop it. You're happily married."

"Doesn't mean I can't notice a job well done on God's part. And you, my dearest friend in the world, are most definitely *not* married." She craned her neck in a not-obvious-at-all sort of way. "And from the looks of it, neither is he."

Ew. "I can't speak for him, but I am not looking. And even if I was, I definitely wouldn't be looking at work. Or in his direction."

"Last time I checked, looking in the conductor's direction was a fairly important part of your job." Joy's eyes gleamed with mischief. "And if any of my past conductors were that beautiful? Or even close? Watching them would not have been difficult at *all*."

Blair rolled her eyes. "He needs a haircut."

"Ehh, I kinda like it. Makes him all broody and mysterious. Like Beethoven."

"Ludwig van Beethoven was not exactly the poster child for healthy relationships."

"Touché."

Callum settled in the row in front of them, three seats to Joy's right, and guzzled coffee as if it were his lifeline. He hadn't waved or nodded or even acknowledged Blair's existence. Fine with her. Though they needed to get along for the kids' sake, they certainly didn't have to be friends.

But Joy, ever the raging extrovert, had already leaned over so far in Callum's direction that she nearly fell out of her seat.

"Hi. Joy Westinghouse." She extended her right hand to Callum. "Orchestra. Eighth year. Married. Two kids, four cats, and a Sheltie."

Callum blinked at the onslaught of information. "Callum Knight."

He tentatively returned Joy's handshake. "Vocal music. Second day. Single. No kids, no cats, no Sheltie."

Joy glanced over her shoulder at Blair, mischief curving her lips. *Told you he was single*, her look clearly said.

Blair made a face back. *And I told you I don't care.*

"And this is my best friend in the whole world, Blair Emerson," Joy said. "Who I think maybe you already met?"

Callum regarded Blair with a cursory glance. "Yes."

Charming.

"Great," Joy said. "And hey, since you're both here and we've got a few minutes, I've been wondering what sort of repertoire the choir might be considering for the holiday concert. In case nobody told you, the orchestra and choir combine for that concert, and it's never too early to start thinking about Christmas."

Callum's brows lifted. "It's August."

"We've been over this. No Christmas talk until at least September." Blair delivered her automatic reply, then pulled up short. Had she and Callum just agreed on something?

Joy had definitely noticed, if her crimson-lipped grin was any indication.

Blair resisted the urge to roll her eyes. *I see what you're doing, best friend of mine. And it won't work.*

Joy's grin grew even more devilish, a clear sign that she'd received Blair's telepathic message and was cheerfully ignoring it.

"The fall concert is only the choirs, yes?" Callum asked over the rim of his mug.

"Yes," Blair replied.

Callum muttered something that sounded suspiciously like "Thank God" as he turned back around, but Ron Cashman, the principal, had stepped to the microphone, which squealed feedback as it always did, so she couldn't be sure.

As Cashman launched into his falsely peppy introduction, Joy shot Blair a glance. A moment later Blair's watch buzzed her wrist, and the tiny screen filled with a text from Joy. Grinning, Blair pulled her phone from her purse. The 2020s equivalent of passing notes.

> You have to get along with him, you know.

Blair's thumbs tapped the screen.

> Who? Cash? We get along just fine.

The screen immediately filled with a string of eye-roll emojis.

> You know perfectly well I'm not talking about Cash. Give Callum a chance.

Blair studied the unruly head of dark hair in the row in front of her. Callum dragged a hand through the mop, then shifted in his chair and drummed long, sturdy fingers against the armrest. His entire being radiated boredom. Superiority. An ego the size of Alaska.

She turned her attention back to her phone.

> I did. He blew it.

> Five minutes in the choir room before a staff meeting does not constitute a chance. You haven't even seen him work with the kids yet.

> I don't need to see him work with them to know I don't like him.

> You don't have to like him. But you do have to get along with him. If not for your job satisfaction and mental health, then do it for the children.

Blair stifled a sigh. The children. That sea of faces she anticipated greeting every morning, whose trenchant observations and unabashed wit often doubled her over with laughter. Whose determination inspired her, whose musicianship drove her to give her all every single day. A bad day at Peterson High was still better than a good day anywhere else.

> Why do they have to be so lovable? 😭

> Right? ☺ SO inconsiderate of them.

Joy paused, her crimson lower lip sliding between her teeth as it did when she was deep in thought, then her beringed thumbs danced over the screen again.

> Please, for me, try being nice to this one. I've got a good feeling about him.

Blair shot her friend a withering glance and tapped out a reply.

> You just have a thing for guys who look like Beethoven.

> You say that like it's a bad thing.
> Beethoven was HOT.

Blair clicked her phone into Airplane Mode and tucked it back into her purse. "We are not having this conversation," she whispered.

"Avoiding the truth doesn't change it," Joy shot back.

Blair stifled a grin and forced herself to pay attention to Cash.

One thing was certain with Joy—Blair couldn't live without her.

But sometimes, some days, she wondered how in the world she would ever live *with* her.

Callum sank into the creaky chair at his desk with a sigh that emanated from somewhere deep in his bones, then reached for the insulated lunch sack into which he'd thrust a hastily constructed ham sandwich and a handful of chips. Three days of meetings, and now his first school lunch—his first "first day of school" in over a decade.

What he wouldn't give to be able to pop around the corner for some ceviche at that place in Somerville, or grab a *chowdah* from Legal Seafood like he had when he'd lived in Boston. But there was no chowdah in Peterson. No ceviche. Probably no one who'd even heard of chowdah. Instead the only restaurants nearby were a mediocre Mexican place, a pancake house that catered to octogenarians, and a dingy burger place that seemed to be open only when the mood struck the proprietor.

On the other hand, the lack of dining options might further his goal of saving every penny so he could walk out that door next May and never look back.

Had he ever been so exhausted in his life? The morning had been a blur of policies and procedures, syllabi and safety instructions, and a dozen other things that didn't involve making music. And though all his new colleagues had waxed rhapsodic about what gems the students of Peterson were, how polite and kind and selfless they were, all the students who had graced his classroom had regarded him with either undisguised loathing or total apathy.

He wasn't certain which he preferred.

And Blair had been only marginally helpful. During the scant few minutes of actual singing during Mixed Chorus, she'd faithfully given pitches and played for warm-ups, but other than that she'd seemed perfectly content to watch him twist in the wind. Her expression at the piano had been one of someone who'd thought they were sipping coffee only to find they'd sipped soy sauce by mistake.

But a funny thing happened when she got around the kids. Her pinched expression morphed into one of the sweetest, sunniest smiles he'd ever seen. And the same kids who'd glared at him swarmed her with hugs and high fives and how-was-your-summers. His ice-cold accompan— collaborative pianist had simply transformed when the kids came in. She'd come to life.

She'd become almost pretty.

But this joyous reunion, this transformation, further emphasized the adversarial relationship between the Peterson choral program and its new director. Obviously the lack of continuity at his position would lead to a certain closeness between the kids and their one constant, but that closeness came across as a concrete wall he had no hope of scaling. An exclusive club he would never be welcomed into.

The office door opened, and he jumped. "What?" It came out as half word, half growl.

Blair stood in the doorway, eyebrow arched, a cardboard coffee cup in her hand. "I'm sorry." Her tone contained no apology whatsoever. "Am I disturbing you?"

Yes. "No." It was her office too, after all. She even had a desk near the upright. Smaller than his but in much better condition. A vase of artificial flowers and a candle adorned its otherwise pristine surface, and the wall behind it was littered with mementos and photos and thank-you notes.

More evidence he was on the outside looking in and always would be.

Not that he wanted in. By no means.

He'd only be here for the year.

"Madrigals is our next class." Her voice was a crisp staccato. "You'll want to start with uniforms sooner rather than later."

"Of course."

"Today, if possible. Especially for the new members. The company we use is wonderful, but they aren't the speediest in the world, so time is of the essence." Her foot wasn't actually tapping with impatience but might as well have been.

"Yes. On it." The beginnings of a headache throbbed at his temples.

"And make sure you remind the afternoon choirs of the deadline for the signed page of the choir handbook. You forgot that this morning."

He dug in his desk drawer for the ibuprofen he hoped to God he'd remembered to bring in. "Anything else?"

She hesitated, her lips tightening ever so slightly. "Only this." And then she held the cup out to him. Steam piped up from the little hole in the lid, and the life-giving aroma of coffee reached his nostrils.

Coffee? For him?

Oh, he could have kissed her.

"They're free for staff today, courtesy of Pat's." His expression must have been quizzical, because she offered an apologetic half smile. "It's our student-run coffee shop. It isn't the best coffee in the world—or even the best coffee in Peterson, for that matter. But it's here, and it gets the job done." She set the cup on the corner of his desk. "They tend to go fast when they're free, so I wanted to make sure you got one."

"Thank you," he managed.

But she'd already turned back toward the door. "I'll let you enjoy the rest of your lunch." And then she was gone, the door clicking behind her.

Did she normally eat in here, needing quiet as much as he did? Or did she have a friend or two she ate with? Did she bring a lunch? Buy one from the cafeteria? Was the Mexican place around the corner better than it looked?

He hadn't bothered to ask.

He'd barely spoken to her at all today, other than to ask for starting pitches.

And yet she'd brought him an olive branch. The cup of coffee he didn't know how badly he needed until it appeared in front of him. He took a sip. She hadn't oversold the brew. It definitely wasn't the best coffee in the world. Likely not even the best coffee in Peterson, although he made a mental note to ask her where said coffee could be found.

But right now, on his first teaching day in a job he still hoped was a bad dream . . . it meant the world.

He had no idea if he could survive the year or not.

But thanks to this coffee, he just might make it through the rest of the day.

CHAPTER THREE

$\mathcal{M}$s. Em!" Thalia Jones, a senior soprano, wrapped Blair in an enthusiastic hug as kids filed into the choir room for Madrigals after lunch.

"So good to see you, Thalia." Blair returned the embrace. "That haircut is perfection on you."

"Thank you." Thalia grinned and fluffed her hair, now much shorter, curlier, and redder. "My mom hates it."

"Which I suspect is part of the appeal for you?"

Thalia's grin widened. "You know it. She—"

"Hey." An ear-splitting baritone yell sliced through the din. Blair and Thalia both jumped. The choir fell silent. And Callum, the source of the sound, stood beside the piano.

"The bell rang," he said to the class. "Though it's clear none of you heard it through that unholy racket you were making."

Unholy racket? It's the first day. Cut them some slack. She bit back the words.

"We'll talk later." Blair motioned toward the risers, and Thalia cast a reluctant glance toward Callum as she ascended to her spot on the top row of the soprano section.

The rest of the choir turned wary attention to the wild-haired man in the center of the room.

"And who are you, exactly?" The question on all the students' minds came, naturally, from the lips of outspoken alto Makayla Barnes.

"I'm Callum Knight." He raked a hand through his mop of hair. "Er—*Mr.* Knight, that is. I'm the new choral director here at Peterson."

Brayden Lee, the tenor section leader, elbowed Jake Ireland. "I heard this one wasn't even the one they hired back in May."

Jake's eyes widened. "Really?"

"Yeah. My mom said they originally hired some other guy but he got a better gig."

Jake chortled. "This one might not even last until the first concert."

"Jake. Brayden." Blair shot them a warning glare. "A little respect, please."

"Ms. Emerson. I'll take care of discipline in my own classroom, if you don't mind." Callum's gaze toward her was level, his voice pleasant, but both were underpinned with unmistakable warning.

She stared in disbelief. She'd only been trying to help, and he'd dressed her down in front of the students. While holding the coffee she'd brought him, no less. How *dare* he?

"I didn't realize you valued discipline so highly." Her voice was heated but low enough so only Callum could hear. He ignored her, but a muscle in his jaw twitched. Had her point landed? She certainly hoped so. More than half the students were on their phones, and a good portion of those still had their AirPods in. Even the ones whose phones were tucked away sat on the risers, their expressions ranging from apathy to suspicion to undisguised loathing.

Not a particularly auspicious beginning. It didn't matter, of course, since he'd be gone after this year.

Check that. Jake might not be wrong. Callum Knight might not even last until October.

"Now." Callum looked around the room, his voice a crisp staccato. "Since all of you seem so intent on running your voices, let's bypass the handbook for now and sing something."

To their credit, at least a third of the choir lowered their phones to reveal eyes glimmering with at least marginal interest.

Callum reached for a yellowed stack of music on a table to his right. "Could I have a volunteer to hand these out?"

Thalia raised her hand, and Blair sent her a glance of thanks. Thalia, a born leader and this year's choir president, could always be counted on to step up. Callum acknowledged Thalia with a nod, and she stepped down from the risers and took the stack from his outstretched hand.

Blair snagged one of the copies off the top of the stack as Thalia passed her, and she almost choked on the sip of coffee she'd just taken. "'Daemon Irrepit Callidus'?" She peered at her new director. "Callum, really?"

He met her gaze with a level one of his own amid the quiet din of choral chatter. "While everyone else played ridiculous icebreaker games, you may be pleased to know that I spent that time reading the choral handbook from the state activities association. A school this size is required to perform a level four for state festival."

Blair's eyes narrowed. "In April, yes. But this is August."

"And these are the famed Peterson Madrigals," he replied with a smirk. "I've heard good things. I believe they'll rise to the challenge."

While she had to admire the director's faith in the ensemble, and while it was true that the Peterson Madrigals likely could have handled a piece like "Daemon" in their glory days, those glory days were long gone, and she highly doubted Callum Knight could bring them back.

Pulling in a breath, she settled back at the piano bench and steeled herself for the impending train wreck, which was putting it mildly. Within ten minutes Callum's cheeks above his stubble were stained a deep crimson, sweat dotted his forehead, and the muscle in his jaw twitched wildly. At least half the kids had given up and checked out, and the ones who still tried gave a frustrated sigh as Callum cut them off.

"Altos. You missed your entrance. *Again.*"

"I'm sorry, Mr. Knight." Makayla's cheeks were flushed with anger and embarrassment.

"Sorry isn't good enough," Callum snapped. "Good enough is good enough."

Makayla's eyes widened, then filled with tears. Makayla normally kept her emotions reined in, but "not good enough" was her Achilles' heel. The girl's father was a raging perfectionist—a cardiothoracic surgeon at Peterson General—and nothing she did ever measured up. Blair had spent the last two years trying to convince Makayla of her talent, to help her see the beauty of her gorgeous alto voice with its velvety tone and natural vibrato.

All that work over all that time, and this pompous blowhard had just undone a fair bit of it.

As calmly as she could, Blair stood from the piano and leaned toward Callum. Twin whiffs of coffee and cologne greeted her. "Mr. Knight."

"Yes?"

"A word, please." She jerked her head toward the office.

"Not now." His blasé, dismissive tone made her even madder.

"Yes. Now." Each word was a dagger. "Or you'll find yourself in need of a new accompanist. And I'm told those are hard to find."

That got his attention. He glanced up from his iPad and lowered his baton. "You wouldn't dare."

Of course she wouldn't. Especially not if it meant leaving these kids with him. But were she a betting woman, she'd place a large wager on him not knowing this about her.

"How confident are you in that assessment?" She locked her gaze on his and refused to blink.

He stared at her, jaw rock hard, stormy emerald eyes narrowed into slits. Finally he set his baton down on the stand, the click of wood against metal the only sound in the tension-thickened choir room.

"Fine." He stalked toward the office.

"Hold down the fort, Thalia," Blair called as she followed Callum inside.

"Will do, Ms. Em."

Callum stood aside to let Blair pass, then shut the door, folded his arms across his chest, and faced her, brows arched. "What on God's green earth is so important that you were compelled to interrupt my rehearsal?"

"It's not *your* rehearsal. It's *their* rehearsal. *Our* rehearsal." Pulse pounding in her throat, she gestured toward the choir room. "They are *children*, Callum. I know you've been conducting professionals for years, but you need to take a step back and understand that these are young people, impressionable people, who are enrolled in your class because they want to be. Because they want to learn to sing."

Callum's lips tightened, the skin around them whitening.

"Makayla Barnes is the one person you should never, ever say 'not good enough' to. She seems tough, but inside she's a fragile young girl with a backstory that'd break your heart, and if you talk to her that way, you'll lose her. And that would be devastating, because if you heard that girl sing . . ."

"I have heard her sing. Just now."

"I mean *really* sing. If you'd heard her rendition of 'Quella fiamma' at contest last year, you'd—"

"If she's already sung 'Quella fiamma,' then she needs to be challenged. They *all* need to be challenged." Callum stepped toward her, close enough she could feel the warmth from his body. "I don't know what kind of kindergarten coddling you all have been doing around here, but this choir is capable of greatness. The talent is there. You know it and I know it. They just need someone to harness it. Channel it. Bring it out from where it's hiding to where the whole world can see."

Blair pulled back, the searing heat of anger cooled slightly by his words. Normally, she'd have a bone to pick with his description of her career as kindergarten coddling . . . but even in a frustrating, ten-minute train wreck of a rehearsal, Callum Knight had seen the talent that lay in their top choir, and something had motivated him to try to bring it out of them. Gone was the burned-out shell of a man she'd met on Monday. In his place stood someone who might have what it took to bring the Peterson High choirs out of the ashes.

"What?" Callum's voice was quieter now, hawkish eyes roving over her face in a thorough, but not unkind, evaluation.

She straightened. "If I didn't know better, Callum Knight, I'd think you might care about this job after all."

Callum dragged a hand through his hair. "Blair, when I was eleven years old, I thought I signed up for robotics as my sixth-grade elective, but a computer error put me in choir instead. And ever since then, choral music has been my *life*. Singing it, conducting it, creating it myself, coaxing it to life, watching people connect with it, with each other . . . making music is what makes me come alive. Sometimes in those magical moments when everything goes well, it just . . ."

". . . seems almost like a glimpse of heaven." Goodness. Two minutes ago she'd wanted to fling her cup of coffee right in his face, but now something hovered between them. A commonality. A connection. One she hadn't had with any of the other choral directors who'd occupied this office. Who'd taken charge of this classroom.

Callum seemed to feel it too, because those narrow slits of eyes had widened. Dark lashes blinked, and tightly folded arms gradually relaxed. One hand slid into his pocket, and the other found that wild mop of hair again.

Perhaps they could salvage the year after all.

"Look, Blair." His voice was considerably softer. A bit rough around the edges. "I'll be honest with you. This isn't where I saw myself at this point in my career. And those kids might be right. I might not even last the year. But as long as I am here, as long as my job is to teach them, then I'm going to demand their absolute best."

"Then may I give you a bit of advice from the perspective of someone who grew up in this community and who's worked with these kids for almost a decade?"

He nodded. "You may."

"If you want their best, you have to give them yours. And that starts with letting them see what you've just let me see. Let them see you care." She flipped a lock of hair over her shoulder. "We've had six directors in six years. Let that sink in. Nobody in this room has had the same teacher two years in a row. Every August there's a new face in front of them. New expectations. New ways of doing things. And just when they think they've got it figured out, just when they start to like that person, they get the rug yanked out from under them and have to start all over again. Frankly, it's a wonder any of them are still enrolled in choir. But the fact that they are means that getting to sing—to make music with each other—is worth putting up with all the other crap they've been through. These kids adore one another, Callum. And for a lot of them, this is the only place they feel safe. Don't take that away from them by yelling and screaming on the first day."

He was silent again, that impossible-to-read expression flitting over his face. Had she angered him again? Gotten through to him? She couldn't wait for the day when she'd understand this expression, because guessing games were the worst.

"I think perhaps I've underestimated you. And been a bit rotten to you." He flashed a slight smile. "Forgive me? Please?"

"Of course," she replied. "Thank you."

"And I think perhaps I've overestimated the choir's capabilities at this point in the semester."

"I . . . don't disagree with you."

"Well, that's a first." And then Callum smiled. The curve of his lips carved a slight indent in his cheek. His eyes crinkled at the corners. And her heart gave a curious thump. It wasn't attraction. Goodness, no. But if she had to spend the rest of the school year watching someone . . . there were certainly less pleasant someones she could be watching.

"Not to push this tenuous truce too hard," he began, his hand on the doorknob of the office. "But might you be available for a bit after school today? I could really use your help."

Blair tilted her head. "With . . ."

"Repertoire selection," he replied. "I'd really like to get going on music, for Madrigals in particular, but I haven't had a chance to explore the choral library, so I'm not sure what's in there and what I might need to order. I want to find something challenging but achievable, and high-quality compositions are an absolute must. Frankly, I'd like to select music for all the choirs. Four per choir to begin, with a goal of learning at least that number, if not more, for the October concert. Does that sound reasonable?"

Reasonable? It sounded like perfection. Not that she'd give Callum Knight the satisfaction of knowing she thought that. Not yet. Not when the idea of not hating him was so new. "Yes. Very reasonable."

His eyes lit. "Wonderful. Then perhaps the rest of the day we go over the handbook?"

"That sounds like a good idea to me."

"And I'll make sure to remember to point out the deadline this time around." He cracked the door and tossed another grin over his shoulder, and her heart did that same funny thing it had before.

She had to get that under control.

If she didn't, Joy would never let her hear the end of it.

CHAPTER FOUR

*C*ALLUM WOULD say one thing for Peterson High School: Their choral library was extensive. Floor-to-ceiling shelves lined the walls of a small, musty-smelling room off the main choir office. Rows of boxes filled the shelves, each box carefully labeled with the title of the composition it contained, alongside a number corresponding to the library's equally extensive and equally well-organized online database. He chuckled at the unfathomable neatness of the handwriting on each label. Blair's, no doubt.

For the last twenty minutes, both tantalized and overwhelmed by the possibilities, he'd combed through the database and jotted down a few ideas for each choir. Now he was pulling boxes off the shelf. Ah. Mozart's "Regina coeli." That might be a possibility. He grabbed it from the shelf and plopped it onto a table in the corner. The resulting cloud of dust made him sneeze.

What next? Ah yes. Kinley Lange's gorgeous "Esto Les Digo." With senior bass Willie Vance's luscious low C, not performing this one would be positively criminal. It was perched two shelves over amid a couple of boxes' worth of Vic Nelson's work. Callum's pulse quickened at the sight of "Death Be Not Proud," perhaps his favorite Nelson composition. A beastly piano part, but Blair seemed to have the chops for it. Probably too easy for Madrigals, though. Could Mixed Chorus handle it? He'd give that some thought.

Wait . . . was that . . .

It was. "The Road Not Taken." One of his own, and earliest, compositions.

He pulled the box from the shelf with a wave of nostalgia. Inspired by the famous text by Robert Frost, Callum had written the piece in a feverish spurt of midnight creativity four days after arriving in Boston, a reflective homage to both his new home in New England and the leap of faith he'd just taken. At the time he'd thought the work genius, and the sales numbers had pleased his publisher, but in later years he'd realized just how basic and beginner it was. As recently as two years ago, he'd been embarrassed by its pedestrian chord structure and predictable melody.

Helpless bitterness clawed his chest and clenched his jaw. Now, writing even a high-school-level song like this—the creativity required to summon even the most basic of harmonies, the most boring of melodies—seemed a pipe dream. *Dear God, what I wouldn't give for another feverish late-night composing session.* Whatever price the Almighty required, Callum would pay double. Anything to get his mojo back. Anything for inspiration, anything for—

A light clicked on behind him, streaming soft warmth across the carpet at his feet. Quickly, he shoved "The Road Not Taken" back onto the shelf, then grabbed the other titles he'd pulled and strode back into the office, where Blair stood at her desk. Lighting a candle.

"Isn't that against fire code?" The question came out far more of a snarl than he intended.

She regarded him briefly, then stuck the lighter in the drawer. "No one's ever complained." *And you'd better not either.* She didn't say the words, but her expression conveyed them all the same.

The smell of cinnamon cut through the stale air, bringing to mind the Cinnabon stand at O'Hare. Blair pulled her long red hair back with one hand, then leaned in to take a deep breath. In the flickering candlelight, with her eyes closed and lips curved, she was almost pretty.

Almost.

"It's my after-the-students-leave ritual." She fished in a drawer of her desk. "Gotta have *some* consistency around here, after all."

Was that a shot? She'd let her hair fall back around her shoulders, obscuring her face, so he couldn't read her expression. Irritated, he turned and thumped the boxes of music onto his desk.

"Looks like you've already got a decent start on the library." Her voice was steady, maddeningly devoid of anything other than cool pleasantry.

"Yes. It's quite impressive."

"Thank you."

He hadn't meant that as a compliment exactly, but the satisfied gleam in Blair's eyes made it clear she'd taken it as one. Or . . . perhaps that gleam had something to do with the bag of mini foil-wrapped peanut butter cups in her hand.

"Guilty pleasure," she said in answer to the question he hadn't asked. "Want one?"

Did he want one? Absolutely. Did he trust himself to stop at one? Not a chance. And based on the way his tux had fit last time he'd worn it, he needed to be able to stop at one. "No"—he held up a hand—"but thank you."

"Suit yourself." She dug another couple of cups from the bag, closed it with a hair tie she slipped from around her wrist, and tucked the bag back into the desk drawer. "Find some possibilities?"

"I've spent the last half hour digging through the database and feel like I barely scratched the surface." He nodded toward the library. "I could lose many, many hours in there if I'm not careful."

"I could too. And have." Blair's eyes took on a mischievous gleam. "Got a few of your pieces in there, if you didn't see."

His jaw clenched. "I saw."

"We did 'The Road Not Taken' a couple years ago. Fall concert. Third on the program." A faint peach blush touched the tops of her cheekbones. "Sorry. I remember every piece on every concert."

Why did she feel the need to apologize? His inner angst must've registered on his face as disapproval. "No, it's not that. It's . . ." Words failed him, and he shook his head. "How was it?"

"Not bad."

Had she meant the piece or the performance? Desperation to dig further clawed at his chest, but he wouldn't give her the satisfaction of knowing just how deep his insecurity ran.

Blair gathered her hair and leaned toward her cinnamon candle again. "Are you composing anything at the moment?"

"No." It came out a growl.

"Wow." Hurt flashed in her eyes. "Sorry I asked."

He pulled in a breath and ordered his chaotic emotions into silence. "No, I'm the one who needs to apologize. I shouldn't have snapped at you."

She straightened and let her hair fall. "Thank you."

"I have creative block." He reached up to rub the back of his neck, the red and blue stripes on gray carpet tiles suddenly preferable to Blair's too-piercing gaze. "Have had for a while now. I thought my muse would come back after the pandemic, but . . ." *But Rayne . . .*

And my life crumbled to dust. My past self wouldn't even recognize me now.

"I'm sorry you're dealing with that." Her voice was just soft enough, just sympathetic enough, that for a terrifying second he wondered if she'd read his thoughts and knew that creative block was the tip of his personal iceberg. "Truly. It sounds difficult and frustrating."

For the first time, someone had accepted his struggles. Heard him without either pressuring him, as his agent had, or giving him a chin-up, God's-got-this speech, as his mother had.

No, Blair had simply heard him.

And until this moment, he hadn't known how much he'd needed that.

"Thanks." The single syllable seemed inadequate, but it was all he could summon.

Clearing his throat, he turned back toward his desk. Back toward the stacks of music he'd be charged with teaching to high schoolers. Perhaps this could be a good thing. Perhaps studying these scores, refamiliarizing himself with music he loved, would start his own creativity flowing.

Over his shoulder, Blair gave a quiet gasp. "Is that 'Death Be Not Proud'?" Without waiting for a reply, she slid an octavo from the box and flipped through it. "Oh, I love this one with every fiber of my being." Her enthusiasm was unexpected. Disarming. Alarming in the way it squeezed his heart. "It's sheer brilliance. That E-flat major chord, right here."

Callum didn't need to look to know what she was talking about, but he did anyway, following a neatly trimmed nail to measure 24, the spot with one of the most beautiful harmonic twists he'd ever encountered in all of music.

"That chord absolutely melts me," he said.

"Every. Time." She caught his gaze and held it, admiration for the music hovering between them, edged with the dawn of camaraderie.

"What I'd give to be able to compose like that." He tore his gaze away, the beauty of it suddenly too much. "And Vic makes it seem so easy."

She gave a chuckle, low and rich. "I know it wasn't. Not this one, anyway."

"You knew him when he wrote this?"

"I was a sophomore." Her expression softened. "He was a total bear for a couple weeks during the fall of that year. I'd been told to expect that during contest season, but this was in September. The year had barely started. One of the seniors warned me that he always got super grouchy when he was composing. It was a commission for an honor choir in . . . Kansas, I think?" She flipped to the first page. "Yup. The Kansas Music Educators Association All-State Choir. But we sang it ourselves the following year, and I fell in love with it." Her eyes sparkled as she scanned the score.

Callum leaned against the desk. "So you grew up here in Peterson, then?"

"Born and raised. My dad owns the Dodge dealership, and my mom is head of every civic organization you could possibly think of." She rolled her eyes. "I'm practically royalty."

"Have you been here your whole life?"

"Other than college, yeah." She waved a hand, years of her life dismissed in a single second. "Happens to the best of us. We spend high school counting the days until we can get out, but a whole lot of us either never do or come right back."

She held up "Death Be Not Proud." "Shall I hold on to this, then?" Hope shimmered in her warm brown eyes, and Lord help him, he didn't want to do a single thing in the world to crush that hope. Not when it seemed the ice queen might be starting to thaw. There was a vulnerability beneath that hard exterior, one that beckoned him. No, *compelled* him.

Not that he needed much convincing to program "Death Be Not Proud."

"You said you've been here, what, six years?" he asked.

"Seven."

He grinned. "And I suppose you'd remember if it's been performed during that time?"

Amusement sparkled in her eyes. "Yes, I would, and no, it hasn't."

"Then yes. Hang on to it. We'll start it with Mixed Chorus tomorrow."

The smile that lit her face nearly knocked the wind out of him. "Excellent." She set the octavo down on the desk and pawed through the box of music. "If memory serves, there's a pianist's copy in here somewhere. Mrs. Cassidy always did come up with the most intelligent fingerings, rest her soul." A soft rustling of paper. "Ah. Here we are." Blair pulled out a copy of the music, and with it came another sheet of paper, which flew across the distance between them and landed on his desk.

But instead of the turquoise-and-white Teal Springs Publishing cover characteristic of Vic Nelson's work, this was a sheet of yellowed staff paper, folded in half, its shredded left side indicative of being torn from a spiral notebook. And instead of crisp printed notes and rests, this music was written in age-faded pencil.

"What's that?" Blair leaned in, bringing a swish of hair across her blouse and a faint whiff of peanut butter and chocolate.

"I'm not sure." Callum unfolded the paper, curiosity creasing his brow. The melody arched across the staff, instantly entrancing him with its twists and turns and soaring intervals.

"There's another couple pages in here." Blair stood at his elbow, but her voice sounded a million miles away, so deep had the thicket of this music pulled him in. Another pair of pages appeared in her outstretched hand, and he took them. They bore the same ivory hue and ghostly pencil markings. A few notes had been erased here and there, replaced with others, and he instantly wanted to sit down with this composer and discuss those decisions—but the result was the same heartrending soprano melody pinned over lush harmonies in the alto, tenor, and bass. The rudimentary piano part consisted mostly of chord symbols, with a few notes tossed in here and there. Perhaps the composer's strength lay in choral music, not writing accompaniments. Or maybe they'd planned to go back in and finish the piano part at some point. Regardless, the faded pencil and yellowed paper indicated a project long abandoned.

But why? It was brilliant. The harmonies and melodies displayed creativity on a level he'd never encountered. The way he could only hope and pray to be able to write someday. There was something innate, natural, God-given about this composer's talent.

If this had been abandoned . . . what had been finished in its place?

And who on earth had written it?

He flipped through the pages, his pulse hammering. "This is genius." He used that word sparingly, but it fit this composition.

A piano sounded. Not the piano in his mind, but the reddish upright in the corner. Blair had slid onto the bench, the first sheet of music open on the rack in front of her. And then she sang—her voice a husky, sweet mezzo-soprano—and the melody reached somewhere deep inside him, wrapped around his heart, and pulled him closer. He couldn't have stopped his progression across the office if his life depended on it. Something about this melody, these chords . . . touched him on a level very little ever had. He needed to meet this composer. Talk with them. Where had they studied? Who had they studied with? Where had these ideas come from? Maybe if he just spent a few minutes in this person's presence, he could find his inspiration again.

Tentatively, not wanting to sully the beauty of the moment or the composition, he propped the two other pages beside the first one on the music rack, then peered over Blair's left shoulder and joined in to sing the bass part. Their voices blended like coffee and cream, and the shimmering he'd felt before now wrapped around him like a blanket. It was magic. No, beyond magic. It was one of those moments he needed to savor, one of those musical highs, those glimpses of heaven that would fade all too soon.

But nothing would erase the memory of this moment, this melody, this making music with Blair. Whether she was part of it or whether it was simply because she happened to be here, he couldn't know. Couldn't guess. Didn't care. It simply existed, and—

What?

No. It couldn't end there. No. No, no, no. It wasn't even resolved yet. The harmony was left hanging.

"That can't be it." Blair's graceful right hand lifted from the keyboard, and she flipped the page over.

Blank.

Why? Where was the rest of it?

"No." Despair burst from him. "No, that can't be the end. It can't."

"There aren't any more pages."

"No. I simply won't accept it." Callum covered the distance between the piano and his desk in two defiant strides and emptied the file box, sheet music spilling over the surface of his desk. He pawed through the mess, frantic. But the only things left were a bright-green concert program from 2005 and a couple dried-up, broken rubber bands.

He felt broken. He couldn't even envy that composer anymore, whoever they were. He *had* to find the rest of that music.

His head snapped up, and he found Blair's eyes. "Who wrote it? Does it say?"

She pursed her lips and flipped the page back over. "Nope. Probably Vic, though."

The most likely scenario, to be sure. But this piece differed quite a bit from anything else he'd written. Much as he loved Vic Nelson's work, Callum had never been touched—moved, *changed*—by a piece of music as he had by this one.

"It's reminiscent of his style in places." He dragged a hand through his mop of hair. "But there's just something about it that's . . ."

". . . not his style at all." Blair looked up at him, his own confusion swimming in her depthless eyes.

"I'll ask him." Callum grabbed his phone, took a picture of the first page, and fired off a quick text to Vic.

"I mean . . . the melody is a bit like some of his." Blair studied the music again. "But the harmonies are rather different. More like Rutter than Nelson."

"Exactly."

Callum's phone buzzed against the desk, and he grabbed it.

Might be an early draft of something I forgot about. I'm afraid my memory's not what it used to be.

Callum read the text aloud, then set the phone on his desk, irritation tightening his neck. "Well, if this is one of Vic's early drafts, he needs to finish it, because it's brilliant."

Blair's brow furrowed. "I wonder . . ."

"Wonder what?"

"Rumor has it there was a student back in the sixties who wrote music. I always assumed it would be singer-songwriter guitar stuff, given the era, but maybe it's this." Blair turned the page over. "The handwriting is pretty juvenile-looking."

Callum's jaw unhinged. "A *student* wrote this?"

Blair shrugged. "Maybe. I heard she was a little bit of an odd duck. Iris . . . something. Can't remember the last name off the top of my head."

He flipped through his mental choral database. "I can't think of any composers named Iris. Maybe she wrote under a different name?"

"If it is her, then she'd have never had the chance." Blair squared her shoulders and met his gaze. "Because Iris died in the spring of 1970."

CHAPTER FIVE

September 1969

*T*HEY DIDN'T tune the bell over the summer.

Not that I'd thought they would, especially with the whole world watching Armstrong take "one small step for man, one giant leap for mankind." Plus, I was probably the only person in the history of Peterson High School to notice that the school bell clanged somewhere between an E—a slightly flat E, no less—and an F, which was, of course, slightly sharp.

I wasn't bragging. Truthfully, I hated noticing these things. I wished I could go about the school day and not have my teeth set on edge and my nerves jangled every fifty minutes. What I wouldn't give to be as oblivious to the sound as all the other students. Sometimes I wondered why God had made me so different from all the other girls, those blessedly normal girls with their straight hair and glossy lips and short skirts, gossiping and hugging and caring for nothing beyond makeup and boys.

And I was always on the outside looking in.

I ducked out of the crowded hallway into the little alcove leading to the music classrooms and double-checked my printed schedule. *Yes.* I had music theory next. Mr. Gilbert, our choir teacher, had finally convinced the administration to add it this year. *"The nuts and bolts of music,"* he'd told us. *"Opening its hood and poking around underneath."* The analogy was meant to make theory more relatable to the other students, but I hadn't needed any convincing.

It was music.

For me, that was enough.

I entered the choir room, cringing once more at the clanging, out-of-tune bell, and took a seat in the small section of desks beside the risers. Close to the back, so I'd be nowhere near the bell, but not so far away that I had to walk in front of everyone.

Not that there was much of a class. Despite Mr. Gilbert's rousing recruitment speech, there were only five others. No . . . make that four. A dark-haired girl in the front row stood suddenly, eyes wide, schedule in hand. She wore a skirt so short that I'm surprised Principal Smith hadn't sent her home to change.

"Oh. This isn't Freshman Choir. I'm not supposed to be in here until next hour." Blushing, she gathered her books and dashed for the door.

"Anyone else?" Grinning, Mr. Gilbert scanned the room. His spectacled gaze landed on me. "Iris Wallingford. Good to see you in here."

Mr. Gilbert meant well, I knew he did, but I also knew what came next. Sure enough, everyone turned to look at me.

That was the only problem with sitting in the back. It was always painfully obvious when everyone was staring at you.

Most of the faces were familiar—Susan and Barbara from glee club. Gary, who played drums in band. And a boy from the trumpet section. Victor, I think. But their stares all converged on me like sunlight through a magnifying glass, intense and concentrated. All my thoughts went up in smoke. My skin burned.

"Okay, class." Mr. Gilbert clapped his hands, and mercifully the students turned toward him instead of me. "Good morning, and welcome to music theory. I'm so excited to teach this course. And while I do have an outline for what we'll cover, I've left room for suggestions from all of you."

My mouth had already gone dry. My stomach knotted.

"So I'd like each of you to tell me *briefly*"—his gaze darted toward Susan, known school-wide for her endlessly long answers to any question from a teacher—"why you enrolled in music theory and what you hope to gain from it."

Susan's hand, naturally, shot into the air. "I want to be a music teacher," she said without waiting for Mr. Gilbert to call on her. "And since theory will be required in college, it makes sense now to get an early start, to learn as much as I can, so maybe I'll do better in college theory and—"

"Thank you, Susan." Mr. Gilbert was polite but firm, then turned to Barbara. "And what about you, Barbara?"

Barbara beamed at Mr. Gilbert. "You're my favorite teacher, so why wouldn't I want to take another class from you?"

Gary rolled his eyes. "You mean you just want another class with Mr. Gilbert because you think he's a hunk."

A hunk? *Mr. Gilbert?* Who on God's green earth would ever think that about Mr. Gilbert? He was a *teacher.* Practically our parents' age.

"Gary," a red-faced Barbara hissed. "I cannot *believe* you just said that."

"That's enough." Mr. Gilbert held up a hand. "Gary, you seem eager to contribute to the conversation. Why have you enrolled in theory?"

Gary shrugged. "Honestly, I needed another elective credit, and this is closest to the band room."

"Well, I appreciate your honesty." Mr. Gilbert glanced between me and Victor, and I knew he'd call on me next. I prayed he wouldn't, but my prayer went unanswered.

"Iris? What about you?"

Because music is always running around inside me. And I want to know everything I can about it. I want to know how it works. Because there are songs I've never heard before that live in my head and my heart, and if I don't write them down, I'll burst. I want to know if what I'm writing is any good, because I feel closest to God when I'm writing, and I like what I write, but I don't know if anyone else will. And my parents don't think music is an appropriate career choice for me. They might be right, but I still want to learn everything I can about it. I want to be the best composer I can possibly be.

Even if it's only ever for God.

But I couldn't say all that. Not in front of all these people. Not in front of anyone. So I shrugged and looked at the floor. "I dunno . . . 'cause I love music, I guess."

"Thank you, Iris." Mr. Gilbert's voice was warm and rich. "And you, Victor? What about you?"

"Like Iris said, I love music." The words sounded strong and confident coming from Victor, not weak and whispery like they had when I'd said them. "I love everything about it. I can't think of a single thing about music that I wouldn't want to know, and that includes how it works. The car guys want to poke around under the hood, the football team could talk about plays for hours . . . and I want to know about music."

"Well said, Victor." Mr. Gilbert's mouth stretched into a warm smile. "And that's a wonderful place to begin. Let's start by discussing the types of music we like. What songs do we love? And what is it about them that makes us love them so much?"

The discussion continued, but I wasn't paying attention. I was studying Victor. I'd known him for a while, but we'd never spoken. Not that I spoke to most people. But I wished I'd spoken to him earlier, wished I'd found out he loved music like I did. Maybe if I had, I wouldn't have been so lonely for all of high school.

He had a thick head of hair, somewhere between blond and brown, that covered the tops of his ears and most of his forehead. Nowhere near as long as some of the boys' hair, though. He wore black plastic glasses like everyone else, but on him they just seemed . . . right. He had a nice profile too. Nothing out of the ordinary. Simply a nice profile.

Then he turned toward me . . . and smiled. His lips were closed, but the smile made it all the way to his eyes. Curved lines bracketed his mouth, and the skin beneath his glasses bunched up.

I turned away, my face on fire. I had to focus on something else before I flipped out.

Like the hardwood floor between my shoes. That would do.

Hmm. Those lines on the floor looked almost like a staff.

G would go on that second line. And then a B on the line above it. D on the line above that. A G-major chord. A piano in my head sounded the chord, just as real as if the big black grand at the center of the room were playing it. Then a choir took over, and the sopranos took the top note from a D to an A. The lovely dissonance and soaring melody calmed me.

And frustrated me. Where was my staff paper? I needed to write this down before I forgot.

No staff paper, but I found some notebook paper. I scribbled a swirl of a treble clef. Wrote down what I heard. It was messy, but it worked.

The pressure in my heart released a little, like the steam from a pressure cooker, after I finished the phrase. With a sigh, I put the paper aside and focused on Mr. Gilbert. Not the music. Not Victor. Just the class I signed up to take.

The bell rang all too soon, and I clenched my jaw against the sound and gathered my books. When I looked up, there was Victor, smiling at me again.

"Y'know, Iris," he said, hazel eyes twinkling, "I really wish they'd tune that bell."

CHAPTER SIX

"SHE'S DEAD?" Callum's gaze was fierce, his brow furrowed. "Are you sure?"

Blair turned back toward the piano, the musty scent of the long-forgotten music mingling with her cinnamon-roll candle. "That's what I heard."

"That's an unspeakable tragedy." Callum picked up the last of the torn-out sheets of music, the sleeve of his crisp cotton dress shirt brushing her upper arm. "Talent like this. Silenced."

"Yeah. She'd have been in her seventies now." Blair slid from the bench in the direction opposite Callum.

"And an absolute institution. Probably one of the top choral composers in the world."

Blair peered over his shoulder. "The voice parts are incredible, I'll give you that. The piano part is a little clunky, though."

Callum waved a hand. "That would've been easily addressed with the proper training. But the sheer talent?" He held up the fragile pages. "I've only seen this kind of thing a handful of times."

His intensity was infectious, and his curiosity drove her to pull her phone from her pocket. "Let me see what I can find out." She opened her browser and typed in a few search terms, then combed through the handful of articles that popped up. "Oh. Here's a news article." Her pulse quickened. "It's from March 1970."

"What's it say?"

Blair spread her thumb and index to enlarge the microscopic newspaper article. "The Peterson community was shocked and saddened yesterday when seventeen-year-old Iris Wallingford was found dead in her bed. Miss Wallingford was a senior at Peterson High School, involved in choir, glee club, and band, and was the daughter of prominent local businessman Reginald Wallingford III and his wife, Genevieve."

"A senior in 1970?" Callum's voice drew her gaze. "Wasn't that around the time Vic graduated? Maybe he knew her."

"If she was involved in all that, doubtless he did."

Callum was already reaching for his phone. "I'll ask. Does the article say anything else?"

Blair turned her attention back to the tiny screen. "A cause of death has not been released, but no foul play is suspected."

"No foul play." Callum leaned in closer to her phone, wafting a not-unpleasant cologne into the air. The flickering candlelight cast a shadow beneath the hollow of his cheekbone. "They think it was suicide."

Something in his voice drew her gaze. Did he know something about suicide?

She clicked on another article from the same newspaper a few days later. "Unfortunately, yes. They ruled her death a suicide."

"Did she give any clues?" Callum's eyes blazed. "What about her friends? Her family? Did someone in her life miss something critical?"

His desperation gave her pause. "Suicide isn't anyone's fault, Callum."

"Yes. You're right." He dragged a hand through his hair. "Of course. I just . . . I wonder why she felt she had no other choice."

"Whatever the reason, it happened more than fifty years ago." Why was he so concerned about a student gone more than five decades? Didn't he have enough to think about in the here and now?

"But people still lose hope today." His voice sounded strained. "Every day people feel they can't go forward. And maybe if I get to the truth about Iris—about this music, even if she's not the composer—then . . . I don't know, but it might help me somehow. Help me unlock my creativity again. Help me deal with . . ." He swallowed hard. "This isn't something I'd normally tell someone I just met. But my fiancée, Rayne, died by suicide. A little over five years ago."

The air leached out of Blair's lungs, and her stomach plummeted. "Oh, Callum. I'm so sorry."

"So to move halfway across the country and to have that come up here, in a job I never wanted, never even thought about . . ." He looked up. "If God really does have a plan, if he really does have a reason for dropping me here, then . . . maybe this is part of it. I want to know why someone so full of life, so full of talent, would be unable to go on. Partly because of Rayne, but partly the universal question as to why. Or what if it wasn't a suicide? What if the cops got it wrong? What if Iris . . . Oh, I don't know what I'm even saying anymore." Gone was the arrogant facade. Pleading took its place. "But music like this is a glimpse of the Divine, and it deserves to be recognized. To be performed. If Iris Wallingford is the one who wrote it, then Peterson—the world—needs to know that. They need to know her. To learn her story. But I'll need your help. You know these students. This community. You're an insider here. I'm not and never will be."

The reminder that this was just a layover for him, not his final destination, needled her. But at least he wasn't filling her head with promises he never intended to keep. There was value in being up-front and honest.

If only everyone in her life had been that way.

Callum's phone buzzed on the desk, and he picked it up and gave it a glance. "Vic says he didn't know her."

"Not at all?" Blair frowned. "That's surprising."

"He says he knew who she was but that she was pretty quiet. Kept to herself. He said if she indeed wrote music, the piece might be hers, but he doesn't have any idea how it got in our library." He set the phone back down. "So Vic's a dead end. But surely someone knew her, someone who would be able to tell us more."

"Probably, but we have to be careful," she pointed out. "We don't want to cause any of her loved ones further pain."

"If her loved ones already know what happened, then they can help me. And if they don't, maybe we can help them." He paused. "Besides, what if something we learn could help one of the kids? Surely you know what a crisis teen mental health is in right now. What if one of them is having the same thoughts as Iris? As Rayne?"

She tightened her arms across her midsection. "It's an awfully low tactic, bringing the kids into this."

"Tactic?" His brows inched together, and he studied her in a way that wasn't unkind but was sharp enough to see through the walls she'd spent years building around herself. "Who hurt you, Blair?"

Her eyes flew open, and she drew back. How did he know? She learned to read every nuance, every gesture, of whichever director she worked with, but that level of mind reading was *not* supposed to be reciprocated.

"It doesn't matter." She studied the carpet. "Besides, it was a long time ago."

"Sounds like maybe not long enough."

The husky tenderness in his voice caressed her wounded heart.

Well. Maybe he wouldn't be here past this year. But they were stuck together for the next nine months.

He needed this, and the kids needed him. And if digging five decades into the past would help him, then that was what they'd do.

"Okay. I'll help you. But you have to trust me and not go barreling into this town guns blazing."

"So . . . the opposite of how I've handled the choirs so far."

His sheepish grin, against her will, tugged out a smile of her own. "Basically, yes."

His smile widened, provoking unexplained warmth in the center of her chest. "Then, Maestra, I will follow your lead."

Blair held back a snort. She'd believe that when she saw it.

"Finally." Stationed by the hallway leading to the parking lot, Joy made an exaggeration of looking at her watch, the band festooned with burgundy alto clefs.

Blair rolled her eyes. "Oh, enough with the drama. I'm not that late."

"Yes, but I've got a schedule, ma'am." Joy shouldered her enormous tie-dye bag and started toward the exit.

No lie. Joy did have a tight schedule. In fact, the only nonwork time the two frequently had together was their 3:30 p.m. gym trip, squeezed between the final bell and when Joy needed to pick up her kids from day care. With Joy's chaotic home life and stressful job, Blair was constantly amazed at how she continually made everything work. It was a busy life.

Busy, but full.

"And I've got a cat." Blair lengthened her stride to keep up with her fast-paced friend. "Who'll get yowly at me if I'm not home in time to feed him."

Joy gave Blair a sidelong glance. "Doesn't Walter have a self-feeder?"

Blair sighed. "You're right."

"Hey." Joy paused and gave Blair's forearm a gentle squeeze. "You've got a freedom I'd kill to have sometimes."

"And you've got a family." The nose-to-the-grindstone approach that had driven Blair through college and graduate school had reaped rewards in her job, leading her to be full-time salaried staff instead of hourly, like most accompanists were.

But the rest of it . . . the husband, the kids, the Sheltie . . . so far all of that had passed her by.

"So what *did* take so long?" Joy shoved the door open, and a blast of humid air hit them both.

Squinting against the summer sun, Blair dug her sunglasses from her bag. "Callum discovered our choral library, and we picked out some music for the fall concert."

"Well, you're still calling him Callum and not Gollum, so maybe there's hope."

Blair laughed. "Gollum?"

"You seriously hadn't thought of that?"

"No, because I'm not a terrible, horrible person." Blair gave Joy a gentle shove. "But I may keep it on file for the next time he hacks me off."

"Speak of the devil . . ."

Across the parking lot, exiting through the front—he evidently didn't know about the shortcut from the music hallway—strode Callum, messenger bag draped over one shoulder, scrolling his phone and walking toward an aging BMW that, despite the luxury label, had clearly seen better days.

Hmm. Maybe he really did have money issues.

In which case maybe his temporary status here was indeed far more about returning to the life he knew and loved than anything to do with Peterson.

A chirp sounded as Blair unlocked her car. "Hey, do you remember ever hearing anything about Iris Wallingford?"

Joy paused beside a maroon, bumper sticker–plastered minivan. "Iris who?"

"Wallingford. She died by suicide during her senior year in 1970. The newspaper said she was a music student."

"A music student. Wow." Joy's expression turned pensive. "Maybe that's why the auditorium is haunted."

"The auditorium is not haunted. You just don't understand the light board."

"That doesn't mean it's not haunted." Joy opened the backseat of her van, strewed as usual with toys, empty juice boxes, and stray french fries. "It's a known fact that every auditorium has a ghost. Or at least a gremlin. Especially if a student who frequented said auditorium was later found dead under mysterious circumstances. That's ghost hunting 101."

"Most people don't watch ghost shows to relax, Joy."

"Most people don't have their career success depend on the cooperation of teenagers either. And yet here we are." Joy tossed her bag onto the floor of the backseat and turned to face Blair. "How did Iris Wallingford come up, anyway?"

Blair leaned against the door of her car. "Callum and I found a piece of sheet music in the choral library today. It's handwritten and unfinished but utterly gorgeous. I got goose bumps when I played it. The piano part is a little clunky, but the choral writing, the harmonies . . . *oh.* They were something special."

Joy's brows lifted. "What makes you guys think Iris Wallingford wrote it?"

"I remember hearing rumors growing up that she wrote music. And if she really was the composer, that might explain why it was never finished."

Joy pursed her lips in thought. "Hmm. Did you guys ask Nelson?"

"Callum did. Vic says he doesn't really remember the piece or the girl, so that's a dead end. But Callum's determined to investigate."

"Poking at old wounds? That won't backfire at all."

"Right? That's what I told him. He didn't listen."

"Of course he didn't." Joy opened her door. "*Conductors.*"

"Well, you're not so bad," Blair replied.

"That's because I'm a teacher, not a conductor. And Gollum over there?" Joy jerked her head toward the far exit, where Callum's car was pulling out of the parking lot. "He is definitely a *conductor.*"

CHAPTER SEVEN

September 1969

$\mathcal{T}$HERE. FINALLY. The assignment for music theory was done. I tore it from my spiral notebook of manuscript paper. Oops. Almost forgot to put my name on it. That would've been a silly ten points to lose. With a flourish, I scribbled my name in the upper right-hand corner, then walked to the front and put the assignment in the wire basket on Mr. Gilbert's desk. He glanced up, brows arched over his black plastic glasses. Small wonder, since there were still twenty minutes before the bell. Everyone else still hunched over their desks, pencils dancing.

"Thank you, Iris," Mr. Gilbert said. "Just find something else to work on until the end of class."

With pleasure. Trying not to smile, I practically skipped back to my spot, then flung myself into my seat, and turned in my notebook to the thing I really cared about. The piece that had invaded two days ago and taken me over body, mind, and soul. The melody God sent had filled my heart, my head, almost to the point of making it impossible to finish that theory assignment.

But I'd finally finished, and I had twenty minutes—twenty precious minutes—to devote to my own music. *Thank you, God.* My pencil scratched across the page. My hand trembled, frantic to keep up with the stream of notes in my heart. Composing was sometimes like this for me. The music seemed to exist outside space. Outside time. It was like God had held it there, fully formed, and chose me to bring it into the world. I'd feel him watching me, beaming as I scribbled notes onto the paper, bringing the music to life. I'd feel his joy as I composed. Writing music was an honor.

But if I was being brutally honest, sometimes the pressure of the melody, the urgency to get it out of me . . . sometimes it felt like a bit of a curse too.

The phrase ended, and the melody was kind enough to pause so I could sketch out a few harmonies. Just to remind myself what I heard. Bare bones now, but I could fill them in later. Harmony was far more patient with me, but Melody stood there, arms crossed, foot tapping, eager to share more with me.

One second, Melody. Harmony needs my attention for a bit. Just need to fill in these—

"I thought we weren't supposed to use parallel fifths."

A voice interrupted the music. A shadow fell across my desk. The chords in my head shattered, almost audibly. My neck grew hot, and my heart leaped into my throat.

Victor stood at my desk, his gaze fastened on my paper. My notes. My melody. My harmony.

I flung my arm across the composition. Had the lunch bell already rung? It must have, since the other students were gathering their things and heading toward the door.

How long had he been standing there? How much had he seen?

"That's some incredible voice leading, though." He seemed undaunted. He slid into the desk next to mine, his eyes fixed on the spot my arm hadn't covered. He kept his volume low. "I love what you're doing in the alto line. That E-flat major chord . . . it's beautiful."

"Oh, it's just . . . this is . . . it's nothing."

"It's not nothing." Victor reached over and touched my paper. *Touched* it.

My grip tightened. "Please don't touch that."

Victor's long, slender fingers slid off my paper and I could breathe again, but he didn't angle away. He was so close I could feel the warmth of his body. Smell whatever aftershave he used. It was strong—all scents were—but not unpleasant.

"Is this part of our assignment?" He grinned at me. "Because if that's the case, then I really screwed mine up."

The grin disarmed me. Teased out one of my own. "No, this isn't . . . it's not . . ."

"Wait, is that your own work? Something original?"

My face flamed. I really, really didn't like talking about my music with anyone. Especially not anyone at school.

"It's not your business."

He leaned in closer and darted his gaze around the room. When he spoke, his voice was lower. Almost whispery.

"I apologize if I came on too strong, Iris. I only asked because"—he palmed the back of his neck—"I compose too."

I laughed. Just a little bark of laughter and probably a rude one, but he deserved it for invading my space like that. For looking at my work.

"I'm serious." His eyes turned earnest. Pleading, almost. It did strange things to my insides. "I write music all the time. Whenever I get the chance. You should see what I scribbled across the top of our last math assignment." That grin again.

"What kind of music do you write?" He was probably another wannabe Paul Simon type.

"Choir music."

I jerked back. Studied his face. Was he making fun of me? He didn't seem to be teasing me, but I'd misread situations like this before.

"I don't tell anyone because I don't expect anyone to get it. I don't expect anyone else—at least, not anyone here at school—to understand how it feels when music just wells up inside and there's no way to get it down on paper. I don't think most other people understand sitting at the piano for hours, plunking note after note until I finally get the combination that's been swimming around in my head. I don't think anyone else knows what it feels like to put pencil to paper and write it down and try to play it and realize that it's finally exactly what you wanted it to be, and that sense of satisfaction that something you created—something you *composed*—is out there in the world. I've never met anyone else who understands that. Until today."

He tilted his head and met my gaze. His eyes were a mesmerizing mix of green and brown. "I've never met another composer before, Iris."

I'd never liked my name. Not really. I didn't know why my parents picked it. There was nothing special about an iris. It was just a floppy purple flower that only bloomed a few weeks a year.

But when Victor said my name, it sounded like music.

It was too much. I had to look away. "I don't know that I'd call myself a composer."

"You write music, don't you?"

"Well, yeah, but I'm not Bach or Beethoven. Or even Paul Simon."

"You like Paul Simon?" A grin shone through in his voice. "Because I *love* Paul Simon."

"Yeah." I smiled. I couldn't stop it even if I wanted to. "I do."

"Well, groovy, then."

My insides did that strange thing again.

"But don't sell yourself short, Iris. From what I saw, I'd say you're a pretty good composer yourself."

I studied my desk, the staff paper fuzzy through my lashes. "Thanks."

"Hey." Victor cleared his throat. "I might be doing this all wrong, because I've never done it before . . ."

I looked up. "Done what?"

"Asked a girl to join me at Sammy's after school for a soda." Hope shimmered in his eyes.

A soda. At Sammy's. "I've . . . never been invited to Sammy's after school before . . . so I guess there's no way for me to know whether you did it wrong or not."

Victor chuckled. "Yeah, guess not."

An awkward pause. He blinked at me. Oh. Wait. I never actually answered his question.

"Oh. I mean, yeah. Yeah, I'll go with you." I blushed again. "I guess neither one of us is very good at this."

"Then we can figure it out together." He stood and tapped my desk with his fingertips. "Meet you right here after the last bell, then?"

"Sure. Yeah. The last bell."

"See ya then." And he walked off to his own desk.

My head spun, my heart pounded. What had just happened? Had I just been asked out on a date?

I'd never been on a date before. But I'd never met another composer before either.

More notes swelled in my heart, and I picked up my pencil and put it back to the page with a smile on my face.

Today seemed like a wonderful day for new beginnings.

CHAPTER EIGHT

CALLUM SANK onto his sofa with a sigh that came from somewhere deep in his bones. Finally, *finally*, the first week of school had ended and he could clear his mind of all things Peterson High. No five thirty alarm tomorrow morning. No hordes of truculent teenagers. No prickly pianist and her perpetually arched eyebrow. Just blissful solitude.

Well, not quite blissful. Not yet. Right now he was exhausted to the point of numbness. The spring poking through the cheap fabric of his secondhand sofa and into his right thigh barely even registered as he reached for the remote and pointed it at the TV. Nothing sounded better right now than a deliciously awful movie. Bad CGI sharks would be ideal. Bonus if it involved a helicopter crash. In fact, maybe he—

His phone buzzed on the table beside him, and Callum's stomach did a nosedive. Probably Ralph again. His agent had been calling and texting since Wednesday, and Callum hadn't had the heart to answer. Ralph Winters symbolized his old life. His creative life, where both music and money flowed and everything was as it should be. Ralph's repeated attempts at communication were yet another reminder of how the mighty had fallen.

The buzzing wouldn't let up, though, and finally Callum glanced through the slew of texts. Yep. Ralph.

> Callum, I need to talk to you. Call me.

> Or don't. Text. Email. Smoke signals. Whatever.

> This is serious. I don't just want you to call me back because I miss the melodious sound of your voice.

> Okay, fine, I DO miss the melodious sound of your voice. BUT ALSO.

> CALLUM GAMALIEL KNIGHT THIS IS A LITERAL EMERGENCY. WITH BLOOD AND EVERYTHING.

As Callum stared at the screen, another message popped up.

> Yes, I know I middle-named you, but that is how DIRE this emergency is and you need to CALL ME RIGHT NOW because obviously you've got your phone in your hand and nothing else to do.

> DID I MENTION THE BLOOD?

Callum sighed again. Might as well rip off the Band-Aid and get this over with so he could get back to his scintillating evening plans with the sharks.

Ralph answered partway through the first ring. "I knew the blood bit would get you."

"It was actually the Gamaliel part," Callum replied. "Not that it was wise to share that information with you."

"On the contrary, my friend, it was brilliant."

"I hate you."

"You love me." A cheer arose in the background.

Callum frowned. "Wait, are you at Fenway right now? Please tell me you're not at Fenway."

"I am indeed at Fenway. Where you'd be too, if you hadn't abandoned ship and moved to the middle of nowhere."

Callum rolled his eyes. "I'm already in agony, Ralph. Don't make me hate you even more."

"Job not treating you so well?"

Callum sank back, another spring poking him in the left side of his ribs. *Lord, haste the day when my budget allows for real furniture again.* "It's fine. It's just . . . it's a lot."

"Trading Red Sox season tickets for a passel of small-town Illinois teenagers?" Ralph made a shuddering noise through the phone. "I can't imagine."

"You know I had no choice."

"Listen." The background noise dulled. Ralph must've escaped into the relative quiet of the concourse.

If Callum closed his eyes, he could almost smell the Tasty Burger.

"I'm not calling as your agent right now. I'm calling as your friend."

Callum let out a chuckle. "Yeah, right. It's a middle-name, claims-of-actual-blood emergency because you're checking on me as a friend?"

"Okay, you got me. I'm mostly checking to see how your creative block is progressing—or not progressing. Because I have a possible commission for you. The University of Illinois Chamber Singers, of all things."

Callum suppressed a groan. "Yes, I'm still blocked."

"A temporary inconvenience. Taking this will resurrect your career. You know that."

He sprang from the sofa. "A career I no longer have. *You* know *that.* I'm not in Peterson, Illinois, teaching high school choir for fun. I'm doing it because I haven't been able to write a note since Rayne died."

"You know it wasn't your fault, Callum." Ralph's lowered tone contrasted with another cheer from the Fenway faithful. "You couldn't have saved her."

Memories surfaced. Memories of raven-hued hair and winter-white skin. Of music and bliss and the feeling that everything in his life was going exactly as it should. Memories of everything before. Before the pandemic. Before Rayne's medication regimen failed. Before her disease convinced her she couldn't go on.

"I know." Callum leaned against the doorjamb, the grief seeming as fresh as it had five years ago. "In my head, at least, I know. But in my heart, I think if I'd just been a little better to her, if I hadn't been so self-absorbed, if I'd tried a little harder, loved her a little more—"

"No one loved Rayne Driscoll more than you did." Ralph's voice was sharp. "Literally no one."

"But it still wasn't enough. And now she's gone, and I've got nothing left. I *am* nothing."

"You're not nothing, Callum. You're a teacher now! Molding young lives and shaping destinies and whatnot."

Callum rolled his eyes skyward. "Not sure how well I'm doing at that either."

"Do you have them singing?" Another cheer. Louder this time. Sox must've scored a run.

"Yes." If it could be called that.

"Then you're doing all that can be asked of you."

His left fist clenched. "Not *all*, Ralph. I'm still not composing."

"Are you trying?"

"Sometimes, yes. Sometimes I stay up all night trying." He palmed the back of his neck, avoiding the brown upright piano on the opposite side of the small living room. "Sometimes I sit and just stare at the wall. And sometimes I plunk at the piano, but all I can think about is how much I've failed."

"You haven't failed. You're just in a rough patch."

"Do rough patches last five years?"

Ralph fell silent for a moment. "In your case, I think they do."

Callum pushed himself off the wall. "Then why are you calling me about this commission when you know I can't do it?"

"Because I believe in you, Callum. I wouldn't still be your agent if I didn't."

"You're my friend. You're required to be my agent."

"Correction." Callum could picture Ralph's raised index finger and no-nonsense expression. "I'm required to be your *friend*. Because you have photographic evidence of me making questionable decisions at the tenor-bass Christmas party in 2009."

That drew a genuine laugh from Callum.

"But I am *not* required to be your agent." The half-step modulation of the ballpark organ punctuated Ralph's declaration. "If I didn't think you could hack it anymore, I'd have dropped you like a hot potato. There's a line out the door of composers clamoring for me to represent them. I'm a busy man."

Callum grinned. "Then why are you futzing around with me?"

"Because you're not done yet. The fact that you're still getting offers for commissions is proof. God hasn't changed his calling on your life. I know you're in a rough patch with him right now too, but you'll get through that one as surely as you'll get through this one. Try to relax, Callum. I guarantee inspiration will strike. You're too talented for it not to."

Callum let out a sigh. "I wish I had your confidence."

"Ehh, that's what I get the big bucks for."

"So what did you tell our esteemed colleagues at Illinois?" Callum was almost afraid to ask.

"I told them you were booked solid—not an untruth, since you're in the trenches with teenagers now—and that I'd have to feel you out on it."

The fist around his gut loosed. "Is there a deadline?"

"Not a solid one, no. But if it's a definite no from you, then I'll need to tell them soon."

"Noted."

Another cheer from the ballpark. Louder this time. The Sox must be having a good night.

"You'll get there, my friend," Ralph said. "I have faith."

"I'm sure glad *you* do."

"God will give you an idea, Callum. Mark my words." Were Ralph here in person, he'd have whipped out his ever-present ballpoint pen and started to tap Callum gently—or not-so-gently—on the forehead with it. "And when he does, it will be my solemn duty as your agent— and your friend—to respond with a big fat 'I told you so.'"

Callum chuckled. "I'd expect nothing less."

The trademark so-mi chime sounded as Blair tugged open the door to her father's Dodge dealership, and the smell of homemade chocolate chip cookies and the sound of classical piano music over the sound system made her feel at home. In truth, she was at home—her home away from home, since growing up she'd spent nearly as much time here at Emerson Dodge as she had at her own house. Her childhood was filled with fond memories of sitting behind the wheel of shiny new cars on the showroom floor, swiping cookies from the plate on the counter when she didn't think anyone was looking, and drawing pictures at her father's big oak desk while he chatted up a customer.

Balancing the two cups of coffee she'd just bought from the shop down the street, she snagged a cookie—*ooh, still warm*—and smiled her greeting to Becky, the face of Emerson Dodge's customer service desk for as long as Blair could remember. Then she headed toward the tall silver-haired man talking with one of the sales associates at the center of the room.

Mike Emerson smiled when he saw his daughter, politely excused himself from the conversation, and pressed a kiss to Blair's cheek. "Well, this is a nice surprise."

She handed him one of the coffee cups. "Hope this is too."

Dad grinned. "You know the coffee here is free."

"And *you* know that a snickerdoodle latte from Teddy's is not the same as Folgers drip."

"That it most certainly is not, for which I thank you." Dad took an appreciative sip, then motioned down the hallway toward his office. "How ya been, pumpkin? How's life with the latest new choir director?"

"Well, I think this one might actually know what he's doing."

"Oh? Think he'll stick around long enough for me to learn his name?"

Blair gave a snort. "Hardly. He's already announced he's leaving after this year."

"Already? Wow."

"Yeah. He's apparently some hotshot composer from Boston who's creatively blocked and can't fulfill his commissions. Teaching is his fallback plan, and he's made it explicitly clear that he's only here for the money—such as it is—and to buy himself time to get his muse back. Pretty sure he's already booked a moving truck for Memorial Day weekend."

"That's unfortunate." Dad pushed open the door to his office, and Blair stepped in, relishing the scene that hadn't changed since her childhood. The collection of coffee mugs with snarky sayings emblazoned across them. The framed childhood photos of a gap-toothed Blair and her two gangly brothers. The rubber figurine of Figment, a souvenir from a trip to Epcot Center. The "Goa Way" desk sign and "Welcome... ish" floor mat. In a world of constant change, at least some things stayed the same.

Dad settled into his big leather desk chair, and Blair sank onto a chair on the opposite side.

"Are he and the kids getting along okay?" he asked.

"They are now that I had a talk with him. He's used to professionals, not kids."

"Hmm." Dad took a sip of coffee. "Do they like him, at least?"

"Against their better judgment, some of them are starting to."

Dad studied her through his silver-rimmed glasses. "And what about you? Do you like him?"

"Doesn't matter, Dad. He's gone in eight months."

She sipped her coffee, and when she glanced up, Dad was still studying her in that all-knowing way of his. "What?"

Dad paused. "Blair, sweetheart, you know I love you. But you've got to stop holding what Derek did against every man you meet."

Blair arched a brow. "You make it sound like cheating on me a month before the wedding is the same level of mistake as playing a wrong note."

"It was far more than a wrong note. I know he broke your heart, and it took everything in me not to tell him just exactly what I thought of that." Dad leaned forward in his chair, his blue eyes rich with compassion. "But what I'm afraid of is that if you keep clinging to all this anger and bitterness, your heart will stay broken. And that's not what I want for you. That's not what God wants for you."

Blair shut her eyes against her memories. "Then maybe God should've stopped Derek before he hopped into bed with Marguerite."

Dad sighed, a signal that he'd let it drop—for now—and patted the back of her hand. "Just know I'm still praying for you. So's your mom."

Blair nodded, the memories fading. "I know. Thank you." She took another sip of maple-cinnamon coffee, then sat up in her chair. "Hey, not to change the subject, but you're the local history expert. Does the name Iris Wallingford mean anything to you?"

Dad pursed his lips, then realization seemed to dawn. "Wasn't she the Peterson senior who died a couple months before graduation? Late sixties?"

"Spring of seventy."

Dad nodded. "She was before my time, but I do remember hearing about her. Why?"

"We found an unfinished composition mixed in with some music in the choir library, and we think it might be hers."

"That'd make sense. From what I heard growing up, Iris was an incredible musician." His eyes sparked. "Did you ask Vic about her? They'd have been in school about the same time."

Blair nodded. "Callum did, but Vic doesn't remember her."

"Mmm." Dad lifted his coffee cup. "Well, I love nothing more than a research project. I can ask around at the next alumni association meeting, if you're curious."

"We are." Blair paused. "Well, Callum is, anyway."

Dad's graying brows lifted. "Callum's the new director, I take it?"

Blair nodded. "He and I were both blown away by the quality of the writing. It's really good, Dad. We thought maybe it was Vic's, but the style isn't quite the same. So yeah, I guess we're both curious."

"Music to my ears, Blair." Dad lifted his coffee cup in a silent toast. "I'll let you know what I find out."

CHAPTER NINE

September 1969

"*I*S THIS okay?"

Victor motioned to a corner booth at Sammy's, opposite the juke-box. Thoughtfully far away from the noisy pinball machines near the entrance and the accompanying crowd of students. The little café was busy, sure, but far less so at the booth Victor selected.

Yes. The word rose from my heart but lodged in my throat. Because next to that cozy little corner booth, with its red leather seats and Formica tabletop and stained-glass overhead lamp casting a pool of light in the center, and Victor standing there pointing to it . . . suddenly it felt very much like a date. Or at least what I'd always imagined a date might feel like.

Victor stared at me, still waiting for me to answer, but I still couldn't talk, because I didn't know if he was asking my approval of the booth or the whole thing—this date thing. If, in fact, it was a date.

Either way, though, it was okay. So was the booth.

Words still stuck in my throat, I nodded, and he slid into the farthest seat, his eyes alight and his smile wider.

I made that smile wider. I made those eyes light up.

What a powerful feeling.

"You hungry?" He grabbed two menus from the little holder near the napkin dispenser and handed one of them to me.

Was I? Normally after school I was half starved, but at that moment so many winged insects zoomed around in my stomach that I wasn't sure there'd be room for even a bite of food. But Sammy's fries were always delicious.

"I like their fries." Oh, thank you, God. Finally. Words.

Victor smiled again. "Me too." Then he just kept smiling. And he didn't look back at the menu. Nope. His eyes were fixed on me. Why? Did I have something on my face? Did I still have some lunch stuck in my teeth? I'd forgotten to check when I used the restroom earlier.

"What?" Another word popped out.

Victor's gaze traveled over my face. "The way the sun's hitting your face right now . . . You have the most incredible blue eyes. And freckles."

Heat rushed to my cheeks, and I covered my nose with my hand. Freckles. I'd always hated them. When I was little, I used to scrub with a washcloth until my face turned red, thinking if I just washed enough, they'd come off. Alas and alack, they never did. But the way light danced in Victor's eyes and a hint of pink shone in his cheeks as he watched me, maybe that wasn't such a bad thing.

"Oh, don't cover them up, Iris," he said. "I think they're cute."

I think you're *cute.* I wanted to say that, because he really was, in a nerdy kind of way. But of course I couldn't. The words stuck in my throat again. I could only stare at him and feel awkward. But . . . not *bad* awkward, like I normally felt. No, this . . . this was the most beautiful, most delicious kind of awkward. Uncomfortable . . . and yet not. All at the same time.

"What kind of drink do you like?" Victor peered at the menu. "Coke? Root beer? Lemonade?"

"Coke." Another word!

"The lady speaks!" Victor used a false British accent, one that drew a giggle from me. "And I like Coke with my fries too." Then he ditched the accent, sounding once again like any other guy from central Illinois. "I'm beginning to think you and I have quite a lot in common, Iris Wallingford."

"I think so too." The voice that came from my lips was quiet, but the voice inside my head was loud. Buzzing almost. Buzzing with thoughts and ideas and plans and dreams and music. So much music. The next line of the melody, in fact.

Oh. Melody. Hello again.

I jerked to my right, where my bag sat next to me. I yanked my notebook of staff paper out and found a pencil. Victor was saying something, but I could barely hear him over the choir in my head.

The melody poured from my head down my arm and into my fingers and into that little stick of yellow wood and gray graphite. Seemingly encouraged by the fact that I'd found a way to write it down, Melody sped up the pace of her ideas. If I squinted, I could almost see smoke coming from the pencil lead as I frantically scribbled. My arm muscles tightened, and my fingers turned white and almost cramped. Would I even be able to read this later? I didn't know, but I still couldn't stop until Melody did, and then she stopped, and oh thank *goodness.*

My muscles relaxed. I set the pencil down. The music in my head faded, replaced by some Beatles tune coming from the jukebox.

"Whoa." Victor stared at me, eyes wide through his glasses. "Did I just give you an idea?"

I was still breathing fast from my efforts to get the melody on paper. "I dunno. Maybe."

Victor's gaze fell to the table, adorably shy. "Can I see it?"

"Sure." I slid the paper across to him and watched his face as he studied it. I'd never cared what anyone else thought of my music before . . . but I'd also never shown it to anyone before. And now that I was showing it to Victor, I suddenly cared.

I cared desperately.

He looked at it for a long time—too long—then blew out a breath and turned his gaze to me. "Wow. Iris. This is . . . this is brilliant."

A smile sprang to my lips. "Thank you."

"And you had this idea? Just now?" He leaned in closer, which brought another wave of that comfortably uncomfortable feeling.

I nodded.

He shook his head and pushed the paper across the table toward me. "You amaze me, Iris. I've never met anyone else who can do that."

My gaze fell to the scribbled-out melody beneath my hand. "It's not much. Not yet. Just a melody."

"Melodies are the hardest part," Victor said. "At least for me."

"For me the hard part is knowing what to put underneath the melody," I replied. "Like, I hear the harmonies, but I can't quite figure out exactly what notes they are. It's a lot of trial and error."

Victor nodded in understanding. "Harmony can be tricky. I'm not great at it myself yet, but I do play some piano, and that helps. And what we're learning in theory class, that'll help too." He craned his neck toward my composition again, and a long finger pointed toward the sixth measure. "But like, right here. What if the harmony did something like this?" He hummed a few notes. "Is that close to what you're hearing, Iris?"

I tilted my head, comparing his version with the version racing through my mind. "Sorta. It's more like this." I hummed my own version. It wasn't quite perfect yet, and my voice didn't sound great, but hopefully he wouldn't judge.

"Ohhhh. Okay, yeah, you're thinking an augmented sixth chord there."

My eyes jerked open. "A what?"

"You'll learn about it in theory class. I took a peek at the textbook, though, so if you want to read ahead, it's in there. But it's basically this." He picked up the pencil I'd discarded and made a few marks beneath the measure.

Did he really just do that? Did he really mark on my composition?

Part of me felt violated. But this was the first real-life composer I'd ever met, and I didn't want to scare him away.

"There." He shoved the paper back at me, his sketched-out chord structure faint beneath my frantically scribbled melody. "See?"

"Huh." I heard the notes in my head. Imagined what the harmony would sound like . . . "Yes, that's it. That's it exactly." Somehow he'd managed to capture the notes in my head and put them on that paper. "An augmented sixth. Thank you."

"An augmented sixth." Victor's gaze drifted to his right, and he issued a low chuckle.

A basket of fries perched on the edge of our table. When did they get here? How had I not noticed? Our Cokes had arrived too. Quite a while ago, if the drops of condensation on the outside of the glasses were any indication.

Suddenly I realized how hungry I was, and I reached for a fry. Victor did the same, and our fingertips brushed in the basket.

"Cheers." He raised his fry to me, a grin on his lips. Giggling, I bumped my fry up against his, and we took a bite together.

It was cold. Sammy's famous piping-hot fries had gone stone-cold.

Our eyes met and we laughed, our mouths full of cold, mushy potato.

"Well, I can't say this has ever happened to me before, Iris." The laughter shimmered in his voice, beautiful music in its own right.

"What? Getting so wrapped up in a conversation you didn't notice your fries?" I laughed again. "That's an awfully specific situation, Victor. I'd be surprised if it ever *had* happened to you before."

His laughter chimed with mine, a rich harmony. "You're a funny girl, Iris. I think I'm really going to enjoy getting to know you."

Then he reached across the table and laid his hand on top of mine. I flinched at first, because I didn't normally like to be touched. But then I relaxed.

Because Victor's touch was like nothing I'd ever felt before.

For the first time ever, I felt like maybe, just maybe, another human being understood me.

And that just might have been the best feeling in the whole wide world.

CHAPTER TEN

*B*LAIR LEANED back in her office chair, plastic container of salad in hand. Usually she ate lunch in Joy's office, but Joy had dashed out the door right after fourth hour, bound for the grade school with a box of Benadryl to bail out her oldest son, Graham. His allergies were always awful in late summer.

Forking up a bite of kale and pumpkin seeds, Blair reached for the gold-embossed blue leather yearbook. A storage closet at the back of the journalism classroom contained a treasure trove of yearbooks dating back to 1924, but she hadn't needed to go back that far.

Just to 1970.

Over the last few days, Blair had reached out to a handful of alumni, but all her inquiries about Iris met the same brick wall. *Iris Wallingford? Sure, I remember her. She was quiet, though. Kept to herself. I didn't really know her. I don't think anyone did.*

And Norman Gilbert, the man who'd been at the helm of the choirs during Iris's time in high school, had unfortunately passed away in 2019.

So here she was with the yearbook, hoping that a name might leap from the page as a possible new lead.

Setting her salad aside, Blair opened the front cover. A large black-and-white photo of a teenage girl stared up at her.

In loving memory of our friend and classmate Iris Jean Wallingford. We love you, Iris. Fly high.

It was *her.*

Short, shiny dark hair.

Dreamy light eyes.

A sleeveless, high-necked blouse and delicate necklace.

She appeared to be looking past the camera, almost as though seeing a faraway future.

A future that had been denied.

The office door creaked open, and Callum gave his usual grunt of greeting as he moved past her toward the minifridge and rooted around inside. Then the microwave door opened and shut, followed by three beeps and its annoyingly loud whir.

Okay, the fridge was community property. Vic had brought it in years ago after his daughter moved from dorm to apartment. But the microwave was *hers*. And Callum had probably been using it the whole time, that fink.

Irritation rising, she turned to snipe at him, but the words died in her throat when she saw him. He sat at his desk, hunched over his iPad. His left hand plunged deep into his mass of coffee-colored hair while his right traced a beat pattern. Was that . . . Yes. That tricky passage of "Dies Irae," the one with the random bars of five-four, where the sopranos always came in late. He beat a few bars, then stopped. Did it again. And again. Changed a gesture and cued his imaginary soprano section with a bit more crispness. He broke off. Shook his head. Practiced the pattern again.

Hmm. For all his blustery arrogance, he certainly seemed to care about the precision and clarity of his conducting gestures.

Quite a lot, if the bags beneath his eyes were any indication. He must still not be sleeping well. And the slump of his shoulders . . . He looked like he bore the weight of the world on those shoulders. He'd shed his tweed coat, and his light-blue dress shirt highlighted his broad, muscled shoulders. The sweep of strength in his upper back.

The microwave beeped, a necessary jolt from a most unwelcome—though annoyingly not unpleasant—reverie. Had she truly been admiring Callum's back? His shoulders? She shuddered. Thank God Joy wasn't anywhere nearby. She'd never let Blair hear the end of it.

Another series of beeps from the microwave set her teeth on edge, but Callum made no move to retrieve his lunch. He was still hunched over his screen. Still conducting an imaginary choir.

When the microwave beeped yet again, Blair rose, opened the door, and slid the plastic tray from the warm interior. Some sort of single-guy microwave pasta dish, no doubt chock-full of sodium and chemicals and smothered in something that may have, at one time, been actual tomatoes. She shut the door and placed the tray of pasta on Callum's desk, near his left elbow.

He glanced up, the expression in his forest-green eyes a mixture of surprise and gratitude, along with a tiny bit of embarrassment.

"Sorry." He slid his iPad to the side and replaced it with the tray of pasta. "I must've zoned out for a bit. Apologies if I hogged the microwave."

Sitting back down at her desk, she gestured toward her salad. "No need. But I appreciate it all the same."

She reached for the yearbook again.

Callum's chair gave a squeak. "Last year's yearbook has you sucked in too, I take it?"

"What?" Oh. Right. Yearbooks had been distributed yesterday morning, and getting the kids to focus on anything but those had been an uphill battle. "No, this one's from 1970. Iris Wallingford's senior year."

"I see." Pasta in hand, he rolled his chair closer. "Anything good?"

"Well . . ." Rolling her own chair, she met him halfway and showed him the picture at the front of the yearbook. "Callum, meet Iris."

He took the book from her, and a subtle whiff of cologne cut through the fake-marinara smell. A not-unpleasant whiff either.

In fact, it was . . . *quite* pleasant.

Ugh.

Callum's hair fell across his forehead as he studied the picture, and suddenly she couldn't look away. Cheekbones shadowed by the office's soft lamplight. A defined jaw shrouded in a hint of dark stubble. And those shoulders . . .

Crap.

Joy was right. Callum Knight *was* handsome.

What a revolting development.

Callum chuckled, low and in his throat, and Blair startled. Had he caught her staring? Did he know her thoughts? He probably did, that eel, and now he knew she—

Oh. His eyes were focused on the yearbook. Good.

"That's Vic?" he said around the baritone melody of his laughter. "My word. I had no idea what he looked like in high school."

"Let me see." Blair leaned in closer, a second whiff of Callum's cologne doing nothing for her concentration.

But the sight of Victor Nelson as a high school senior caused her to erupt in her own giggles. Heavy, dark-blond hair combed over his forehead, Beatles-style. Thick black plastic glasses. And a smile not unlike Sheldon Cooper's Joker-like grin in *The Big Bang Theory*. "Wow. Just . . . wow."

"At least we know the man didn't peak in high school," Callum said. "That's comforting."

"Right?" Blair chuckled her agreement. "Never peak in high school."

Their eyes met then, and their laughter died. Something hovered in the pasta-scented air between them. Something warm and wonderful, yet also alarming. Callum looked as uncomfortable as she felt.

Were they . . . having a moment?

He broke eye contact first and handed the yearbook back. "Thank you, Blair. I needed that laugh."

"You're welcome." She turned back toward her desk, gulping a bite of salad and turning another page in the yearbook. Iris should provide a needed distraction.

Except . . . huh. This was Vic's *senior* picture. In 1970.

Had he and Iris really graduated the same year? With both of them being involved in music and in the same hundred-member graduating class . . . no way did he not know her.

So why would he claim otherwise? She turned another page in the yearbook and froze.

Because front and center on the marching band page, feathered band uniform hats pressed together, mugging for the camera, were Iris Wallingford and Victor Nelson.

"Callum?"

"Mmm?" He sounded distracted. Must've gone down the "Dies Irae" rabbit hole again.

"Didn't you say Vic told you he didn't know Iris?"

Callum glanced up from his iPad and met her gaze. "Yeah. Why?"

She held the yearbook out to him, and he took it from her. "Because I don't think that's entirely accurate."

Callum stared at the picture, then looked back up at her, eyes wide. "Nope. Not accurate at all."

The lunch bell rang then, and they both jumped. Was their break really over? How had time evaporated so quickly?

Callum handed the yearbook back, then shoved an unseemly amount of microwaved pasta into his mouth, picked up his iPad, and headed out to the choir room. She turned back to her desk, set the yearbook aside, and wolfed down the rest of lunch, her mind in overdrive.

Vic Nelson had always been above reproach in all he did. She'd never known him to lie about anything. So why would he tell them he hadn't known Iris, when that yearbook photo seemed to prove otherwise?

Maybe the yearbook photographer had been roaming the sidelines and decided to snap a picture of the marching band. One of those random "Okay, folks, grab the person next to you and say cheese" sort of situations.

Or perhaps the years were catching up to Vic, poking a few holes in his legendary memory.

Blair grabbed the thick blue music binder off the corner of her desk as the final bell rang.

There had to be an innocent explanation. Had to be.

Any other possibility simply wouldn't be worth entertaining.

"No, no, it's not 'haaaaal-le-lu-*juh*.'" Callum drawled an exaggerated short A sound on the first syllable and all but grunted the final syllable. "It's hah-le-lu-JAH." Opening his mouth wide and dropping his jaw practically to his sternum, he placed his hands on the sides of his face. "Drop your jaw."

Normally his exaggerated accents and fish faces drew a chuckle or two from the kids—or at the very least a few halfhearted grins—but on this day, the Friday before Labor Day weekend? Crickets. In fact, the only sound permeating the dead-quiet choir room was a literal cricket chirp, though whether it came from an actual insect or just someone's phone, he couldn't be certain.

"Again," he said. Blair gave the pitches, and he raised his right arm and cued the choir. Better, but only marginally. Still, this close to a long weekend, it was about as good as he could expect.

The bell rang as he cut them off, and Callum slumped onto his stool, relief coursing through him. A three-day weekend. Three whole days away from this place. The very idea sounded like heaven itself. His Netflix queue was stocked and ready to go, and the DoorDash gift card his mother had sent him was fully loaded. With any luck at all, maybe he'd even sleep.

Not that luck had been on his side lately.

"Take care of each other and yourselves. And don't be idiots," he called in farewell to the eager teens shouldering backpacks and streaming toward the door. His own high school choir director's weekend sign-off sounded odd coming out of his mouth rather than Mrs. Bailey's. Not that any of the kids heard him. In their minds Callum had ceased to exist.

Blair had made her way from the piano bench to the door, her dimpled smile wishing them all a happy weekend. "Have a great weekend, Miss Emerson," several of them said, and a few even hugged her. She seemed to soak in their attention, her cheeks creasing and her eyes crinkling, her affection and enthusiasm warm and genuine.

Unexpected envy pricked his spirit at how much the kids seemed to love Blair. And why shouldn't they? Through all the chaos and constant upheaval, she'd stayed. A needed source of continuity in the choir department and the one person the kids could count on to always be there.

That bond was probably for the best, as Callum wouldn't be here any longer than anyone else who'd tried to fill Vic Nelson's sizable shoes. The minute he got his life back together, he'd hightail it back to Boston where he belonged. He wasn't part of the Peterson choir family, nor would he ever be.

But in this moment of temporary insanity and exhaustion beyond belief, he wished he were.

A bittersweet ache bloomed in the center of his chest as he gathered his iPad and baton from the black metal music stand. But then the ache morphed into sound. A snatch of melody sung in the soprano register.

He froze, breath suspended, heart beating a staccato counterpoint, baton clutched in his shaking hand.

Music.

Music had come to him.

An effortless fragment of melody—not like those in recent years that surfaced only after hours of work and never amounted to anything. No, this was like the ones *before*. Those that sprang to him unbidden, fully formed, fluttering in from somewhere outside himself. He never knew where they came from—only that when they did, they usually blossomed into something beautiful.

And this one came while watching Blair.

She still hovered near the door, making small talk with an earnest, nerdy-looking freshman tenor, and the melody expanded. Lengthened. Spun its gossamer strands around his heart.

Slowly, as though approaching a timid baby deer, he moved toward the piano. Set his iPad and baton to the side and found the ebony and ivory notes that matched the ones in his head. Yes. There. That.

Blindly he reached for his iPad and turned on the voice memo app. Played the theme through a couple of times. And what if it did this? What if he went here? What if he added a harmony?

Yes. Yes. *Yes.* It was *happening.* A song was taking shape in his brain.

He was composing again.

Bitter experience stifled his enthusiasm. It had been five years since he'd finished anything, and this might end up doomed to the same fate. But how long had it been since he'd had even this much of an idea? How long had it been since he'd had something new to play around with? Something to color this way and that, something to explore, to—

"What's that?"

His inspiration became his distraction. Blair stood in the crook of the piano, reaching up to free her hair from its large tortoise claw clip. It tumbled over her shoulders, and with it more notes tumbled, unbidden and unconscious, from his fingers. Thank God he'd thought to record this.

He'd never thought of Blair as pretty before—never thought of her as much of anything, really, except a pain in his rear end. But right now, even with her arched brow and sharp, quizzical expression, she was one of the most beautiful sights he'd ever laid eyes on. Because—whether he liked her or not—she was the source of the first good idea he'd had in God alone knew how long.

"I don't know," he replied. "It might not be anything."

"Hmm." She watched him for a second, her expression indecipherable, then retreated to the office to gather her things.

And with her movement, with the trace of sweet fragrance in her wake, came more notes. Callum noodled around at the piano, tossing and turning the melody, testing out harmonies, tinkering with it like a child surprised with a new toy. A few minutes later, she emerged from the office, long hair corralled over one shoulder, briefcase, purse, and lunch bag draped over the other, and met his eyes with a weary yet satisfied smile.

He grinned at her. "But . . ."

That arched brow again.

"Then again, it might be something after all."

Was he still talking about the music? Or whatever was happening between the two of them? Because something had shifted. Rotated. His world had just tilted on its axis in a way it hadn't in quite some time. If ever.

He couldn't identify how, exactly. Or what might come of it. All he knew was that it was because of Blair and the snatch of melody she'd inspired, the snatch of melody that meant he would still probably use that DoorDash card tonight but the Netflix queue could wait.

And sleep? Ha. Who needed it?

Had all these thoughts just flashed across his face? They may well have, if Blair's expression was any indication. Her head tilted to the side, her lips quirked in an odd, mystified grin, and the skin beneath her eyes bunched slightly, as though she'd momentarily burst into a full-on sunny smile.

She didn't, though. She just adjusted her grip on her bags and started for the door.

"Have a good weekend, Callum." She tossed the nonchalant farewell over her shoulder as she slipped through the door.

"Right," he replied. "You too. Good weekend."

Thank the Lord his musical abilities were functioning a bit better than his verbal ones.

But having a good weekend? For the first time in ages, that might actually happen.

CHAPTER ELEVEN

October 1969

𝒶 COOL GUST of wind hit my cheeks as the referee blew his whistle to end the second quarter of the football game and announce the beginning of halftime. I was in the line of mellophones, pressed between Jacob Whittaker and Larry Schmidt, who both stood at attention, their gleaming horns positioned perfectly. But beneath their navy-and-white silver-embossed hats, their eyes communicated the pair's usual brand of mischief.

Someone bumped my back with the slide of a trombone. Will Garrison, no doubt.

"Sorry," Will mumbled, and I rolled my eyes.

The crowds, the noise, the funky smell of band uniforms . . . all these made me detest marching season. But it was a required part of the class, so if we wanted to sit onstage wearing elegant black dresses and tuxedos, performing music by real composers instead of bad arrangements of radio drivel, we had to spend the first quarter of the year marching in formation and putting up with the occasional clonk on the head from stray footballs.

But as we took the field tonight, I had at least one glimmer of enjoyment.

Victor.

As drum major, he marched out first onto the white-striped field. He strutted with confidence, leading the parade of majorettes, all flash and fringe and silver batons. Pride swelled in my heart. Victor was such a natural at everything. He never seemed nervous in a crowd. Never robbed of speech around someone he liked. Not the least bit unsure of what he wanted to do after high school. No, Victor's goal was clear: He wanted to become a world-renowned choral director and composer. And his path to achieving that goal was equally clear. Even before high school, he'd set his sights on the Whitehall Conservatory of Music in Chicago. As I watched him, his baton moving up and down with expert precision, his head held high, every movement a concerto of choreographed confidence, I couldn't imagine him not achieving all those dreams and then some.

Men had it easier, of course. Victor's mother hadn't sat him down repeatedly and encouraged him to come out of his shell, to put away his sensitivities and shyness and just *"Smile. Smile, dear, you're so much prettier when you smile. Not like that face you always make. You mustn't look at a man that way, darling, or he'll think you're criticizing him."*

"And what if I am, Mother? What if he's doing or saying something that deserves to be criticized?"

"Iris, you mustn't. Certainly never in public. If you absolutely cannot hold your tongue, then it is imperative that such a conversation take place in private and with the utmost in respect. Otherwise you'll never find a husband."

And what if I didn't care about having a husband?

Of course, I never asked Mother that. Whatever I might want didn't matter. Never mind that women were achieving more than they ever had. Money talked, and most people thought if you came from money, you could do whatever you wanted. But in my case, money was precisely why dreaming about the future was painfully pointless. Why, if Mother had her way, I'd be trapped in a prewritten life, a boring composition with no dissonance, no development, and no hope of improvisation.

No hope of improvisation now either. It was time for the halftime show.

A few minutes later, it was over, and I made my way back to the band's spot in the stands. A variety of sounds assaulted my ears. The *blaaaaaaattttt* of a trombone. An unnecessarily loud rim shot from one of the snare drum players. The seal-like laughter of Jacob and Larry.

I sighed into my mellophone's mouthpiece and opened the spit valve.

Only four more home games, and then I could leave the Peterson High Marching Patriots behind forevermore.

"Hello, gorgeous."

The deep voice startled me, but in a much more pleasant way than all the previous noises had. Victor stood at my right.

Gorgeous? Not possible. Not in this ridiculous navy-and-white band uniform, complete with a cape, with my face half covered by the chin-strap of my hat, my hair mashed into a frizz bomb underneath.

"Hi." There was so much noise—and my voice so quiet—that Victor probably didn't even hear me.

He removed his hat, his dark-blond hair damp and pressed to his forehead from a slightly-too-tight hatband, and his pale skin flushed, but the smile he aimed at me could've melted ice. He made this dumb, itchy band uniform seem dapper and sophisticated. Like he'd been born to wear it.

He leaned his baton against the front of the bleachers. "Hungry?"

Actually, yes. I'd only gotten half an hour at home before I'd had to get ready for the game, and I'd spent that time working on another melody that wouldn't leave me alone. "Gosh, I—"

"Because I'm starving," Victor declared.

I smiled up at him. "Me too."

"Well then, milady"—Victor gave an exaggerated courtly bow, complete with a flourish of his cape—"would you care to accompany me to the purveyor of concessions?"

Giggling, I set my horn down. "Of course, my liege. I particularly fancy a cylinder of their finest processed beef, grilled to perfection and served piping hot in a nest of freshly baked bread, topped with a pinch of Dijon and an array of chopped pickles."

"That does sound delicious." Victor beamed, pleased that I'd joined in his game. "I have my eye on that as well. It would be even more scrumptious with a side order of potatoes, sliced into strips, salted, and fried to a crisp." He leaned in, brows arching with mischief. "Perhaps they won't go cold this time."

Our eyes met and our laughter increased, the shared moment at Sammy's shimmering in the chilly air between us.

"In fact," he continued, "perhaps later we could—"

"Hey! You two!"

We turned at the sound, and a long-haired kid in a pair of bell-bottoms and a bunch of necklaces aimed a camera at us.

"Smile," he said. "Say cheese. Whatever."

"Sure," Victor replied in his normal voice. "Just let me put my hat back on."

The rest of the band streamed past on the way to the snack stand as Victor replaced his hat and leaned in close. His hat clunked against mine, and his arm found its way around my waist.

His arm.

Was around.

My waist.

Someone was touching me.

Victor was touching me.

And unlike touches from most people, Victor's felt nice. Comfortable. Like I belonged to him.

I slipped my arm around his waist too. And it didn't feel as weird as I thought it would.

He tightened his grip, and that didn't feel weird either.

In fact, it felt . . . good.

"Okay," the photographer said. "One . . . two . . . three!" The camera clicked, and the flashbulb popped. "Far out." His feet crunched against the gravel around the field as he headed toward a cheerleader.

What was I supposed to do now? Spots from the camera flash still danced in front of my eyes, and Victor and I still stood there, smiling at nothing, our arms around each other. But he slid his away, and I did the same.

Phew. Okay. Good. It was over.

Wait, *was* that good? Was I truly glad it was over, or did a large part of me wish it would happen again?

Okay, all of me wished it would happen again. But maybe not at the orders of a half-stoned photographer.

As though summoned by my thoughts, Victor slipped his hand into mine. He still wore his gloves, and so did I, but I could feel the warmth of his skin through the thin layers of white fabric.

We were holding hands. And . . . that felt good too.

"Let's see." Victor no longer sounded like he was from London. "We've been out to Sammy's together. And we've been photographed together. And now we're holding hands."

Curious, I glanced his way. "All of that is true."

"Well then. I think that makes you my girlfriend, Iris Wallingford."

I stared. *Girlfriend.* I'd never been anyone's girlfriend before. The word sounded weird, especially if I thought about it too much. Girl. Friend. Both were true of me, so the combination made sense. But Victor's expression indicated he had a lot more than "friends" on his mind.

I did too. Victor Nelson made me feel like nobody else ever had. Weird and warm and tingly, but not in a bad way.

If I made him feel anything close to that, then I probably was his girlfriend.

My smile made my cheeks ache. "I guess that makes you my boyfriend."

He answered my smile, then led us toward the snack stand. "Brilliant. Talented. Gorgeous in a band uniform."

This made me giggle.

"You amaze me more every single minute."

Once again he'd managed to put my feelings into words.

CHAPTER TWELVE

*B*LAIR LIFTED the lid of the temperamental Xerox machine in the faculty workroom, set the choral octavo on the glass, whispered a silent prayer, and pressed the button to start the copying process. Elaine Hagenberg's "Tyger" contained a couple of beastly page turns, and a well-placed Xerox would ward off potential disaster.

That was, as long as the machine cooperated. But the disapproving beep indicated that today would not be that day.

"Paper jam?" Blair lifted the lid. "Oh, come on." Wiggling the blank paper free from the machine's clutches, she replaced the lid and pressed Start again. Mercifully, the machine whirred to life.

"I'm telling you, iPads will solve all your page-turning problems." Joy bustled into the workroom and tossed an empty can of Diet Dr Pepper into the recycling.

Blair rolled her eyes and slid her fresh, warm copy from the print tray. "Yes, but what if the battery dies in the middle of a performance? What if the Bluetooth pedal screws up and turns too many pages?"

"What if an asteroid crashes into the auditorium while the kids are onstage? There's always something to worry about." Joy turned toward the rows of faculty mailboxes. "Technology is the way to go."

Blair turned to another page in the octavo. "I'll stick with the low-tech solution, thank you very much."

"Suit yourself." The machine whirred, papers rustled, and then Joy let out a groan. "Oh *no*."

"What?"

Joy held up a sparkly silver envelope, her eyes rolling skyward. "I forgot that was this year."

"That's right, darlings." Camilla Lewis, drama teacher and Student Senate sponsor, fluttered in, all fake lashes and dangly earrings and oversized scarf. "It's the fine arts department's year to chaperone fall homecoming."

Blair's heart sank. "So that means . . ."

"And of course I didn't forget about you, Blair." Camilla paused, manicured hand on the refrigerator door. "It's in the choir mailbox, ready and waiting for you."

"What's in the choir mailbox?" This from Callum, coffee mug in hand.

"One of *these* bad boys." Joy jiggled the envelope, and sparkles showered the gray carpet below.

Callum regarded it with an arched eyebrow. "It looks like the aftermath of a glitter-factory explosion."

"Why, *thank* you, my dear." Camilla made her way to the exit, blowing kisses in Callum's direction, and the door clicked shut behind her.

Callum moved toward the mailboxes. "That wasn't meant as a compliment."

Laughing, Blair retrieved "Tyger" from the Xerox machine. "Camilla Lewis is . . . very special."

"That woman's DNA sparkles." Joy stuffed the envelope in with the usual plethora of music catalogs and college recruitment letters that awaited her in her mailbox.

Callum sorted his mail, and more glitter puffed up, making him sneeze. "So I see."

"Welcome to Peterson, Callum." Joy gave an exaggerated courtly bow.

"What is this monstrosity, anyway?" Callum held the missive by one corner, eyeing it with suspicion.

"It is your *invitation*"—Blair framed the word with air quotes—"to chaperone the homecoming dance."

Callum tilted his head. "And I suspect this is an *invitation* I am not allowed to refuse?"

Joy snorted. "Not unless you want Camilla Lewis and her fake eyelashes to be on your case from now until prom."

Callum shuddered. "No, thank you." He turned his attention to the envelope. "Tell me, ladies, what on earth does this involve?"

Blair rolled her eyes. "It involves getting paid an infinitesimal amount to dress to the nines and stand around in a hot, overcrowded gymnasium, listening to endless Taylor Swift songs turned up way too loud while also making sure our lovely students don't grope each other unnecessarily or sneak off to do inappropriate things in inappropriate places."

"With an endorsement like that, how could I possibly say no?" He tucked the envelope in the pocket of his jacket, unleashing another shower of glitter over his shoes, which he regarded with a disgusted expression. "Guess I'd better clear my bustling social calendar." He slipped out of the room.

Blair sighed at the carpet that was significantly sparklier than it had been five minutes ago. "I feel sorry for Henry and the rest of the custodial staff, having to clean all this."

Joy regarded her with an odd smile.

"What?" Blair asked. "Why are you looking at me like that?"

"This could be *fun.*"

"What, chaperoning homecoming?" Blair held the back of her hand to Joy's forehead. "Are you feeling okay?"

"Never better." Joy's grin morphed from slightly odd to full-on Cheshire Cat–like. "Because you'll be at homecoming. And so will he."

"Who?"

"Callum." Her eyebrows wiggled. "In *formal wear.*"

An unwelcome but not unpleasant shiver made its way down Blair's spine. She had yet to see Callum in anything except everyday school clothes, since their first concert wasn't until the week after homecoming. But she had seen his headshot. And if real-life Callum looked anything like that picture . . .

"Well, clearly you don't hate the idea." Joy sounded satisfied with herself.

"I said nothing," Blair protested.

"And you said it very loudly." Joy patted Blair's cheek. "Your cheeks turn the most adorable shade of pink when you're crushing on someone."

"What?" Blair lowered her voice. "I am not *crushing*"—more air quotes—"on him. Or anyone. Other than Hugh Jackman, of course."

Joy peered closer. "Oh. Wait. No. You're not just crushing on Callum. You actually *like* him."

Blair avoided her friend's gaze. "I do not. We work together. That's the extent of it. Besides, he's made it abundantly clear that he's only here this year, and then I have to start over again in August with someone else. Just like always. So there's no point in investing in him."

"Uh-huh. You should wear that bronze dress."

"The one I wore for Luke and Cassi's wedding last year?" Two former students who'd hated each other in high school but found their way into each other's arms in college.

"The one with the lace-up back and the slit? Yes. That one."

"I'm there to chaperone, not compete with high schoolers for who can show the most skin."

"Oh, come on. That dress is tasteful and you know it." Joy grinned. "Practically a nun's habit compared to what some of those girls wear."

"Hence the need for chaperones. And I don't want to look like I'm trying too hard. Or at all. I'll just wear my blue dress."

"That boring navy thing you trot out for everything that doesn't require concert black?" Joy shook her head. "Sweetie, I love you more than life itself, which is why I'm telling you that dress ages you at least ten years."

"So?"

"So it's something you'd wear to a funeral. And Callum Knight will be there."

"Again, so?" Another shiver.

"So I'm almost positive that man absolutely smolders in a tux. And he *knows* it." Joy fixed Blair with an intense expression. "Are you gonna let him outshine you?"

Her competitive urge kicked in. "Good point." She *would* wear that bronze dress. The one she'd almost bypassed as being "too much." Urged by the saleslady and an uncharacteristic impulse, she'd tried it on and had never felt more beautiful in all her life.

"As always." Joy smirked.

Blair shot her friend a halfhearted glare. "I hate that you know me so well."

"Hate it and love it."

Callum retreated to his office. When he dropped into his chair, glitter spilled from his invitation-slash-prison-sentence over the keyboard of his school-issued laptop, still open to the glut of emails about homecoming week.

During his own high school years, homecoming week meant little more than popularity contests he ignored and dances he avoided. It seemed the universe would have the last laugh, though, because now he couldn't avoid homecoming if he tried. Themed spirit days. Pep assemblies that screwed up the schedule and cost him rehearsal time. And Difference Makers Day, whatever that was. He hadn't read the email thoroughly yet. Doubtless still more rehearsal time down the drain, time they couldn't afford to lose with the fall concert rapidly approaching.

Callum gripped a fistful of hair and let out a groan. How had it come to this? What his old self would think of him now. The twentysomething dynamo who'd, given enough coffee, could function fine on four hours of sleep. The one who'd spent his days and nights making a name for himself in the composing world. Who'd had so many ideas he could cheerfully toss them around like preteen pranksters toilet-papering a tree. Who'd even heard one of his works on a Boston-themed Netflix series, which had led to Ralph taking him on as a client. The one who'd planned a future with Rayne and had easily been able to afford the diamond to prove it.

Well. He might not have his conducting career back yet. Might not reassemble the Cambridge Chamber Chorale anytime soon. But at least his composing brain had come back online, at least in part. That idea Blair had inspired was taking shape into an actual piece. Nowhere near finished—not yet—but it was there. Percolating. That alone wouldn't be enough to get him out of Peterson and back to Boston, but it was a start. After five years of wandering in the desert, he'd take that start and run with it.

He tossed the homecoming invitation to the side, where it landed near the yellowed page of staff paper covered with Iris Wallingford's pencil scratches.

Iris. Callum reached for the score, then leaned back in his chair and studied it for what must've been the hundredth time. The girl could've been a legend had she lived. And if she and Vic had known each other, if they'd been able to collaborate on music? Callum ached thinking of what the choral world had missed out on.

But had Vic truly not known her? That seemed to stretch the bounds of credibility. Both talented composers, both in the same graduating class, both residents of the same small town. Plus that yearbook picture and those cheesy grins. How could he *not* have known her?

Maybe Vic's memory really was failing. Shame if that were true. Or maybe discussing Iris was too painful. Callum could certainly relate to that. He'd made progress in his grief, but he still didn't talk about Rayne much. Even if Callum were able to move on someday, to rebuild his career, to eventually love someone else—if such were even possible— Rayne Driscoll would forever be tattooed on his innermost being.

Music bloomed in his heart the way it always used to, and Callum's breath caught. The harmonies moved forward, the melody full of urgency and passion. Exactly what his piece in progress lacked. He set Iris's score back on his desk, next to the to-do list that would have to wait, and wheeled his office chair toward the upright piano. Fumbling for his iPad, he turned the recorder on and set it on the stand, then pounced on the keyboard, his fingers finding the notes surfacing in his mind and heart. No, that wasn't . . . Oh. Yes. There it was. There. And oh, there it went, tumbling down a musical pathway like an overeager dog yanking on a leash. Callum had no choice but to follow and hope his hands could keep up.

The phrase came to a natural end a few moments later, and Callum breathed a sigh of relief, turned off the recorder, and listened back to his musical exploration. He'd have to tinker around with it, see how he could develop it, but the secondary theme he'd needed had finally arrived. He'd nicknamed the first one "Blair," since she'd inspired it. Should he call this one "Rayne"? Had his memories of her caused it to take shape?

No, this didn't sound like anything she'd inspired. Those motives were always ardent and full of yearning, as though his subconscious somehow knew his dreams involving her were doomed to an early death.

This one was full of determination. Hope. Forward motion.

"Moving On." That's what he'd call it. Because he intended to do exactly that. And this rapidly forming piece would begin that journey. His skills were coming back. He might even be able to fulfill that commission for the University of Illinois after all. In fact, this piece might be perfect for it.

He wouldn't call Ralph just yet, though. Not until he knew for sure that his muse had returned.

But for the first time in years, that possibility seemed more than just a pipe dream.

CHAPTER THIRTEEN

November 1969

Y SHOES crunched through a pile of dead brown leaves beneath the tall oak on Sixth Street. Beside me, Victor's shoes crunched in a slightly different rhythm, but not the usual syncopation with mine. Usually we fell into step every fourth beat. Our very own downbeat, as I'd started to think of it. Victor called it a sign of our deep connection. How even our footsteps made their own music.

But today he took a faster tempo. Our steps aligned irregularly. I'd even tried to come up with a mixed-meter pattern for them, but if there was a pattern, I had yet to see it.

And those fast footsteps were the only sound he'd made since he'd picked me up at my house to walk downtown for a soda.

It wasn't unusual for us to be quiet when we were together. A companionable silence, I'd heard it called. But this silence seemed different. Victor's jaw was set, his eyes straight ahead, and his stride so long, so fast, that if I didn't know better, I'd think he was trying to get away from me.

Wait, *was* he? Had I done something to upset him?

I flipped back through the few minutes we'd spent together, but I couldn't come up with anything. Maybe it had nothing to do with me. He'd been in this mood before. Preoccupied, like his mind had ventured to another planet.

Well. He wasn't the only one having a bad day. Mother and I had argued again just before Victor arrived. But Victor's issue was clearly more than a little parental disagreement. I'd learned over the last few weeks to read his moods, how to be just what he needed. In fact, he'd told me several times that I was the only one who truly understood him.

And he understood me too. Sometimes I felt exposed around him, like his gaze was a spotlight and I stood at center stage. Maybe that was just part of being in love. Caring so very much what Victor thought of me. I didn't feel this way around anyone else, that was for certain.

No, best not to bring up my argument with Mother. I didn't want to add to whatever burden Victor carried.

"Victor?" My breath came fast from trying to keep up with him. "Are you okay? You've barely said a word."

He stopped at the entrance to Sammy's, his eyes strangely blank. He looked in my direction, but it didn't feel like he truly saw me. "You haven't heard?"

I frowned. "Heard . . . what?"

He tugged the door open and gestured for me to walk through. "The protests yesterday in Washington. Some say it was the largest anti-war demonstration yet."

Oh. Right. The protests of the war in 'Nam. Anti-war demonstrations had been happening more and more lately. Lots of students had even missed class Friday so they could participate in a protest on campus in Champaign. My parents had talked about it at breakfast this morning, but I had so much music in my head that I'd tuned them out. Not that this was unusual.

"I'd have given anything to be part of it." Victor balled up his fists as we waited for a table. "Because the war is pointless. So many thousands of lives sacrificed, and for what? We have no reason to be there. Nixon promised to pull out the troops when he took office. You know as well as I do, he hasn't done it. Guys leave here to go over there and then come back in boxes. Like Richie Martin."

Victor walked toward our usual booth in the corner, and I followed him. I knew Richie—though not well. He was three years ahead of us, into sports and not much else. But I still remembered the day they brought his casket back to Peterson. All the flags in town and the patriotic ribbons tied around lampposts and porch railings seemed to make a mockery of the prayers that had been offered up on his behalf.

We slid into the booth, and Victor leaned across the table, his gaze intense. "And now there are rumors that Nixon wants to send even more. That he wants to lower the draft age to nineteen."

I glanced up. "But you're not nineteen."

"I turned nineteen in September." He avoided my eyes. "We moved around a lot when I was young, and I had to repeat first grade."

I gulped. I hadn't realized Victor was almost a year and a half older than me. Nor had I realized how dire his situation truly was. "But that doesn't mean you'll automatically get drafted. Not everyone does."

"With my luck, I will be. And that's why I need to get into Whitehall. Why I have to write the piece of a lifetime. But I can't come up with an idea that's good enough."

I placed my hand on top of his. I'd never seen him this agitated. "Even if Whitehall doesn't pan out, surely you have other options. We're not that far from Champaign—doesn't the U of I have good composition professors?"

"I'm sure it does. But it's not an option."

"Why on earth not?"

"Because not everyone has the same advantages you do, Iris." He smacked the table, making the silverware jump. "Not everyone was born with a silver spoon in their mouth."

"What is *that* supposed to mean?" My family had money, sure. But it wasn't like we were the Kennedys or the Bouviers. What was going on with him?

The waitress returned to take our orders, and Victor was all smiles and politeness with her. When she bustled back toward the kitchen, he turned his gaze to me. "I'm sorry, my flower." His voice was sweet as honey, as though his mini-explosion never happened. He laced his fingers in with mine, and his touch was so soft, so tender, that I wondered if it *had* happened. Maybe it hadn't. Maybe I'd overreacted.

"The truth is, my parents can't afford to send me to college. Anywhere. Not even U of I." He glanced around, but nobody was paying any attention to us. "My father has never been able to hold down a job. He drinks. A lot."

The last traces of my irritation melted away. "Oh, Victor. I had no idea." He'd alluded to his family not being as wealthy as mine, though honestly that applied to a fair percentage of families here. But it explained why I'd never been to his house. Why I'd yet to meet his parents.

He reached for his straw wrapper and coiled it around his index finger. "It's not something I share with most people. With . . . anyone, really." His eyes met mine. "But you are where the other half of my soul lives."

I melted into the booth. Utterly melted.

"My mother says my dad was a totally different man before the war. She's spent her entire marriage trying to coax him back to life. Iris, the war changed him. I think the things he saw over there, the things he did . . . I think the man he used to be is gone forever, and he drinks to try to escape the memories." His eyes shone with unshed tears. "And I don't want that to happen to me. You get it, don't you?"

I rose, slid into the booth next to Victor, and took his hand in both of mine. "Of course I do, Victor. Of course I do." My heart ached for him.

"And I'm not an athlete. I'm not popular or on homecoming court or student council or any of the other things a college like Illinois would look at. And the worst part is, as much damage as the war did to my father, he still thinks it's my duty to go if I'm drafted. No one should get out of serving after all this country has done for them. That's what he always says." His voice sounded choked. "So unless I run away to Canada or figure out how to be a conscientious objector, college is my only option. And since Whitehall is tuition-free, that's my only option for college."

Tears stung my eyes. This meant far more than a degree for Victor. It might mean his very life.

"So you understand, then, just how important this composition is. Why I need this." The tears spilled from his eyes. "I just . . . I don't know how I'm going to make it happen."

"You will, Victor." I pulled him into my arms, wanting to absorb his pain into my own body. I'd never seen a man cry before. "You will. I believe in you. You have the notes inside you. And I'll be right here. I'll support you. I'll encourage you. Anything you need—all you have to do is ask."

Victor pulled me to him, clinging to me as if I were the only thing keeping him upright. "Oh, Iris. Thank you. I have no idea what I'd do without you."

Nobody had ever said that to me before. Nobody had ever said anything like that to me before. My parents were mostly indifferent. I'd never had many friends. But here, the smartest, most talented guy I've ever met . . . wanted me. He needed me.

I leaned my head on his chest. "I hope you never have to find out."

CHAPTER FOURTEEN

*T*HE STRAINS of students sawing on stringed instruments met Callum's ears long before he cracked open the door to the orchestra room later that week, and the cacophony only grew louder as he slipped in the back, behind the double bass section.

On further consideration, *cacophony* wasn't quite the right word. Not anymore. Joy's freshman orchestra had improved considerably since the last time he'd heard them.

From her spot on the podium, Joy's eyes met his. She acknowledged his presence with a nod, guided the orchestra to a dramatic crescendo with her baton, then cut them off with a flourish. "Good job today, everyone. Pack up a couple minutes early."

Kids exchanged surprised glances, then moved almost as one to stash violins in cases and cellos on stands at the back of the room. Callum chuckled, recognizing that *quick, move before she changes her mind* energy permeating the classroom. He'd never seen it from his choirs. Then again, when had he not rehearsed until just past when the bell rang?

Joy wove her way through the mass of music stands to where Callum stood. "Mr. Knight." She greeted him with a smile. "To what do I owe the— Brax! Jayden! Viola bows are not light sabers, for the love of all things Mozart." She glared fiercely at a couple of gangly boys paused mid-bow battle, who appeared chastened and packed up their instruments with murmured apologies. Joy sighed, rolled her eyes, and offered a rueful grin. "Welcome to my world."

Callum repressed a shudder as he surveyed the chaotic scene and thanked God that teaching choir didn't involve trusting students with anything expensive. "Could I borrow you for a moment? It won't take long."

"Sure." Joy turned toward her students and shouted, "Okay, you squirrels. Pack up and behave like civilized humans, or so help me, I will never give you free time again." The sternness gone from her voice and her smile bright, she gestured toward her office. "Right this way."

Callum followed her into a small, intensely cluttered office, where Joy closed the door most of the way and eyed him, her right brow arching above her colorful glasses in a gesture eerily like Blair's.

"What can I do for you, Callum?"

Was every female faculty member here at Peterson this intimidating? He'd never found Joy to be so, especially since he had at least a foot on her in height, but right now, as she stood with her arms folded across her chest, eyeing him thoroughly, he felt like beating a hasty retreat back to the choir office.

"Well." He stopped and cleared his throat. "That is, I wondered if you might . . ."

"Spit it out, Knight. I haven't got all day, and neither do you."

"Coffee. Blair." The words leaped from his mouth like scared kids off a high dive. "I want to know what kind of coffee Blair likes. Like, what does she order from a coffee shop?"

"Ooooh, *interesting*." Joy's eyes lit. "Why?"

Callum held up a hand. "Whatever you're thinking, it's not that. I just . . . I need to get along with her, and I know she likes coffee, so I'm going to bring her one tomorrow. You know her much better than I do and thus are more likely to know her usual order. Because Blair does not seem like the sort of person who'd be happy with just anything."

Joy let out a bark of laughter. "No, she's pretty particular. About practically everything."

Callum resisted the urge to roll his eyes. "I've noticed."

"She has high standards, Callum. Nothing wrong with that. And I suspect she's not the only person in the choir department to whom that applies."

Callum studied the carpet between his shoes. "Yes. Well."

"Okay, coffee. Listen up. If it's before lunch, Blair likes—"

"Wait, she has a different favorite drink depending on the time of day?"

"You asked. I'm answering. Kindly wait until I'm finished before you complain," Joy replied, in the same tone of voice she'd used with the kids, although thankfully at a lower volume. "Now. If it's before lunch, she likes a hot butterscotch oat milk latte with an extra shot and whipped cream. After lunch, half-caf iced latte with skim milk, a shot each of coconut and vanilla, and about an inch of cold foam on top."

Callum blinked. A mocha or something he could remember, but this?

"Should I write it down for you?" Joy asked.

"No need." On sudden inspiration, he pulled his phone out from his pocket and opened up his voice recorder app. "Just say it again."

Joy lifted her chin and repeated the order. When he switched off the recorder, she nodded toward his phone. "Good idea, Mr. Knight."

"It's how I remember things when I'm composing." He tucked the phone back into his pocket.

"Oh, you compose?"

"Not as much anymore. It's been a rough few years." His standard answer. But now, blessedly, thank the Lord, he could elaborate beyond that. "But the muse is starting to return. It's slow going, but it's coming back. And Blair, well, she inspired the first musical idea I've had in half a decade."

He knew he'd made a mistake as soon as the words left his mouth, but Joy's mischievous grin confirmed it. "Oh, she *did*, did she?"

"She doesn't know, and this coffee is a way of thanking her. A small down payment on the debt I owe."

His attempt at mitigation did nothing to dim Joy's smile. "I *see*." She also must've seen something untoward going on in the orchestra room, because she banged on the window of the office. "Hey. You three. Cut. It. Out."

"Anyway." Callum moved toward the door. "Thanks for the tip."

"She's pretty special, y'know."

Joy's words at his back stopped him, and he turned. "I'm sorry?"

She was eyeing him again. Sizing him up, as though deeming him worthy. Or possibly unworthy.

"Blair. She's one in a million. Don't hurt her."

He held up a hand. "It's just coffee, Joy."

"Mm-hmm. That's what they all say."

They all? Who were they all? Did Blair have a steady stream of men wanting to buy her coffee? And why did he care, anyway?

He kept his tone and expression carefully neutral. "Sometimes coffee is just coffee."

The bell rang, and kids streamed by the window on their way out of the classroom. Callum put his hand on the doorknob but waited for the hordes to pass.

"She is single, just so you know," Joy added, her tone rich with mischief.

Callum sighed. Blair? The ice queen? Not seeing anyone? He was going to have a heart attack and die from that particular surprise. Best not to say anything, though.

"Again, thank you." He strode from the office behind a couple of straggling students. Never had he been so grateful for his third-hour music theory class and an excuse to get away from Blair's meddling mother hen of a best friend.

It really was just coffee.

A cup of coffee sat on Blair's desk.

Cardboard. Decorated with the unmistakable teddy-bear logo from her favorite shop and a little plastic stopper in the lid to keep the heat in.

She shed her jacket and hung it on the rack by the door, then picked up the cup to investigate. It wasn't her birthday, nor any sort of professional milestone. Had Joy woken up extra early this morning? Had Dad brought a surprise?

CAL, the handwritten name on the cup read.

Cal? Did she even know anyone named Cal?

Well, whoever Cal was, he knew her exact morning coffee order. At least, if the weird shorthand beneath his name could be believed.

BTSCTCH OAT LATTE XTRA SHOT WHIP.

"Morning, Blair." Callum strode into the office, a smile on his face and his own Teddy's coffee cup in hand.

Callum.

Cal.

"Morning." She held up her coffee. "Is this ... did you ... are you Cal?"

He grimaced. "I've never gone by Cal, not once in my life, nor will I ever. Teddy's was busy this morning, so the girl behind the counter must not have heard me correctly."

"But this is ..."

"Your standard morning order? Yes. Joy told me what you like." He pulled out his desk chair, looking very pleased with himself.

Joy told him? Did Joy volunteer that information? Did she put Callum up to this in an effort to get Blair to like him? Or had he *asked* her? And if he had, why?

"Thank you," she said. "Truly. I didn't sleep well last night, so this is very, very necessary." She took her first sip and closed her eyes in bliss. "And delicious."

"Glad you like it." His voice had gone soft. "Plus, I figured I owed you one from a few weeks back."

She lowered the cup and smiled at him. "Oh, that was just ... it was nothing."

"Maybe not." He met her gaze and matched her smile. "But it was something to me."

Blair settled into her chair and took another sip. "You're in an alarmingly good mood this morning. You have been for ... several mornings, actually."

"That idea I got a couple weeks ago actually turned into something."

"So that composer's block is a thing of the past now?"

He angled his chair toward hers and leaned back. "I don't want to get ahead of myself, but I will say that this is the furthest I've gotten since ... well, since Rayne died. Feels good to make progress."

Genuine happiness bloomed in her heart. "I'll bet it does. I'm glad for you."

"Thanks. My agent will be too, when I tell him." Callum's smile widened. "Glad for himself too, of course."

Her happiness vanished as quickly as it had come. The man who currently shared the office wasn't really a teacher. She had to remind herself of that. Oh sure, he had a teaching certificate and an education degree, but his heart lay elsewhere. He'd only come here to get back on his feet, and once he did that, he'd vanish in a puff of smoke, just like all the others had.

But this impending departure hit different. It felt less like irritation, less like the resignation of having to start over yet again with the umpteenth new director, and more like . . . sadness. Genuine sadness.

Was she actually going to miss *him*?

Oh, surely not.

"And I have you to thank for it," Callum was saying.

She blinked. "Me?"

"My idea came when you were saying goodbye to the kids that day." He leaned forward in his chair, his words tumbling out in a rush of enthusiasm. "They're crazy about you, Blair. They adore you. And I—I could feel it. I envied it, frankly. And that love you all share turned into a melody, and that melody turned into more."

Those green eyes stared into hers so deeply she wondered if he could see her soul. She felt exposed, but not in an unpleasant way. He'd seen beyond her piano skills to her passion for the job, and not only had he admired that, he'd also been inspired by it.

Had she ever inspired anyone to do anything before?

"Wow." She sounded breathy, like a teen girl staring at her crush. She cleared her throat. "Really?"

"Really." His voice was a caress, almost as though he'd reached out and covered the scant few feet between them. She felt the same as if he'd touched her . . . but what would it be like if he actually did? If one of those strong, capable hands brushed her arm? Her shoulder?

And gah, he was still watching her, but now he seemed curious—amused, even—and she had to say something.

"I'm glad I could help." Standard collaborative pianist response.

"Me too," he replied. "You have no idea. I could buy you a thousand coffees and I'd still be in your debt."

Callum's computer dinged with an email notification. He turned away to check it, and Blair could breathe again. A second later, her phone buzzed, and she pulled it from her purse. A text from Joy.

> Enjoying your coffee?

> Yes. Did you put him up to this?

> Nope. He asked yesterday. Completely on his own.

> He says I inspired a piece he's working on.

> LOL. My spidey sense tells me he's inspired to do more than just write music.

Joy had punctuated her last text with some grinning emojis. Blair texted back an eye-roll emoji of her own and set the phone down.

"Looks like we've got our assignments for Difference Makers Day," Callum remarked.

"Yeah?" Blair clicked into her email and scanned the missive from Cashman. *Peggy Sue Weldon, 621 North Court Street . . . Peterson High alum . . . recent widow . . . yard work, painting both exterior and interior . . .*

"Do you know Peggy Sue Weldon?" Callum asked, and Blair turned to face him.

"Not well, but we've met. Why? Is that where your group is going?"

Callum reached for his coffee. "Seems that way."

"Huh. So's mine."

"Guess she needs quite a bit of help."

"Makes sense. The email said she's a recent widow. If she's who I think she is, her husband was quite the handyman." Blair scrolled through the email. "Hey, since we're going to the same place anyway, I can supervise your group if you don't want to mess with this. Call in sick. I won't tell anyone."

Callum frowned at her. "You think I can't handle it?"

"No, I just think you don't *want* to handle it. I highly doubt you did this sort of thing directing professional choirs in Boston."

"You're right. I didn't," he replied evenly. "But I wish we had."

She studied him. "I'm sorry?"

"My high school choir director said she wanted us to be good singers and good musicians, but more than that, she wanted us to be good humans. 'Most of you aren't going into music as a profession,' she always said, 'but you are all members of the human race, so I'm going to do everything in my power to make you good ones.'" He chuckled. "I can still hear her voice like it was yesterday. So as long as I'm here, whatever influence I have on these kids, I'd like to make them better people than they were before I got here. So, yes, I'm all in on Difference Makers Day. I'll be there with bells on."

Just what had they put in his coffee at Teddy's? Who was this cheerful, unselfish person, and what had he done with the grumpy Callum Knight she knew and didn't love?

"Are you sure?" she asked.

"Of course I'm sure. You all have a good community here. Solid. Close-knit. You don't get that kind of thing in places like Boston." He glanced at the clock on the wall behind her, then reached for his iPad and stood. "It's a nice change of pace. See you in there?"

She nodded, and he strode past, leaving a hint of cologne in his wake.

Still a couple of minutes before kids started coming in. She had time to savor a few more sips of coffee.

A nice change of pace indeed. All the way around.

CHAPTER FIFTEEN

$\mathcal{S}$TRIPES OF sage-green paint spread from Blair's roller onto Peggy Sue Weldon's living room wall—not a color Blair herself would have chosen, necessarily, but a vast improvement over the original washed-out pink. The tarp beneath her bare feet crackled with her every step, and the aroma of paint permeated the entire room, along with mercifully quiet strains of the Top 40 radio station the students in her group had agreed to in a semi-grudging compromise.

Perhaps the agreement wouldn't last long, though, if the mostly good-natured muttering was any indication.

"One more song and we're switching it to the *good* station," Thalia piped up from the stepladder above Blair.

"Yes. Thank you." Jake ripped off a strip of painter's tape on the other side of the room.

"This *is* the good station," Makayla argued. As if to illustrate her point, Taylor Swift's latest single came over the airwaves, and Makayla aimed a pointed finger and a triumphant grin at her naysayers. "See? I told you. Turn. It. Up."

Jake gave a dramatic moan and clutched his chest while Thalia gave a quiet groan. "You had to agree to five songs on this station, didn't you, Jake?" she said.

"Hey, Makayla plays hardball. It was either five songs or *all* Taylor Swift."

"You're not wrong." Makayla cranked the volume and sang along with T. Swift at the top of her lungs.

A breakup song, of course. A song about being used, then abandoned.

ECHOES OF A SILENT SONG

Unbidden memories surfaced. Memories of Derek professing his undying love. Getting down on one knee and presenting her with a rock of a diamond on that sunny July day.

Six months later, the sunshine had turned to clouds.

Had they ever truly lifted? She was over him, that much she knew. She could no longer imagine a life with him. Painful as the discovery had been, at least God had revealed her fiancé's true colors to her before she walked down the aisle and pledged herself to him for life.

But was she over *it*? The pain? The betrayal? The knowledge that although she'd once thought him the love of her life, to him she'd just been a stopgap? A way station on the road to something he perceived to be better? She'd been a happy, sunshiny person once upon a time. Naive, perhaps. But happy.

Was she happy now? Legitimately, deep down? Was that sunny girl still in there, but frozen? Or was she gone forever, having seen how the world really works?

Could she ever open her heart to anyone else again? Could she trust again?

And God help her, was she really thinking this deeply about a Taylor Swift song?

Finally, mercifully, the song ended, much to the delight of Jake, who dove for the radio and changed it to an alternative rock station.

"My goodness, you're all working so hard in here."

Blair turned, and an elderly woman entered, her arms laden with two boxes of doughnuts. "How about a snack break?"

"Yes, please." Thalia had already climbed halfway down the ladder.

"Mrs. Weldon, that's so sweet of you." Jake moved to take the doughnuts from her arms, and Makayla took advantage of the distraction to turn the radio down. Brightened by the prospect of sugar, though, the other two didn't seem to notice.

While the kids pounced on the doughnuts, Peggy Sue Weldon glanced around the room, a wide smile creasing her cheeks. "Those kids are doing an amazing job."

"Thank you," Blair replied. "They're great kids."

"I can't tell you how much I appreciate this. The place has just gone to pot since Roland died, God rest his soul." Peggy Sue crossed the room to the large picture window. "Oh, honey, at least let me give you some light." She yanked on the cord to open the blinds, flooding the room with daylight and providing a view of the sunny backyard, where Callum's group was focusing on the exterior. A group of girls raked leaves near the center, and four guys—two from choir, a tall and broad-shouldered one in a dark-blue T-shirt and ball cap who probably played basketball, and a football player—were repairing a broken fence.

"It's our pleasure." Blair picked up her paint roller and ascended Thalia's stepladder to finish the spot the girl had been working on before the doughnuts arrived and . . . wait. Wait a minute. That guy in the blue T-shirt. That was not a basketball player. Wasn't even a student. No, that was *Callum*. He was the one hammering the fence, the motion pulling the shirt tight across his back.

He wasn't just supervising. He was pitching in. For a community he didn't belong to. Yet he worked as hard as the kids, if not harder.

Her heart warmed and softened.

He wasn't just paying lip service before. He really did care. And he cared about more than just the music.

He cared about the community.

"Did you say something?" Peggy Sue asked.

"No," Blair replied quickly. At least she hoped she hadn't.

"Stupid contraption." Peggy Sue reached beneath silvery curls and fiddled with her hearing aid. "Still can't quite get used to this."

Outside, Makayla appeared with the second box of doughnuts, and Callum set down his hammer, lifted his cap, and drew an arm across his forehead, and Blair could *not* just stand here staring at him.

She slapped the paint roller onto the wall and started rolling it more aggressively than before. "You're an alumna of Peterson High, right?" she asked Peggy Sue.

"Yes, ma'am. Class of 1961. Went away to school and came back to Peterson as soon as I graduated. I was the librarian. Would've stayed here forever, but Roland got transferred to Decatur, so we moved there in seventy-two. But as soon as he retired, we moved back."

Blair turned. "Were you here in sixty-nine to seventy, by chance?"

"Sure was." Peggy Sue snapped her fingers. "That's right. Your father mentioned when I saw him at church last week that you were curious about Iris Wallingford."

"We found a piece of music in the choir library we think might be hers."

"Oh, I wouldn't doubt it. That girl was always writing music. Usually she ate her lunch quickly and then came to the library for the rest of the period. She never said much more to me than hello, and she never asked for books. She just sat at a table by the window with that notebook of hers. At first I thought she was drawing, but once I was shelving books near her and saw the music. Don't know whether it was any good or not." Peggy Sue grinned. "That's above my pay grade."

Certainty thudded in Blair's chest at Peggy Sue's confirmation. It *was* Iris's music they'd found. Outside, Callum had popped the last of a doughnut into his mouth and reached for the hammer again. She couldn't wait to tell him.

"One time, toward the end of her life, though . . ." Peggy Sue continued, "Iris came in with a boy." Blair tore her gaze from the window. "A boy? Do you remember who?"

"Like it was yesterday," Peggy Sue replied. "It was that tall boy, Victor Nelson."

November 1969

My pencil flew across the staff paper on the table in the library. Victor and I had met there after school to work on our theory homework together, but I'd finished mine a few minutes ago. It was an easy assignment about secondary dominants. Mr. Gilbert had even made up a song to help us remember that they're chromatic, and that song had launched another thread of melody that welled up inside me, demanding to be poured into my pencil and set free on paper. Demanding to live outside me.

Ideas blossomed everywhere now, with Victor and me spending nearly all our free time together, and my brain constantly hummed with music. I'd written so many scraps of songs the last few weeks. Sometimes they were destined to remain just that—scraps—but some held the promise of much more.

I needed to finish something, though, and soon, because the application deadline for Whitehall was just two weeks away.

Yes. Like Victor, I'd decided to apply to the Whitehall Conservatory. I hadn't told my parents yet. Not much point really, since I doubted I'd get in. And even if by some miracle I did, my parents probably wouldn't think a music career a suitable future plan for "a woman of our social stature."

But even if I didn't go, just getting admitted would prove to me that I had real talent. That I was actually good at this. Whether I became a student or not, if some faculty member saw something in my work, it might put my name out there. Establish some connection with the world outside boring little Peterson, Illinois.

And if I wasn't any good? If I didn't get in? Then I'd know a career in music wasn't worth pursuing. Perhaps that would give me some peace about following the path my parents planned for me. Marrying some rich or socially prominent man—ideally both—and settling down to a vapid, meaningless, moneyed life of clinking champagne glasses, trilling laughter, and empty conversation.

If I did get into Whitehall, though, even if I couldn't go, somehow that would reassure me that God hadn't forgotten me. That he saw me and knew me and loved me as I was, not as others wished I were. That he had a plan for my music. That maybe people were meant to hear it. That maybe it didn't exist just for me.

But first I needed to finish my audition piece.

Victor sat across the table from me. His black plastic glasses sat in a shaft of sunlight on the scarred table. The same shaft of sunlight fell across his face—the sharp angles of his cheekbones, the little divot in his chin, the smattering of pale-brown freckles across the bridge of his nose. He was so handsome, my Victor. And now I could call him mine.

I am my beloved's, and my beloved is mine.

The verse from Song of Songs popped into my head. I'd always been inspired by the book, ever since my parents told me it was too mature for me. Of course I sneaked away to read it the second I could. It was beautiful poetry, but I'd never understood it. Not really. Not until now.

I was Victor's.

Victor was mine.

The words formed themselves into a melody, shifting and swirling in my heart until they crystallized. This melody differed from my other ideas. It felt more solid. More permanent. *I am my beloved's, and my beloved is mine.*

I am my beloved's. The phrase came to the sopranos first. Repeated then, with altos in harmony.

Then the tenors and basses echoed the second line. *My beloved is mine.*

Then maybe they—

A snap. A splintering.

That wasn't in the music. It took a moment to process. To absorb the reality of the small tip of graphite that shot across my staff paper. A slight grayish smear in the upper left-hand corner.

But it wasn't my pencil. My lead was intact.

Victor's wasn't, though. The pencil was broken in two. Snapped in half. In anger? Frustration?

"Victor?" I sought his gaze. "Are you okay?"

He looked up, his eyes like twin flames. Despite their heat, a chill shot through me.

"Victor?"

"I'm fine." And as quickly as it had appeared, the anger vanished. His eyes became placid again, like the lake behind my grandparents' farmhouse.

"Theory going okay?"

"Yes, until I got distracted."

His gaze was pointed, and I blinked. "Distracted?"

"You were humming," he replied. "And I don't think it was from our theory assignment."

"It wasn't." A smile pushed at my cheeks. "I got a new idea. One I think might actually be something. I'm setting a text from Song of Songs. I am my beloved's, and—"

"But you distracted me." His voice cut like a knife, and my joy tumbled back down into my heart.

"I'm sorry, Victor." I reached for his hand, balled up in a white-knuckled fist. "I'm so sorry. I didn't mean to. I had no idea I was even humming anything."

He placed his other hand on top of mine. "It's all right . . . beloved." Color bloomed in his cheeks, and his smile carved a deep parenthesis in the left side of his mouth.

Beloved. He called me *beloved*.

Was that an accident?

No. It was on purpose. I could tell by the look in his eyes. I'd never seen that expression before, not from anyone, but it left no mystery. He'd used the word on purpose. He'd received my message. And from the way he leaned across the table toward me, it seemed like he intended to send one of his own.

Time slowed to a near crawl. A good thing, because I needed to remember this moment. In a couple of seconds, Victor's lips would be on mine, and I would know what it was like to be kissed. And kissed by him.

I was thrilled. Scared. Self-conscious.

And most of all, deeply aware that this moment would define the rest of my life. This moment would tear the curtain between before and after.

Because this, right now, was the last moment before my first kiss with Victor.

His lips brushed mine. Soft at first. Tentative, as though asking permission. But when I granted it, he pressed his mouth more firmly against mine. His hands slipped behind my neck and into my hair. I tilted my head to the right. Was that what I was supposed to do? It must have been. And moving my lips against his . . . that must've been the right thing to do too.

A full choir burst into song in the center of my chest.

I am my beloved's, and my beloved is mine.

And . . . I needed to write it down. Now. In the magic of this moment, before I forgot this wonderful sparkly, soaring feeling.

I pulled back.

Victor frowned. "Did I do something wrong?"

"No. Quite the opposite." I beamed at him and picked up my pencil. "You inspired me."

"I did?"

"Yes." The pencil raced across my paper. Sopranos here . . . altos here . . . yes. This was exactly it. Exactly right. Exactly what I heard. What I felt. What my heart wanted to say.

I'd never felt more alive.

Before long the whole page was filled with notes. With the outpourings of my heart. With the feeling of belonging. Of being wanted. Of being loved. Of loving.

When I looked up, he was watching me. A smile played on his lips. I returned it briefly, filling my tank of inspiration, then dove back into my work.

I am my beloved's.

And my beloved is mine.

Half a chocolate-frosted doughnut lingered in the box in Peggy Sue's foyer. Callum peeled off his work gloves and glanced around, but the students were nowhere to be found. Blair had probably eaten the first half. It had certainly been cut neatly enough, and exactly down the middle. And she definitely seemed the sort of person who'd only allow half a doughnut's worth of indulgence rather than just eating the whole thing.

His growling stomach prevented any further consideration of the matter, and he popped the half doughnut into his mouth all in one bite. He'd woken up late this morning and had skipped breakfast, but three hours of repairing fences and raking leaves had made him regret that decision.

"So she was working on music that day" came a voice from the living room. "You're sure."

"Sure as shootin'," came the reply.

Callum rounded the corner to find Blair rolling green paint onto the far wall. Peggy Sue sat on a folding chair in the center of the tarp-covered floor.

"And they were kissing?" Blair asked.

"They sure were." Peggy Sue's voice held a laugh. "A second or two longer and I'd have had to break it up."

Callum froze. "Who was kissing?"

Blair turned at the sound, and he froze for an entirely different reason. Her normally pale cheeks were flushed, her red hair was tied up in a messy bun, and she'd traded her usual work wear for a Fighting Illini T-shirt and a pair of worn jeans. Distressed? Was that the term? In any event, they were still in one piece. Just a few little holes where pale skin could peek through.

"Callum." Her voice jerked him back to the matter at hand. "Iris and Vic. It was Iris and Vic. Mrs. Weldon was the librarian back then, and she saw the two of them kissing."

"Kissing." It was important information. Earth-shattering, perhaps. But Blair had a smudge of green paint just beneath her lower lip, and for some reason it made her even more adorable.

Adorable? Had he just thought of the ice queen as adorable?

Well, her lips were, at any rate. They were pink and plump, devoid of their usual lipstick, and . . .

. . . and he was staring at his coworker's lips, and the last words either of them had spoken involved kissing.

He really should stop staring at her.

"Yes." Her lips moved, the word bursting from them. "Why would Vic say he didn't know her?"

"He said what?" Peggy Sue sounded startled. "Oh, he knew her, all right. I think he—"

Whatever she might have been about to say was cut off by the sound of frantic barking, the kind that nearly always belonged to a small, excitable dog. Sure enough, a little white purse poodle, barely large enough to even qualify as a dog, careened around the corner, scrabbling on hardwood and nearly falling on the tarp.

Peggy Sue bent down. "Oh, what's the matter, Gigi?"

Of course its name was Gigi.

"Do you need to go out?" Peggy Sue hoisted herself from the chair and started for the hallway. "Okay, come on. This way. Don't want to get paint on your paws. Come on, Gigi. Out." She and the comically tiny dog disappeared around the corner.

Blair's frown deepened. "Okay, something's not adding up. Vic told you he barely knew her, but the yearbook photographer caught them together, and Peggy Sue just said they were *kissing*."

There was that word again, and there were her lips again.

"But why would he lie?" she asked.

"I . . . I don't know." *Stop staring at her lips. Stop it.*

"Callum? Are you okay?" She stepped closer, the tarp crinkling under bare feet.

"Yeah. Fine. I just . . . it's been a minute since I fixed a fence. Raked leaves. Cleaned gutters. Didn't have any of those in Boston."

Blair smiled. Had he thought of her as the ice queen? Because this smile was warm and soft. Nothing icy about it.

"I had no idea fixing fences was part of your skill set," she said.

He shrugged. "My granddad used to be a carpenter. In all the years I knew him, I don't think he ever hired anything out. Did it all himself. He was always grumbling that my father, the physics professor, didn't have any useful or practical skills, so he made sure I did."

She had paint on her cheek too. Right at the top of her cheekbone. Just a little drop, but the fact that the normally primped-and-polished Blair had let herself get even a little bit messy was apparently his undoing.

Her brows inched together. "What?"

Busted. "You've, uh . . . you've got a little paint . . ." He indicated the spot on his own lip where her worst smudge was, and her eyes followed. Now *she* was staring at *his* lips.

Just for a split second, though. She tried to wipe off the paint with the back of her hand, but she also had paint there, apparently, because the little splotch turned into a smear.

"Oh no," she groaned. "It's worse, isn't it?"

"It's okay. It's a good color on you. Besides, it's Difference Makers Day. We're bound to get a little messy." He gestured toward the paint tray, where an extra roller lay. "Need a hand?"

Blair cast a wary glance outside, where the kids were staining the freshly rebuilt fence.

"I think they've got it under control out there," Callum said. "And our view from this window means if those knuckleheads try anything, they'll wish they hadn't."

"Yeah. Okay. Sure." Blair handed him her roller, then moved the extra out of the way and poured more green paint into the tray.

Difference Makers Day? Yeah. Today was definitely making a difference.

CHAPTER SIXTEEN

O'ER THE la-aand of the freee . . .

Callum held out a hand to indicate the fermata, and a chilly breeze buffeted his cheeks. *Okay, good. They're not closing the E vowel. They're keeping it open, just like I told them.*

Then Zara, their top soprano, popped up to the high B-flat, and Callum resisted an urge to pump a fist. *Yes.* She nailed it. And she even dropped her jaw on that high note. Again, just like he'd instructed. This a cappella performance hadn't been perfect. But the kids were listening. They were paying attention. And by the gleams in their eyes, they knew it was paying off.

And the home of the braaaaaaave.

The crowd started cheering before Callum cut off the final chord, but even the packed stands at the homecoming football game couldn't drown out the excellent "vuh" on the end of the word "brave." A textbook shadow vowel. Those kids really *had* been paying attention. Joy and exhilaration surged through him. He couldn't have fought off his smile even if he'd wanted to. Granted, the national anthem at a high school football game was a far cry from the Rutter Requiem at a cathedral in Cambridge—the last time he'd directed a choir—but it brought the same post-performance high.

No . . . actually, this was a different level of satisfaction. Letter jacket–clad teenagers looked at each other, the *wow* evident on every face. They hadn't known what they were capable of until now. Some had just tasted the magic of music for the first time. And he'd facilitated it. He'd guided them through. He'd taught them things. His professionals in Boston hadn't needed to learn much. They'd merely needed a director. These kids needed a *teacher*. And he had the privilege of being that teacher.

Only for the rest of the year, though. Then he'd be back in Boston, and someone else would be teaching the kids.

Was Boston really what he wanted anymore? As the choir moved off the track and he reached for the microphone stand to pull it out of the way, his heart twinged at the idea of leaving them. Those kids who'd greeted him with such suspicion in August were starting to like him. To buy into his way of doing things. To believe they were capable of more than they thought possible. They were just six weeks in. What magic could the rest of the year hold? How would they react next year when they had to start over—yet again—with someone new? Would this new person challenge them to meet their capabilities? Would the kids continue to work hard? Or would they slide back into apathy and reluctance?

And then there was Blair. Sitting in the stands. Not that he'd been looking for her, of course. But that red hair was hard to hide, even when she'd tucked half of it into an adorable knit beret. She clapped gloved hands together, and her smile was like nothing he'd ever seen. The woman was utterly beaming, and when their eyes met, he smiled back. Blair knew better than anyone the chaos these kids had been through, and if that performance had made her happy? Well, that was even more reason for him to be.

"Sounding good, Mr. Knight."

Callum turned at the deep voice to his right, and there stood Vic Nelson in the flesh. He extended a hand, which Callum shook.

"Vic. What a pleasant surprise."

Vic's free hand found Callum's shoulder and pulled him into a bro hug. "I'm always here for the homecoming game. Of course, I've been retired long enough now that I don't know the students as well anymore, but I still wouldn't miss it."

"Well, it's nice to see you. Big shoes to fill, though."

"Bah." Vic waved a hand. "So many people have come through those doors since I left, I don't think anyone even knows where to find my shoes anymore. But you're doing a fantastic job."

Callum blinked at the praise. "Thank you, sir. That means a lot coming from you."

Vic's dimple deepened. "Wouldn't have sung your praises to administration if I didn't believe you could do it."

"And if you weren't totally desperate."

Vic chuckled. "Well, desperation did have something to do with it. But even at the eleventh hour, I'm not leaving my choirs in the hands of someone who doesn't know what they're doing. And you, my friend, know exactly what you're doing."

"I wouldn't go that far." Callum crouched to corral the extension cord. "There's a big difference between professionals in Boston and teenagers in Peterson."

"That may be, but choir is choir. And that choir sounds significantly better than it did this time last year."

Callum straightened. "Really?"

"C'mon. You know I wouldn't lie to you."

Callum's smile froze on his face. A couple of weeks ago, this comment would've passed without notice. But now? Now that an eyewitness had claimed something happened that Vic had claimed didn't happen? Now, he wasn't so sure.

Callum lowered his voice. "Vic, can I ask you something?"

"Sure. Anything."

"Are you sure you didn't know Iris Wallingford?"

Vic blinked. "Come again?"

"Iris Wallingford. The two of you were in the same grade. You were in choir together. In band. There's . . . there's even a picture of the two of you together on the band page in the 1970 yearbook."

"Is there?" Vic pursed his lips. "Huh. Well, I'll be. I never saw that picture. My parents never bought yearbooks. Couldn't afford it. But I'll take your word for it."

"And that's not all. A former school librarian told us she saw the two of you in the library together. Working on music. She thinks the two of you were an item."

"An item." An odd expression crossed Vic's face. "I suppose you could call it that. Iris and I went on a couple dates. Nothing serious, though.

I wasn't her type. Not good enough for her. Or her parents." His gaze shifted to something behind Callum, and he smiled and waved. "Sorry, Callum, I just spied some alumni I haven't seen in a decade. If you'll excuse me?" Without waiting for a reply, he clapped Callum on the back and strode away.

Callum watched him leave, the stadium lights reflecting off his satiny Peterson Patriots jacket. It was entirely plausible. The librarian could have interpreted events one way, while Vic's version could be the real story.

But why would Vic have first claimed not to know Iris at all? Why not just come out with the truth? They'd dated briefly and ended things. That happened often enough in high school. And maybe Iris meant so little to him, maybe the relationship had been so brief, that Vic truly hadn't remembered it. Not until something jogged his memory.

But what didn't happen every day was someone's high school significant other passing away while still in high school. Surely that would've been worth at least a little bit of brain space.

Blair was still up in the stands, clutching a Styrofoam cup of something and leaning over to talk to Joy. Her puffy coat and her adorable hat were the same shade of Peterson blue, and her fingertips were peeking out of a cute little pair of white gloves, and why did the words *cute* and *adorable* continually spring to mind when he saw her outside of work? It was bad enough Wednesday with the T-shirt and jeans, and now, with her all bundled up like a snow princess despite the fifty-degree temperature . . .

At least he didn't find her cute at work yet. That would make things wicked awkward.

Well, cute or not, he needed to talk to her. Tell her what Vic said and get her read on it. She knew Vic far better than he did. And he wanted to believe Vic.

But right now, he wasn't quite sure he did.

"Blair!" Joy grabbed Blair's left arm, practically vibrating with excitement. "They sound fantastic!"

"Don't they?" Blair returned the embrace as best she could with a right hand that clutched a mostly empty cup of hot cocoa. "I'm so proud of them."

"You should be. I've never heard the national anthem sound that good."

"I have." Her senior year at Peterson had been filled with core memories: an ambitious combined work with orchestra, a performance at the regional choral directors' convention, even a trip to New York. Vic had pulled out all the stops that year, and the results had been nothing short of amazing. She remembered exchanging glances with her fellow sopranos. *Did we really do that? Yes. We really did.*

And now she saw those same expressions on the faces of her students. These kids for whom she'd do anything, these kids who'd had nothing but instability and chaos in choir, were now experiencing the true magic of making music together. Tears pricked the back of her eyes, and she turned her attention to her hot chocolate. "But it's been a long time."

She had to hand it to Callum. He knew his stuff. His methods were still sometimes questionable, but they were paying off, and the kids had noticed. Zara walked by Callum on her way up to the student section of bleachers. Smiling, he leaned in to say something to her. She beamed, said something back, and practically skipped toward the stands.

Oh, crap. They were connecting with Callum. They were starting to *like* him. They were getting attached.

And he was leaving after this year. They didn't know that, but Blair did. And now she hated the temporary nature of Callum's presence in Peterson even more. Because his departure wouldn't just hurt the choir from a musical standpoint. It would be a personal loss for the kids.

Her warm, fuzzy feelings gone as quickly as they'd come, she stood and drained the last of her lukewarm cocoa. "I'm going for more hot chocolate. Want anything?"

"I'm good." Joy turned her attention back to the football game. "Thank you, though."

Blair descended the stadium steps, rounded the corner, and almost ran straight into Callum.

"Whoa." He reached out to steady her, his hands lightly grasping her elbows, then met her eyes. "Blair. Hi."

"Hi." His eyes were extra green tonight. Maybe it was the deep emerald of his jacket. Or the stadium lights. "They, uh—the choir—they sounded amazing. Best I've heard them sound in a long time."

Callum smiled and his eyes gleamed. "Thank you. Couldn't have done it without you."

Standard conductor throwing the pianist a bone. She waved a hand. "No, Blair, I mean it." He sought her gaze. "I truly could not have done this without you. And I'm not just talking about your collaborative piano skills."

Her eyes widened at his use of her preferred term for her job.

"These kids haven't had much they can count on the last few years," he said. "But they've had you. Thank you for being there for them."

The compliment struck her with almost physical force, landing exactly where she needed it most. "You're welcome." Wow, those eyes were green. They could see through to the depths of her, to the insecurities she tried so hard to hide, to the fear that everyone she loved would eventually get sick of her, that she was both too much and not enough. In a single moment, his expression provided the reassurance that—in his mind, anyway—she was the exact right amount.

"Hey," he said. "I was about to head to concessions. Want to come with me? I had something I wanted to ask you about."

"Sure." She yanked her head out of the clouds and shook off the stardust. "I need some more hot chocolate anyway."

They started walking, Callum to her right, their feet crunching across the gravel between the football field and the concession stand.

"I just talked with Vic," he said. "Asked him about Iris again. He said the two of them dated briefly but weren't serious."

Blair raised an eyebrow. "That's a little bit different than 'I didn't know her at all.'"

"That's what I thought."

She tossed her empty cup in a nearby trash can. "Do you think Vic's lying?"

"That's what I wanted to ask you."

"I don't know why he would. Unless Iris is just too painful for him to talk about."

"It's still difficult for me to talk about Rayne sometimes." The hint of a shadow passed over his features. "I certainly wouldn't deny knowing her, though. She's a big part of who I am."

"But you and Rayne were together for quite a while, weren't you?" And why did she find the idea of Callum looking at anyone else the way he'd just looked at her so bothersome?

Callum nodded. "Three years."

"So maybe Vic truly did only have a couple of dates with Iris. Maybe he really didn't know her all that well."

"But don't you remember the guys you had even one or two dates with?" Callum pressed. "Especially in a town like Peterson, where you probably knew them at least a little bit beforehand?"

"There weren't that many. Especially not in high school." She glanced up at Callum. "Do you?"

"Remember the girls I only had a couple dates with? Yeah. I do."

There was that bothersome feeling again.

"Maybe Vic was a player," she suggested.

Callum burst out laughing, his face radiating surprise and joy. He had a wonderful laugh. And she didn't really think of herself as a particularly witty person. She didn't make people laugh often. But for her to have made him laugh like that? She felt like she'd won something.

His laughter was contagious, and she joined in, ignoring the curious stares of the people in line in front of them.

When they reached the front, Callum turned to her. "My treat."

Blair frowned. "Are you sure? What about your master plan to save up and get back to Boston as soon as possible?" She kept her voice light, but the question weighed on her heart.

An indecipherable expression crossed his face. "I don't think a two-dollar hot chocolate will make much difference."

"Well. Thank you."

He was leaving. She had to keep reminding herself of that.

Otherwise she just might find herself starting to fall for him.

CHAPTER SEVENTEEN

CALLUM STOOD along the wall of the Peterson High School commons, marveling at the transformation. All the lunch tables had been folded up and hidden somewhere out of sight to make way for an entire garden full of artificial trees and twinkle lights. Scattered benches and a fake pond formed a photo area—complete with a waterfall made from some type of fabric and still more twinkle lights. Ivy and lights were even woven into the rafters. He had to hand it to the decorating committee—they really had gone all out in their pursuit of the mystical woodland theme. It truly did resemble an enchanted forest.

Or at least, an enchanted forest that contained a dance-remix soundtrack and a healthy population of overly fragranced adolescents. Instead of fauns, teen boys galloped around in attire ranging from rented tuxes to Hawaiian shirts and jeans to—in one memorable instance—a velvet tux jacket and formal tie combined with cowboy boots, jeans, and a Stetson. Callum had to chuckle. You sure wouldn't see *that* in Boston.

As for the girls, most wore skirts that were either too short, way too short, or way, way too short. Many paired their formal dresses with sneakers—was that the trend now?—while a few others teetered on heels that were at least two inches too high for them. They looked like baby horses—or perhaps unicorns, given the theme—learning how to walk, all wobbly and tentative. All these kids were trying on adulthood for the first time, and for the vast majority, it was a suit they had yet to grow into.

Then a pair of open-toed black heels glided past with a stride far too graceful and practiced to belong to a teenager. And the dress she wore was long, unlike those of the students. Long and formfitting with a slit up the side, and—wait, was that a tattoo? It *was*. Dainty and delicate musical notes snaked up a shapely ankle.

His gaze traveled upward, catching creamy pale skin and burnt-auburn hair, and he almost choked.

That was Blair.

That was *Blair.*

All week the word that had surfaced to describe her had been *adorable*, but that adjective no longer applied. In that glittery bronze dress, she was ... gorgeous? Stunning? Neither seemed sufficient. No, the only thing that could appropriately describe her was music. A tune swelled in his chest, chords and harmonies and things he'd have given his eyeteeth for a month ago. Maybe he'd remember it later. He sure hoped so. Because no way could he tear his eyes away from Blair long enough to find his iPad or a piano. Besides, who needed to write it down? She was music itself. The personification of song.

"I told her to wear that dress."

Joy appeared to his left, clad in a full-skirted vintage-style dress covered in eighth notes. Her crimson lips curved upward in a grin not unlike that of the Grinch. "And I see it had the desired effect," she said.

"Joy!"

He turned, and there was Blair herself, even more breathtaking up close.

She didn't seem to have noticed him yet, though. Her eyes were squarely fixed on her friend. "Your dress!" she exclaimed. "It is so *cute*."

"Thanks!" Beaming, Joy lifted both sides of her dress. "It has pockets."

"*Jealous.*"

"Yours doesn't have room for pockets."

Joy's comment drew his attention to the part of her dress where pockets would be, and indeed it did not have pockets, nor did it have room for pockets, but it did have a pair of hips that looked fantastic in said dress, and dear goodness, he had to stop staring.

"Good thing they invented garter purses," Blair replied, a grin in her voice.

He choked again. Perhaps audibly, because her wide-eyed gaze found him.

"Callum. Hi." Her cheeks stained pink.

"Hi." He sounded froggy, so he cleared his throat and tried again. "Hi. You look . . . incredible."

"Thank you." The delicate flush deepened. "You, uh . . . you look like your headshot."

He flashed what he hoped was a devil-may-care grin. "That a good thing or a bad thing?"

She paused, lips pursed in thought. "Yes."

"Okay." Joy's voice was way perkier than it needed to be. "I just spied one of my bass players twerking, so I gotta go put a stop to that. You kids have fun." She leaned in close to Blair and said something he couldn't make out, then bustled across the commons.

He had an odd feeling that there was no actual twerking going on, but he wasn't inclined to investigate that too closely.

"Wow, Ms. Em. Looking *good*." Thalia swept by on the arm of Ryden, a junior bass from Mixed Chorus.

"Thank you." Blair turned, then indicated Thalia's dress, a frothy lavender creation festooned with flowers. "And oh my goodness, Thalia, that dress is *amazing*. You look just like Rapunzel."

"That's the goal." Thalia chattered on, something about sewing on the flowers herself, but her words went in one ear and out the other, because he was still too focused on Blair.

After a moment, Thalia and Ryden departed, waving at someone across the room.

"Have fun tonight," Blair called.

"Don't be idiots," Callum echoed, with what fragment of his brain remained a teacher.

Blair turned back to him, her eyes sparkling like diamonds. "I'm guessing you never had to do anything like this in Boston."

"Wear this?" He indicated his tux. "Dozens of times. Wear it in a crowded commons full of hormone-crazed high schoolers? Shockingly, no. Not once."

Blair chuckled, and the sound hit him square in the solar plexus.

"I, uh . . . I didn't know you had a tattoo," he ventured.

"A moment of youthful abandon in college. My piano trio all got matching tattoos after a recital." She glanced over his shoulder toward the refreshments table. "Have you tried the punch? Camilla was bragging about some secret recipe."

He shrugged. "Meh. Tastes like one of those foil-packed juice boxes from grade school."

"Mmm. Tempting." She grinned at him. "I'll probably wait until later, then. Savor the anticipation."

"You actually liked those?"

Her grin widened. "Not even a little bit."

Had she been trying to set him at ease? Well, whether that was her goal or not, she'd succeeded. He wasn't relaxed—not with her right here, looking like that—but he could at least remember that beneath the bronze dress and the makeup and the piled-up curls, this was still his sometimes-prickly, always-exacting, frequently-annoying-yet-somehow-enchanting coworker. His . . . well, his friend. They were friends now, right?

The song shifted to a much slower tempo, and before he could consider the wisdom of the idea, he'd opened his arms to Blair. "Care to dance?"

"Dance?" Long dark lashes blinked at his suggestion.

"It is, after all, a dance."

"Which we are supposed to be chaperoning."

"Exactly." He smiled. "What better way to blend in and be unobtrusive? Besides, this way we can both have eyes on these little heathens."

She nodded. "Yes. Great idea. For the kids."

"For the kids."

Then Blair stepped into his arms. His left hand found her right, her cheek grazed his, and she smelled like vanilla and cinnamon and everything else wonderful about fall. He wrapped his free hand around her waist. Too late, he realized her dress was basically backless, so half his fingers were grazing bare, silken skin. He should probably move his hand, but where could he move it so it wasn't awkward—or worse, indecent? Clearly he was overthinking this, and he should relax and enjoy, but he couldn't. Because right now he held Blair Emerson in his arms. Suddenly his world made all kinds of sense and no sense at all.

And all his senses filled with nothing but her.

Callum was touching her back. He was *touching* her *back*. Bare skin on bare skin, sending a delicious electric current up the length of her spine. Granted, they were holding hands too, and the stubble of his cheek grazed her temple . . . but those were perfectly innocent touches. They could happen with anyone. If she'd had any inkling she'd end up dancing with Callum, she absolutely would have worn that navy sheath, boring though it might be.

But then he wouldn't be touching your back.

He really did look like his headshot. And she'd meant what she'd said, when he'd asked her if that was good or bad. Because it truly was a good thing—he was so incredibly handsome, all chiseled and coiffed in that effortlessly perfect way characteristic of all handsome men.

But it was a bad thing too. Because now she had no choice but to admit that Joy was right. Blair had a crush on Callum.

Wait. No. More than a crush.

She *liked* him.

He was her closest coworker. Her boss, if you wanted to get all technical about it. He was leaving at the end of the year.

And she liked him.

He shifted and pulled her closer, and now his fingers touched slightly more of her back. His other hand held hers just a bit tighter. And his cheek pressed against hers just a little closer. Her lungs filled with his cologne—fresh and woodsy and musky and male. She snuggled closer and breathed him in and stopped coming up with all the reasons she shouldn't like him. Instead her mind paraded before her all the reasons she should. The reasons she did.

Callum Knight had come into a situation that was at best humbling and at worst humiliating and was giving it his all. Putting in effort. He'd been intentional about learning the kids' names. Remembering who played on which sports teams. He'd pitched in for Peggy Sue on Difference Makers Day. Though he'd never planned on this job, or even wanted it, he'd jumped into it with both feet, dedicated and determined. He had given these kids the one thing they'd needed most: someone who cared. He was passionate and funny and had—to her alarm—chipped away at the block of ice that encased her heart, and he'd done it like he'd tackled everything else these last two months. Gradually. Patiently. Persistently. Doggedly, even. Not always perfectly, but when he stumbled, he always got back up, dusted himself off, and tried again. And that just might be what she admired most about him.

Was God trying to pry open the slammed-shut door of her heart? And was Callum the reason why?

All too soon the slow song was replaced by some annoying pseudo rap that caused the kids to separate from their dance partners and launch into a ridiculous series of moves they'd no doubt learned from social media. Callum pulled back, and she expected him to step away . . . but he didn't.

His hand was still on her waist—though no longer on bare skin—and his other hand still held hers. He'd frozen in place, as though letting her go was the last thing on earth he wanted to do.

Wait. Did he have feelings too?

Oh yes.

Oh *no*.

This could get complicated.

A one-sided crush she could handle, but by the way he was looking at her, it was definitely not one-sided. Smoky-emerald eyes fixed on hers, his expression as helpless as she felt. As though he'd spent the last four minutes figuring out the same things she had, and now the thing between them—this thing they'd either ignored or fought off or been blissfully unaware of—was now a *thing*, and what on earth were they going to do about it?

Well, that last bit he didn't seem to be wondering, because those green eyes had shifted to her lips, and he inched closer. Her breath caught. *Are we really about to do this?* The question hovered in her throat, but she swallowed it. She didn't want to break the spell, because this sort of magic might not happen again. In fact, she—

"Ms. Em? Ms. Em? Oh thank goodness, Ms. Em."

Blair's eyes flew to a frantic Thalia standing to her right, tears smearing her eye makeup.

"I think Ryden's drunk," she choked out.

Callum had increased the distance between them to something professionally appropriate. "Drunk?"

"I didn't notice it at first. I . . . I think some of the guys maybe sneaked something in and he started drinking after we got here. But now he smells like booze, and he's acting really stupid."

"That's an understatement." Blair rolled her eyes. A few feet away, Ryden stood on a table, doing a wobbly sprinkler dance for a small yet enthusiastic crowd.

"I'm on it." Callum was already elbowing through the crowd, making a beeline for Ryden.

"This is so embarrassing." Thalia flung her arms around Blair.

Blair wrapped an arm around her student. "I know, sweetie. I'm so sorry. Thank you for telling us. This is too big for you to handle on your own."

"I've had a crush on Ryden all year and been looking forward to tonight so much, and then he does this."

Blair's heart went out to Thalia. "I'm sorry he disappointed you."

A group of sympathetic girls—most from Madrigals—surrounded Thalia then, and Blair surrendered the girl to the care of her friends. As they departed, she glimpsed Callum escorting Ryden gently but firmly out the side door and into the cool night.

Maybe the fresh air would knock some sense into Ryden. If not, then perhaps a ride home with his parents or a jaunt in the back of a police cruiser would do the trick. Much as she loved these children, they were still children, and sometimes they made incredibly stupid decisions.

But if she were honest, she was grateful too. Because Ryden's stupid decision might have just saved her from making a colossally stupid one of her own.

CHAPTER EIGHTEEN

December 1, 1969

$\mathscr{I}$ SAT BESIDE Victor on his worn, floral-patterned living room sofa. The small black-and-white television set flickered from its cabinet in front of us. His mother bustled around the kitchen, putting dishes away. In the corner stood a weathered aluminum Christmas tree draped in ornaments and tinsel.

At first glance it would seem like any ordinary Monday night. Instead it was anything but. I constantly wiped my hands on my skirt. Victor seemed a million miles away. I could only guess at his thoughts— knowing that in just a few moments, when the first-ever draft lottery went live over the airwaves, his life could change forever.

Even if they did draw his number, he wouldn't have to go right away. He and I both knew that. But a deferment would only get him through graduation in June. If he didn't get into Whitehall, then what would become of him?

The SPECIAL REPORT logo flashed across the screen. Beside me, Vic gasped. I squeezed his hand.

"Is it starting?" Mrs. Nelson poked her head in from the kitchen, still wiping a dish with a threadbare towel.

"Yeah." Victor's voice croaked.

The announcer was still talking, sounding way too perky, but it didn't matter what he said or what explanation he gave. Nothing, no matter how eloquent, could make this anything other than what it was. All I could do was pray with everything in me that September 7—Victor's birthday—would be the very last number they called. Onscreen, old men in suits milled about. Men far too old to fight and likely far too old to care about the lives that would change—the lives that would end—based on what they did. One introduced another, some congressman or something, but I could barely hear over the roar of blood in my ears. The congressman walked over to a huge clear container filled with little capsules. He had to reach way, way in to choose one but still plunged his hand deep. Under any other circumstance Victor would've probably made some wisecrack about how this old fuddy-duddy was almost too short for the task at hand, but he was silent. If he was anything like me, he couldn't summon the oxygen to speak.

The congressman chose a capsule and handed it to the man who'd introduced him. The camera zoomed in on the man's hands as he opened it and unrolled a tiny scroll of paper. He wore a large ring, and . . . were his hands shaking? They looked a little unsteady. Or was it just that my entire body trembled and so everything seemed a little wobbly?

"September . . ." the voice said, and my heart stopped. He paused for what felt like an entire year. *Not the seventh. Not the seventh. Please, Lord God, not the seventh.*

"Fourteenth," he finished. "September fourteenth, zero zero one."

All the air whooshed out of my lungs. My hand tightened around Victor's. He'd dodged the first birthday bullet. I turned to him with a smile, but he still stared at the screen, stone-faced. The men in suits were reloading. It was far, far too early to celebrate.

Another, younger man drew the second number. "April twenty-fourth."

I could breathe again, just for a moment. The announcer handed the little scroll to another man, who pasted it onto a large bulletin board just beneath the first date—002, the number to the left read, and the announcement confirmed it. "April twenty-four is zero zero two."

"December thirtieth."

"December thirty is zero zero three."

"February fourteenth."

"February fourteen is zero zero four."

With each date they called that wasn't Victor's birthday, my lungs opened just a fraction. They hadn't drawn the number I'd dreaded. His birthday was only one of 360 or so left in that bucket. Each time there was a less than 1 percent chance that they'd call his. A greater than 99 percent chance that he'd get to stay home.

October eighteenth was next.

Then they said the month I longed not to hear. "September..."

Not the seventh not the seventh—

"Sixth. September six is zero..."

I folded in on myself. September 6. The day before Victor's. It felt like fate. A sign. Like God had answered all my fervent prayers for Victor's safety.

"October twenty-sixth..."

"It's still going on, Iris." Victor sounded annoyed.

"Well, yes, of course. But they just called the sixth. There's no way they'll call the seventh. Not with over three hundred fifty dates still in there."

"September seventh."

What?!

No. No. They didn't just say that. They didn't just say September 7. No. They picked the sixth. Just two dates ago they picked the sixth. It couldn't be the seventh. They couldn't *do* that. Not Victor. No. They couldn't do that to Victor.

The sound of breaking glass, loud as gunfire, jolted me. Victor's mother was still standing in the doorway, still holding the towel. But the dish she'd been drying shattered at her feet. Pieces of it flew every which way, skittering across the floor. When they stopped, she clapped her hand over her mouth and started to sob.

That was when I knew this was real. They'd just called Victor's birthday. He'd been drafted. And unless he got into Whitehall, then the minute after we walked across that stage in June, he'd be shipped off to the jungle in Vietnam.

God, why? Why Victor? Why?

"You can't go." I clung to him. "There's got to be a way to get out of this."

"And I'll find it, Iris. I'll . . . I'll go to Canada. I'll flunk my physical. I'll—"

"You'll go to Vietnam."

We turned at the deep voice behind us. Victor's father stood in the doorway, a bottle of beer clutched in his hand. Based on what Victor had told me, that beer was likely not his first.

"No, I won't." Victor's voice was quiet but firm.

"Yes, you will."

"No, Dad. I'm not going to 'Nam." He stood, fists clenched, as if ready for a fight. "I'm going to the Whitehall Conservatory of Music in Chicago. I'm a musician. I'm not a warrior. I won't go be cannon fodder for a war we shouldn't even be in."

"You'll do whatever your country needs you to do." Mr. Nelson stepped toward his son. "That's what I did. It's what your grandfather did. It's what every Nelson man has done since we arrived on these shores. It's bad enough you won't volunteer. No son of mine will be a draft dodger. I manned up and served this country, and so will you."

"But look what it did to you," Victor argued. "What you became. You're an embarrassment. Why would I ever want to become like you?"

With a vicious swear word, Mr. Nelson flung the beer bottle directly at Victor's head. Victor ducked, and the brown glass burst into pieces against the dingy wallpaper.

Followed a second later by my heart.

Victor muttered something under his breath, crossed the living room in about two steps, and left. He slammed the door behind him, and a picture fell off the wall. The wooden frame split in half.

A second later, I tore out the door after him. "Victor! Victor!"

He was sliding into his father's beat-up Buick. "Go home, Iris."

"No." I didn't stamp my foot like a toddler, but it took effort to contain the urge. "I'm not leaving you like this. I'm not leaving you alone."

"But being alone is exactly what I need." Without waiting for my response, he peeled out of the driveway and down the street at a speed much faster than was proper. His taillights rounded a corner, then disappeared into the night. The rumbly motor faded to nothing.

Frustrated tears pricked my eyes. It wasn't like Victor to just leave me standing in the middle of the street. But he wasn't in his right mind. And now, having seen what his family was like, I knew exactly why. Draft or no draft, the Nelsons weren't okay. It was a miracle Victor had become the smart, talented man he was.

And now I stood on the street outside Victor's house in the part of town my parents always told me not to go to. No way could I go back inside, not with Victor's weeping mother and his raging father. And I couldn't call my parents either, because they thought I was at the library studying and they would not be pleased to have to come to the wrong side of the tracks, as Mother put it, to fetch me. I could just hear her. *Oh, Iris, what will the neighbors think? Have you no shame?*

Well. At least it wasn't raining or snowing. It was chilly, but not as cold as December in Illinois could get. It was only a mile and a half or so to my house. I'd just walk. It'd give me a way to burn off my frustration. My anger. My helplessness that the United States government could just sign death warrants for gifted young men, and for what?

Victor had to get into Whitehall. He just had to.

I didn't know what would become of him—of us—if he didn't.

CHAPTER NINETEEN

*C*ALLUM KNIGHT!" Ralph's voice filled Callum's car through the speaker as Callum pulled into a parking space outside Peterson High School that clear, crisp Monday morning after homecoming. "To what do I owe the pleasure?"

"Top of the morning to you, Ralph." Callum shifted into park. His car faced east, toward the football field, and the sky filled with the last pinks and oranges of sunrise.

"What on earth is happening? You're calling me at seven fifteen on a Monday morning, and you're forming complete sentences? Wait, are you sick? Dying? You're not dying, are you? That would be very bad for business."

Callum chuckled. Ralph always was inclined toward melodrama. He'd been that way since college, and apparently it had only gotten worse.

"No," Ralph continued. "You can't be dying. Because you're in a good mood. Unless you're—"

"Ralph?"

"Yes?"

"Could you please stop playing wild guessing games and let me tell you why I called?"

"Yes. Of course. Apologies."

"And maybe cut back on the espresso?"

"That will happen on the twenty-first of never."

Callum grinned. The day Ralph Winters quit coffee was the day Callum would wonder if *he* was sick.

"Anyway." Callum took a deep breath. "I wanted to let you know that

I've thought about it, prayed about it, and yes, I will take that commission for Illinois."

"Excellent. Oh, that is *excellent* news. Just fantastic." Ralph's words tumbled out in their usual rapid-fire manner. "I couldn't be happier, Callum. Really. You're absolutely making the right decision. Your career will thank you. Your future self will thank you."

"My agent will thank me."

"I was getting to that. Especially since your agent already told Illinois you'd take it."

Callum hastily swallowed a sip of too-hot coffee from his Celtics travel mug. "I'm sorry, *what?*"

"I told them you'd take it. I knew your muse hadn't deserted you for good. I just told them we needed some flexibility with the deadline, and they went for it. I decided not to tell you until you came to your senses."

Callum stared at the arched entryway to the football stadium. *Welcome to Patriots Country*, it read. "I should fire you."

"You probably should. But you won't. You know you love me."

Callum shook his head. "Sometimes I wonder why."

Ralph laughed. "So what gave you your groove back? Was it the stunning motivational speech I gave you? It was, wasn't it?"

"Not even a little."

"Then you probably *should* fire me."

Callum shifted in the driver's seat. A couple more cars pulled into the lot. "I just . . . got this idea a few weeks ago. A melody. It happened at the most random of times, when I wasn't even thinking about it. It was a Friday afternoon, I was wrapping up the week, and it just . . . hit me. I honestly feel like God chose that moment to hand me a gift from the heavens. And I've been playing around with it, and it's actually turning into something. My compositional mojo is coming back."

"I knew you still had it in you, Callum." Ralph's pride shimmered through the phone.

"It feels different this time around." Callum turned his mug around in his hands, watching the steam rise from the hole in the lid. "More mature. Seasoned. Battle-tested, I guess. I appreciate it more, now that I know what it's like to live without it." True of everything since the pandemic, not just composition.

"It's the best work you've ever done." Ralph's voice was uncharacteristically quiet.

"How do you know that? I haven't sent it to you yet. It's not even finished."

"I can tell by the way you talk about it." The caffeinated pep returned to his agent's voice. "Now. The question is, What changed? What inspired you? I don't have five years to wait through your next rough patch, so I need the express route to unlocking your mojo."

Callum grinned. "I don't think that's how this works, Ralph."

"Well, just in case. What's different now?"

"Everything," he replied. "I'm in front of a choir every day again. Making music. Digging around in scores and finding what I want to bring out and then figuring out how to communicate that to the group. Seeing the kids make progress, watching them come alive, watching them fall in love with it, watching Blair and how she is with them, and the love these kids have for each other, and—"

"Aha! I should've known you met someone."

"I've met lots of people."

"Don't be daft, Callum. It's a woman. Of course it's a woman." He could picture Ralph slapping his own forehead. "That's what got you your muse back. I should've guessed. Blair, is it?"

"It's not a woman."

"Blair's not a woman?"

Images of Blair in that formfitting bronze dress surfaced. The memory of how perfectly she fit in his arms. Her sweet fragrance filling his lungs, the ends of her hair tickling his fingers as he held her . . .

"No, she very much is a woman."

"Callum." Ralph's voice held a grin. "You sly dog."

"It's not like that, Ralph. We work together." *And we talk about everything, and we danced together, and in a moment of temporary insanity I almost kissed her, and I spent all of yesterday wondering what would've happened if I actually had.* Not that he'd admit any of that to Ralph.

"Callum, you can prance around under that giant banner of denial all you want," Ralph said, "but I have not seen you this inspired, this on fire for music, this on fire for life, since you were with Rayne."

"But when I met Rayne, I was also in Boston directing choirs and making music every day. You can't separate the two."

"And you can't ignore the fact that I've known you since you were nineteen years old and I've seen you with women who didn't inspire you. Rayne did. And Blair clearly inspires you too."

Crap. Ralph was right. Callum had dated a few women, a couple he'd even really liked. But Rayne was the only one to inspire the music that came from his heart, not his head.

Well, the only one until Blair.

"Hey, I've got to run, Callum. Do something about the feelings you so obviously have for this woman. Or don't. Whatever works for you and your muse. Just grab hold of these musical ideas you've got back in your corner and don't let go of them. God has clearly answered your prayers and my prayers and your mother's prayers. Whatever you're doing, don't stop now."

The line went dead, and Callum sat in his car, sipping coffee and watching students trickle in from the parking spaces around him. He had feelings for Blair, obviously. He enjoyed her company. He found her attractive. He liked her.

Ralph thought it went beyond that, though. Ralph was comparing Blair to Rayne.

Rarefied air. And air he wasn't certain he was ready to revisit.

But his agent was right about one thing. Callum's prayers had been answered. Gratitude filled him, and he sat there in his car and thanked God for giving him back his creative muse.

God's plan for doing that was certainly not one Callum would've come up with. Bringing him to the middle of nowhere. Forcing him to take a job he'd have never considered otherwise.

But through that circuitous route, God had introduced him to the people and the music that would give him his inspiration back. Would give him his career back.

And that, in turn, would be his ticket back to Boston and back to his real life.

Blair parked her car on a side street rather than using the staff parking lot, and she entered the school through a seldom-used side door.

She wasn't avoiding Callum, necessarily. She just wasn't quite prepared to deal with him. Not yet. Not this early. Not when thoughts of him had occupied all her waking hours yesterday, and some of her sleeping ones. She hadn't even been able to focus at church, for goodness' sake. The pastor would talk about an answer to prayer, and she'd see Callum. He'd talk about how God has a way of bringing the people you need into your life at the exact moment you need them, and she'd think of Callum.

When he'd talked about the desires of one's heart and she'd still seen Callum, she'd forced herself to rein it in. *He's leaving. This is temporary. Nothing good can come of this.*

He hadn't texted her yesterday, which wasn't unusual for the weekend, and she usually turned her phone off on Sunday afternoons anyway. Doubly so yesterday, since that would also give her an opportunity to avoid an inevitable barrage of questions from Joy.

But when she turned her phone back on and hadn't heard anything from him, it was both a relief and an aggravation. He wasn't even going to mention the dance? The fact that they'd almost kissed? Had it meant so little that there was no explanation forthcoming? Or maybe it had meant something—so much that he wanted to discuss it in person.

And what if he did? What if he asked what it meant to her? What would she say?

Those were questions she couldn't answer. And that was why she'd parked off-site and come in through the side door. Why she wouldn't go into the choir room until the bell rang.

Mercifully, the commons had returned to normal. Twinkle lights had given way to the usual fluorescent. Fake trees had been replaced by lunch tables. Nothing remained of homecoming except a spirit-week poster still taped to one wall.

Okay. Maybe things with Callum could go back to normal as quickly as the commons had. Maybe there wouldn't be any discussion or mention or anything. Maybe they could just sweep whatever happened under the rug and go back to the way things were.

Or maybe she should've taken a sick day.

"Ms. Em!"

She looked up at the sound of her name, and there was Thalia, sitting alone at her usual table. A mostly full iced latte from Teddy's sat to one side, and the girl's ever-present sketchbook lay open on the table.

Blair approached and patted her student on the shoulder. "How are you, my dear?"

Thalia popped out her earbuds. "I'm okay." Then she tilted her head to the side, considering, as she stashed the earbuds in their little white case. "Well, maybe not yet. I'm still kinda mad."

"As you have every right to be." Blair pulled out a chair across from Thalia and eased into it. "Have you talked to Ryden?"

"He texted to let me know he got suspended today and tomorrow. He apologized."

"Good for him."

Thalia reached for her latte. "Whatever. I'm done with him. Done with boys in general, at least for a while. Boys are awful."

Blair smiled. "They can be."

"Besides, I'm graduating this year. I want to get into a good college and make something of myself." She offered a shy smile. "Lately I've been thinking I might even want to be a teacher."

Affectionate pride swelled in Blair's chest. "You'd be a wonderful teacher, Thalia."

"You think so?"

"Absolutely."

Thalia gave a crisp nod. "Then I don't have time to waste with Ryden or anyone else right now. Relationships are a distraction, anyway."

As if to illustrate her point, Callum chose that exact moment to stride through the commons, coffee in one hand, his head bent over his phone. Of course he'd worn that deep-green dress shirt of his, the one that brought out all the beautiful shades in his eyes. And of course his hair was tousled just so in that effortlessly perfect way handsome men had about them.

And then their eyes met.

Suddenly it didn't matter that there weren't any twinkle lights or fake trees. Just a glimpse and she might as well have been right back in his arms, breathing him in, and—*oh for the love, Blair, you have got to stop thinking about him like that.*

"You're absolutely right." She forced her gaze back to Thalia and put on a bright smile before the girl could grow suspicious. Thankfully, the early bell rang, and students around them reluctantly gathered their things and headed toward the hallways. "You better get to class, and so should I. But I'm really glad you're doing okay."

Thalia headed for her locker, and Blair squared her shoulders. She couldn't avoid it any longer. Time to face the proverbial—and literal—music. Time to enter the choir room and spend the day somehow not looking at or thinking about the guy who occupied 90 percent of her brain.

She definitely should've taken a sick day.

CHAPTER TWENTY

December 2, 1969

*T*HE NEXT morning, the hallways at school were buzzing.

"*Kenneth's number got called ninth. It's so unfair. He's already got an older brother over there.*"

"*Thank God my brother's in college. His birthday was the first one called.*"

"*My cousin Bill says he's never been so glad to have been sick all the time as a kid. He thinks maybe that'll get him out of it.*"

"*I'm just going to go ahead and enlist as soon as I graduate. Maybe then I can have some say in what happens to me.*"

"*No way, man. I'm going to Canada.*"

"*We should organize another march.*"

"*Yeah, like that'll do any good . . .*"

Last night's draft lottery was all anyone could talk about. All anyone could think about. And I was no exception. I hadn't slept at all. The sheer helplessness of it, that a government had the power to decide who lived and who died just by reaching into a container and drawing out plastic capsules . . .

But around two in the morning, it had hit me. Maybe I wasn't powerless after all.

The rest of the night had passed in a blur of notes and harmonies and playing chords on the piano as quietly as I could. And at the first light of dawn, I drew the double bar line at the end and sat back. There.

Finished. The piece Victor had inspired. The piece I'd been planning to use for my audition for Whitehall.

The piece I carried in my bag now as I entered the library.

Victor had already arrived. He sat at our usual table near the window, his head bent over a notebook of staff paper. He glanced up when I walked in, but he didn't smile. He just went back to his work.

My stomach churned as I approached. I hadn't heard from him since last night. I knew my parents wouldn't have let me take a call—nothing after 8:00 p.m.—but I'd at least thought I'd have heard the phone ring. I thought he'd have at least wondered how I'd made it home.

"Hello, Iris," he said.

"Hi." Was that it? Just *Hello, Iris*? No *I'm sorry about last night* or *I'm glad you got home safe*?

His lack of concern hurt. But however much I hurt, Victor hurt more. He'd just been told that unless he got into Whitehall, he'd probably be doomed to the jungles of Vietnam. And I'd glimpsed a little of his upbringing last night too. No way in the world could I understand what he was feeling. He needed my support, not my pettiness.

As if confirming my thoughts, he let out a frustrated snarl, tore the piece of manuscript paper from his notebook, and crumpled it into a tiny ball.

I sat down across from him, opened my bag, and pulled out my notebook. I flipped to the finished piece, then opened it and laid it in front of him. *I am my beloved's, and my beloved is mine.*

"You finished yours. Good for you." His voice was as cold as the weather outside. "Is that supposed to make me feel better?"

Heart pounding, I pulled in a deep breath. "Take it."

He blinked at me, his eyes unfocused through his glasses. "What?"

"Take my piece. For your audition. I finished it last night after . . ." Probably best not to bring up last night. "Anyway, it's done. You can have it."

He stared at me. His expression was almost totally without feeling. "I don't need your pity, Iris."

What? In all the times during the night I'd envisioned his reaction to my gift, not once did I predict this. I thought he'd be grateful. I must not have explained this very well. Wouldn't have been the first time. Words weren't my thing. I did so much better with music.

"It's . . . it's not pity."

"It's not?" He tilted his head. "Sure sounds like it to me."

How could I make him understand? "Victor. My parents will never let me go to Whitehall. I never even told them I was going to apply. Mother thinks the only reason for a woman to go to college is so she can find either a husband or a job to tide her over until she *does* find a husband. And her reasoning is that since we have money, I don't need a job, so . . . what's the point of college?" I laughed, hoping the sound would cover the shattering of my heart. "So even if I got in, I wouldn't be able to go. And I guess I'd rather the work I did not go to waste."

"You think I can't come up with something on my own?" he challenged.

Oh no. This was going from bad to worse. "I never said that, Victor. But you look like you're having trouble—"

"I am having trouble. But I have to do it on my own. That way my father will know beyond a doubt that I'm talented. That I deserve this and that I can make a living at it."

I laid my hand on top of his. "You can, Victor. And you will. Whether your father ever believes those things or not, I do. You'll achieve whatever you set your mind to. That's . . . part of what inspired me to write this piece. It's for you, Victor. I wrote it for you. You inspired every part of it. The music, the text . . . everything."

Finally he seemed to come back to himself. "Oh, Iris. I'm such an idiot. I'm not in my right mind." He glanced through the music, and his lips curved. "You'd do this for me? You'd offer me your work?"

"Of course I would. In a heartbeat. I'd do anything for you, Victor." I drew a breath and met his gaze. "I . . . I love you."

His eyes widened. "You do?"

The love in my heart bloomed into a smile. "I've never been more sure of anything in my life."

He answered my smile with one of his own. "I love you too, Iris. You're . . . an angel from heaven."

"I don't know if I'd go that far." I beamed across the table at him.

"Maybe that could be the text of the brilliant piece you write someday. I know you'll have an amazing career."

"With you by my side, Iris? There's no way I can fail. You'll see." He talked fast, and his cheeks turned pink. "And when I get into Whitehall, I'll write to you all the time, and I'll tell you all the amazing things I'm learning. And when I graduate, we'll get married, and we'll both compose. We'll be the next Rodgers and Hammerstein." He gestured toward an imaginary sign. "Victor Nelson and Iris Nelson. Can't you just see the marquee?"

He went on talking a mile a minute, and my heart welled with joy. It seemed I'd given him exactly what I'd wanted to. Hope. Enthusiasm. A ticket out of Vietnam. All because of the piece that lay open on the table between us.

And he'd promised me everything I wanted. A future with him. Making music together as husband and wife. Surely that was worth sacrificing my composition. I wrote it for him, anyway, didn't I?

So why were the chords in my soul so dissonant?

Why did part of me feel like I'd just made a terrible mistake?

CHAPTER TWENTY-ONE

*L*ET'S GO, people. Move with a purpose. We've got a lot to do today, so let's get after it." Callum greeted Madrigals before the bell even rang, while they were still filtering onto the risers in the auditorium. Rehearsals had been moved from the choir room for the entire week leading up to Thursday night's concert, and he was eager to see how the auditorium's acoustics would change the sound of the choir.

His good mood from the morning had gradually faded over the course of the day. A post-homecoming funk afflicted all the students with a lack of energy and focus—the exact opposite of what they needed for concert week. As a result, the knots in Callum's stomach tightened with each passing minute. The national anthem at a football game, as successful as the performance had been, was small potatoes. Besides, two-thirds of the choir were returners from last year and thus already knew their parts for the anthem—and the "Star-Spangled Banner" was nowhere near as challenging as the program he'd selected for the fall concert.

"Hey, hey, Mr. K." Zayden, a skinny tenor, loped across the stage toward the risers, tossing his folder to himself as he walked.

Callum had never sanctioned the abbreviation of his last name to a single letter, but Zayden marched to the beat of his own drum.

"Afternoon, Zayden." Callum's greeting was punctuated by the high-pitched drone of the bell, which hovered between an E and an F but was annoyingly neither of those pitches.

"Saw you and Miss Em gettin' your groove on at homecoming Saturday night." Zayden took his spot, front and center, with a mischievous wiggle of his eyebrows. Predictably, student gazes bounced from

Callum to Blair and back again, grins appeared, and a whisper wound its way through the choir.

"We were chaperoning," Blair replied coolly, at the same time Callum stomped his foot on the stage floor to regain order.

"That is in the past." Frustration bled into his voice. "It's concert week. We have four rehearsals left, and we are not where we need to be with this music. We do not have time for chitchat."

Zayden elbowed Jake. "When have we ever had time for chitchat?"

"Bruh. Shut up," Jake hissed.

Callum leveled a lethal glare, which he then swiveled to the rest of the choir, just in case anyone else felt like trying anything.

"For time's sake, let's skip warm-ups and go directly to page eight of the Lauridsen." Callum tapped the screen of his iPad. "We have a lot of work to do yet on that middle section."

He avoided making eye contact with Blair, because he knew she'd have that eyebrow raised again. She hadn't said anything about his repertoire selection since the first day. At least not with her voice. But her pointed expressions and silent, sniffy disapproval communicated clearly enough. She still thought the music was too difficult.

To his chagrin, she was probably right. But he wasn't about to admit that and give her the satisfaction. Especially not today, when she'd seemingly retreated into her deep freeze. Blair had barely given him the time of day all day. Just crisp nods and sharp angles and as few words as necessary. And as much as that had bothered him before, it bothered him doubly now, because the ever-perceptive Ralph had brought up a valid point: Callum had feelings for Blair.

At least, the version of her he'd seen these past few weeks, and especially Saturday night, all warmth and softness and curves.

Theoretically her return to cold and angular should make it easier for him to focus on his job. Irritatingly, though, it did not. Every time he had to glance toward Blair to give her a cue, he remembered her in that glittery dress.

She wore a thick brown sweater today, but thanks to Saturday night, he knew the graceful sweep between her neck and shoulder. She hadn't gotten close enough today for him to smell her shampoo, but its delicious scent was still seared in his brain. He knew what she felt like in his arms, the delicate touch of her fingers on his shoulder, the tickle of her breath on his ear—and he couldn't un-know those things.

And she acted like none of that had happened. Like it meant nothing. Which it probably didn't. Who was he kidding? This was Blair the ice queen. Any heart she had was doubtless poured only into the music and the kids. That was all she had room for. No space left for anyone else. No space left for him. And that was just fine. Perfect, even. The last thing he needed was to get mixed up with someone in Peterson when his mission had always been to return to Boston.

But Blair's softer, warmer side had kicked his compositional muse back into gear. It had given him the confidence to accept that commission.

If she had forever shut off that side of herself, though, then where did that leave him? Would he require a constant supply of inspiration to be able to complete his commission, or was that kick start last month enough?

No wonder he was grouchy today. But at least he could use the concert as an excuse. Any director would be stressed the week of a concert, especially if it was their first one at a new school.

It was 100 percent believable, and no one would look too closely.

No one had to know that the concert wasn't the only cause.

Blair's cinnamon-roll candle flickered to life beneath the flame of her stick lighter. Its golden glow and homey scent soon filled her corner of the choir office but did nothing to calm her jangled nerves. With a sigh, she plopped into her chair, jammed the lighter back into the desk drawer, and tore into a fresh bag of peanut butter cups.

Seeing Callum in normal work clothes, keeping a professional distance from him, and not having his hand graze her bare skin should have yanked her back to reality. Sadly, they had not. She'd even gotten lost in the music during Women's Choir this morning—something she never, ever did—because she couldn't stop staring at him. He hadn't said anything, mercifully, but the look he'd pinned on her meant he'd definitely noticed.

But the post-homecoming fog had quickly given way to irritation as the day wore on and rehearsals progressed. The choirs always lost a little bit of momentum over the weekend, and the first few minutes of every Monday rehearsal were spent reteaching everything Saturday and Sunday had made them forget. And she'd known to expect a slight lack of focus from everyone after homecoming. But, true to form, Callum expected more of the kids, not less. He was impatient with their lack of focus. Frustrated that he had to reteach. All the feelings you'd expect from a new director staring down the barrel of the October concert.

He cared about the job—and the kids—more than she'd expected after that first stiff handshake. And she was grateful. But her esteemed colleague had yet to entirely grasp that these were children, not professionals.

The door creaked open, and Callum strode in, iPad in hand. He gave her an indecipherable glance as he passed her desk, and she responded by defiantly stuffing a peanut butter cup into her mouth.

He set the iPad down on his desk, then turned to face her. "Blair . . ."

Finally. The *what on earth was that* conversation she'd been dreading since Saturday night.

"We don't know each other all that well yet," he said. "And God willing, we only have to work together until May."

The knife-edge of his words cut swiftly and unexpectedly deep.

"But we do have to work together until May, so . . ." He ran a hand through his hair. "Are you upset with me about something?"

The peanut butter cup slid down her throat as her defenses ratcheted up. "Why do you ask?"

"I thought things were going well. You know, between us. But today you've been a little . . . frosty."

Of course I'm frosty. Because we danced together Saturday night and I felt things I didn't want to feel, especially for you, and it sure seemed like you felt the same things, and yet we're not going to acknowledge that, which is probably just as well since you're counting the days until you can get out of here, so there's literally no point to exploring those feelings we had. If, in fact, you weren't just faking it.

Oh, that she had the courage to actually say those words. Instead she reached for her water bottle. "Surely you understand concert stress. Especially when the choir isn't ready."

"There it is."

She turned to face him, water halfway to her lips, her voice still sticky from the peanut butter cup. "There what is?"

"Could've guessed it." He tossed his high-tech pencil onto the desk beside the iPad. "You might not say anything, but your expression always gives you away. You still think this music is too hard for the choirs."

"It's great music, Callum. But these kids haven't had any sort of meaningful choral experience for the last five years. Going from zero to a hundred is giving them whiplash."

He looked skyward. "I see. So you just want me to stay with safe, easy, *boring* music."

"If that's what they need for a successful performance, then yes." She set the water bottle back down on her desk. "A successful performance will give them the confidence they need to tackle more challenging music, and that's something we can build on. For this year, anyway. Then we have to start over again."

"With all due respect, Blair, that's not really my concern."

"Clearly." She unwrapped another peanut butter cup, the crinkle of the foil filling the cinnamon-scented air.

"But it is my concern this year. They're my choirs. And what's become very obvious to me over the past two months is that no one has challenged them. No one has stretched them."

"How can they be stretched when nobody sticks around longer than a year?"

"They're good singers, Blair. Despite everything they've been through, they're good. Madrigals especially. Those kids have a ton of talent. But if no one ever takes them out of their comfort zone, they'll never know what they're capable of." He leaned toward her. "Don't you want to see how far they can go?"

"Of course I do. But not if it means they're going to humiliate themselves Thursday." She punctuated her argument by popping the unwrapped peanut butter cup into her mouth.

Callum didn't reply, just sat down at his desk and clicked into his email program. *Wow. Well then. Guess we're done talking.* She woke up her own laptop and scrolled through the dozens of emails she'd received that day, deleting them or filing them one by one.

She must've spent too much time around high schoolers if she'd truly thought a homecoming dance would change things. Clearly it hadn't. Whatever had happened Saturday was a flash in the pan, and now they were back to being at loggerheads over what was best for the kids. And his approach wasn't best. The frustration on the kids' faces in rehearsal today. The fact that they were still, three days before the concert, unsure of their individual parts. And memorization? Ha. That would take a miracle.

But whether she agreed with him privately or not, publicly she had to support him. He was the choral director, after all. The decisions about the direction of the program weren't hers to make. They were Callum's. The most she could do was offer her opinion and then outwardly support whatever he did. Even if—even though—he was dead wrong.

"Huh." Callum broke the tense silence. "I got an email from Peggy Sue Weldon."

Blair had just reached the same one in her email queue. "Yeah, I got one too." She clicked on the message.

Mr. Knight and Ms. Emerson,

Please share with your students how grateful I am for all the hard work at my house last week. My backyard hasn't been this beautiful since my husband was alive, and I can't tell you how happy that makes me. And the new paint color in the living room is just so peaceful and calming. You are all truly messengers of the Most High, even if you're unaware. He chose you to bless me, and if there is anything I can ever do to bless all of you, know that I stand ready and willing to do so as much as I am able.

Thank you again for preserving the legacy of generosity and service that the Peterson community is known for. You are truly outstanding young citizens, and I can rest assured that the future is in excellent hands.

PS: You'll probably be getting a phone call soon from my granddaughter Keira McLane. You may recognize the name, as she is a reporter for Channel 6 News in Champaign. Her passion is investigative reporting, and when I mentioned the two of you were looking into a former student's story, she lit up like a Christmas tree. I don't know how you feel about media attention, so if this is something you prefer to keep under wraps, I'll do my best to dissuade her. I will warn you, though— she is very persistent. She gets that from my side of the family.

Blair stared at the screen until it blurred from her lack of blinking. "An investigative reporter?"

"This could be huge," Callum replied. "She might get people to talk about Iris who otherwise wouldn't. And who knows? There might be people who don't live in Peterson anymore who'll see the story online and remember something about her."

Oh. He thought this was a good thing. "Well, yes, that's one possibility, but—"

Callum's desk phone rang, and he raised one finger. "Sorry. Hold that thought?" He picked up the phone. "Callum Knight. Oh. Yes. Hello, Keira. I've just been told we'd be hearing from you."

Blair gulped. Like it or not, their curiosity about Iris Wallingford had just reached another—very public—level.

She reached into her desk drawer once again. Some days called for a third peanut butter cup.

Today was definitely one of those days.

CHAPTER TWENTY-TWO

December 2, 1969

ℐ ARRIVED HOME just past five that chilly evening, though it was already dark as midnight. My father's Cadillac quietly gleamed in the driveway. Pushing my glove aside, I checked my watch just to be sure. No, he really was home early. Usually he stayed at work until six, or even later. He only came home early when Mother invited company for dinner.

My heart sank as I opened the front door and hung my coat in the foyer. Sure enough, our maid, Flora, had put in another long day. The house was even more spotless than normal. A picture-perfect fire crackled in the fireplace, and the huge Christmas tree in the corner cast flickering light over the grand piano. Our formal dining room, which we hardly ever used, was polished to a sheen and set with our best china.

I suppressed a groan. Not only were we having company, we were having company whom Mother wanted to impress. That meant an evening of boring conversation and constant needling from Mother to be charming and social and all the things she wanted me to be. All the things I was not.

Mother burst through the doorway, bearing a large ceramic Christmas tree. She wore a green dress I'd never seen before, and her dark hair was coiffed to perfection as always. Flora was at her heels, a professional, pleasant expression on her face and a tray of appetizers in her arms. Flora had worked for our family for as long as I could remember, and sometimes I thought my parents liked her better than they liked me. *Why can't you smile like Flora, Iris? Why can't you stand up straight like Flora does, Iris? Why can't you be exactly who we want you to be, just like Flora is?* In fact, once I heard my mother refer to Flora as the daughter she never had.

And then there was me. The daughter she actually had.

"Iris Jean Wallingford. Why are you home so late?" Mother eyed me with a steely glare as Flora slipped into the living room.

"I . . . I went to the library." Not entirely untrue, since I began my day in the library. But after school Victor and I had found a practice room, and . . . well . . . we had not practiced music. I could still taste his kisses. Best not think about that too much, though, or I'd blush.

Mother heaved a gusty sigh and moved toward the buffet, where the tree's light-bulb base sat. "I could've used your help this afternoon. The Stuarts are coming over for dinner."

"The Stuarts?"

"From church? Surely you remember their son, Robert." She set the tree on its base and switched it on. The little bulbs on the branches lit up in a dazzling multicolored array.

Yes, I remembered Robert. He graduated a couple of years ago and was now attending Northwestern. He'd been class president, homecoming king, and all the other inane high school status symbols that made people like my mother salivate.

"I told you just this morning." Mother turned toward me, her voice tight with exasperation. "Honestly, Iris. You've always got your head in the clouds. Go upstairs and change. Wear your nice red floral blouse. Red is a good color for you."

Of course she wanted me to wear my red floral blouse. I hated that blouse. So stiff and scratchy.

"Oh, but don't wear the white skirt. It's much too short." She checked her hair in the mirror behind the buffet. "Wear the navy jumper instead. And put on some rouge for once. You look like a ghost."

Maybe I should've allowed myself to blush. "Mother, I have an English exam tomorrow, and—"

"*Now,* Iris." Mother turned a fiery glare on me. "The Stuarts will be here in ten minutes."

I waited until she turned back toward the mirror, then rolled my eyes to the ceiling. "Why is this such a big deal?"

"Because Robert Stuart is a wonderful young man, and last time I talked with his mother, she told me he was interested in you."

Robert Stuart? Interested in *me*? Not possible. We had nothing in common. I wasn't even sure he knew I existed. He'd certainly never spoken to me or even acknowledged my existen—

Wait. Mr. Stuart was the president of First National Bank downtown. Mrs. Stuart was related to the Roebucks of Chicago. The Stuarts were the richest family in Peterson, and I knew my mother and Glenda Stuart played bridge together. Those two must've been matchmaking. Planning a family alliance. That was literally the only reason Robert Stuart would have any interest in me whatsoever.

"Robert intends to become a lawyer, then go into politics. Run for governor someday. Maybe even president." She turned to me, her eyes sparkling like a teenage girl with a crush. "Just think of it, Iris. First Lady Iris Stuart."

The name landed with a decidedly unmusical thud. Nothing like *Iris Nelson* in lights on a marquee.

"Mother, I—"

The doorbell chimed, and my mother jumped. "Oh! They're early. Go upstairs and change right now." She gave me a gentle shove toward the stairs. "Join us in the living room for hors d'oeuvres."

"Fine." I started up the stairs. Dinner smelled delicious, but I'd lost my appetite. I had a sneaking suspicion that before the evening ended, I'd have to come clean with some secrets.

That sort of thing usually didn't end well.

Flora slid a plate of beef Wellington before me. I murmured my thanks as she moved to my left, where Robert was sitting. His aftershave was so strong that I could barely smell the beef, and that irritated me. Flora's beef Wellington was delicious. Anything that covered up its aroma was a crime.

Robert hadn't changed much since high school: blond, blue-eyed, and so impossibly handsome he may as well have been made of plastic. He looked like a human Ken doll, and he'd obviously been well programmed. He smiled at the exact time and to the exact degree that he was supposed to, no matter the situation. He made conversation with ease, as though he were born doing it. There was not an ounce of awkwardness in this man, but there wasn't an ounce of realness either.

Maybe the Stuarts had ordered him from a lab. They'd certainly have been able to afford it.

Robert turned to me, and his smile notched up to a 6.5. Flirtatious but Still Family Friendly seemed to be his current setting. "I forgot how quiet you are, Iris."

"She's always been a shy one," Father commented from the head of the table. Beside me, opposite him, my mother gently nudged my ankle with the toe of her pump, her socially acceptable way of ordering me to say something witty and charming. Even when I was with someone I wanted to impress, witty and charming didn't come naturally. And I had no desire to impress Robert Stuart, or charm him, or do anything whatsoever with him except endure this forced dinner.

Because he wasn't Victor.

"It's fine, Mr. Wallingford." Robert turned his smile up to a 7.2. "I don't mind, I assure you. Lots of girls, you can't get a word in edgewise. Iris here is a breath of fresh air."

As if a conductor had just cued them, all the adults at the table laughed that light, humorless laugh the wealthy had perfected: *What you said wasn't funny, but you're a high-status individual, so I shall reward you with an expression of humor and delight.*

I only laughed when something was genuinely funny. So I didn't laugh.

Mother leaned over. Her expression was perfectly pleasant, but her teeth were clenched. "Would it kill you to smile?"

I met her gaze. "I fear it just might."

"So, Iris." Robert speared a bite of sautéed asparagus. "What do you like to do for fun? I hear there's a new Bond film coming out in a couple of weeks. Are you excited to see that one?"

"No, I . . . I don't go to the movies much." I took a bite of beef to have a ready-made excuse for not making further conversation.

Another nudge on my ankle from Mother. "Iris is much more interested in music than movies."

"Oh, that's right. I remember now." Robert's manufactured smile was at a level 8. "And that's wonderful, because so do I. Tell me, Iris. Who's your favorite Beatle?"

I swallowed. None of them, honestly. "Well, I—"

"Wait, I'll bet you're more of a Rolling Stones girl, aren't you?"

"Actually, Robert, I like Chopin."

The smile faded to a 7.5. "Show . . . who?"

"Frédéric Chopin. A Polish-born French composer most famous for his piano works. Of course, I also love Bach and Beethoven, but who doesn't?"

I sensed Mother getting ready to kick me again, so I moved my right foot out of the way. Sure enough, there came a gentle tap against the table leg as her toe connected with wood. She shot me a brief glare.

"Oh, of course." Robert's smile had dimmed to a 7. "Obviously Bach and Beethoven. I meant besides them."

A devilish idea seized me. Putting my fork down, I turned to Robert and batted my eyelashes. "I could listen to Bach all day long. Especially his seventh Brandenburg Concerto."

"Ah, yes. The seventh." He dug his knife into the Christmas tree–shaped pat of butter on his plate and buttered his dinner roll. "That's my favorite one, Iris. Especially the beginning."

"The beginning of which movement?"

Robert still wore that manufactured smile. Did anything deter this man? "The first one, of course."

For the first time all evening, my own smile turned genuine. "Trick question, Robert. There is no seventh Brandenburg. Bach only wrote six."

Mother set her fork down on the table with enough force to slosh water over the edge of my glass. "Iris. May I please speak with you in the kitchen? *Now?*"

"With pleasure, Mother." I tossed my napkin aside and charged into the kitchen. Flora glanced up, startled, and bustled around the corner toward the laundry room.

Mother whirled to face me, hands on her hips. "You will apologize to the Stuarts immediately."

"I'll do no such thing."

"How many times do I have to tell you, Iris? Men don't appreciate it when women one-up them."

"Then men should be smarter," I retorted. "Honestly, who doesn't know there are only six Brandenburgs? Victor's probably known that since kindergarten."

It wasn't until Mother's penciled brows inched together that I realized what I'd said. I never meant for the name to slip out, but it had, and now it hovered between us.

"Victor?" Her mouth twisted uncertainly around the word. "And who on earth is Victor?"

"Victor Nelson. The drum major." I lifted my chin. "We've been seeing each other."

"*Seeing* each other," Mother scoffed. "Well. The least you could've done is bring him to meet us. Is he of the Chicago Nelsons?"

"No." My lips curved. "He's of the Second Street Nelsons."

"Second Street?" Mother drew back as if she'd been branded. "Oh, Iris. No. Absolutely not. You can do better than Second Street. What kind of life can this boy give you? Don't you want better for yourself?"

"What I want is Victor," I snapped. "Because he loves me. He understands me, which is something no one has ever done."

"Oh, *please*, Iris." Mother folded her arms across her chest.

"Everyone thinks I'm weird, Mother. I don't like loud noises or scratchy fabrics. I don't like movies or rock bands or crowds or parties. I like music, because it's the only thing that makes me feel alive. It doesn't matter whether I'm singing it or playing it or writing my own. And Victor is the only person I've ever met who has the same talents. Who loves music the same way I do."

Mother reached out to touch my arm, but I backed away.

"Well, of course, Iris." She offered a smile. "Music is wonderful. There's nothing wrong with it. But, darling, it's simply not a sensible career. For you or for him."

"Victor's going to make it one." An idea crystallized in the center of my chest. "And so am I."

Mother arched a brow. "I see. And how are you planning to make this happen?"

"We're applying to the Whitehall Conservatory in Chicago." Never mind that I just gave Victor my audition piece. I could write another one. I still had almost twenty-four hours before the postmark deadline. "It's very exclusive, and tuition-free for those who are accepted."

"Mmm. Then they must not accept many."

Courage hummed through my veins. "They don't. But we'll both get in. And we'll soak up all the knowledge we can, and then we'll go on to graduate school. Maybe we'll even get doctorates. Become university professors. Well-known composers."

Mother patted her hairdo. "You think this is the life you want, Iris? Then go make it happen. But you'd better get into that conservatory, because if this is the direction you're choosing to take your life, you'll not get a penny from us."

I'd already started up the back stairs. "I don't need your money, Mother. I'll make it in music with or without your support."

"And just where do you think you're going, young lady?" Mother demanded.

"Upstairs." For the first time all day, something felt right. "Give the Stuarts my regards. I have an audition piece to write."

CHAPTER TWENTY-THREE

*T*HE AUDITORIUM was dark and empty when Callum arrived for the concert an hour and a half before curtain. Good. He'd come early enough, because the auditorium was the way he wanted it. Devoid of any human presence but his own.

Aided by his phone flashlight, he found and activated a series of buttons on the back wall, flooding the house with golden light. The wicked noisy stage lights he'd save for later. Those things made such an unholy racket that he didn't want to deal with them any longer than he had to. If he were going to be here long-term, he'd march into the next school board meeting and demand they do something about the lighting situation. As it stood now, he'd just grit his teeth and put up with it until May.

Standing here, at the back of an empty hall on concert night, brought a wave of nostalgia and an unexpected lump to his throat. He'd always shown up early and alone before concerts in the past, practically giddy as he walked the aisles, praying over the patrons, the podium, and the piano. Concerts were the culmination of weeks and months of hard work. He'd trusted the choir and they'd trusted him, and that combined with years of experience on everyone's part had resulted in performances that were as close to heaven as anything he'd ever encountered.

Back then his heart was bursting with joy and hope and the dazzling possibilities his future presented. Rayne was alive and well. His creative cup was full to overflowing. The world was his oyster.

Then those news reports surfaced—some weird new virus in China—and it all came crashing down. Faster than he could've ever imagined.

Now here he stood, alone at the back of a hall, wearing a tux, preparing for a concert. Green tendrils were shooting up from the blackened, ashy soil of his former life. He had a choir again. He had inspiration again.

But those tendrils were still a far cry from the forest that had once been there.

Looking back on his past with new perspective, though, had that forest been as thick and lush as he'd once thought? His prayers had been little more than surface-level thanks. A formality. A superstitious ritual to put the finishing touch on his concert preparation. He hadn't truly depended on God, because he hadn't felt like he needed God's help. He'd trusted far more in his and the choir's preparation, their professionalism, than in God. No, back then prayer had been a mere rubber stamp. A good luck charm. Nothing more.

Now he was moments away from a concert with high schoolers. Immature, inexperienced, unpredictable high schoolers. He couldn't depend on them to come through for him the way his Boston professionals had. And his faith in himself had taken a beating too. For the first time in his entire career, God was his only hope.

His prayer was a simple one, but it came from the very depths of his being.

Jesus, help.

The door at the rear of the auditorium opened, and his head snapped up.

It was Blair, clad head to toe in concert black, carrying her blue binder full of choir music. She looked as startled as he felt.

"Hi," he said.

"Hi." She brushed a lock of red hair away from her face. "I . . . didn't expect anyone to be here yet."

He stuffed his hands into his pockets. "Well, that makes two of us."

"I usually warm up before concerts. In here." *Alone.* She hadn't said that last word, but it hung in the air just as clearly as the last echoes of a final chord.

"Then I'll get out of your way." He turned and strode up the aisle, catching a crazy-making whiff of her shampoo as he passed her. A moment later, scales filled the auditorium at a near-dizzying pace.

Her technique was so crisp and clear. Mozart and Haydn would've been right up her alley as a soloist. Early Beethoven too. By contrast, his piano teachers had quickly realized that he excelled at things like Rachmaninoff. Thick, juicy chords and a ton of passion.

But Blair's delicate precision worked for her. Disciplined and exacting, just like her personality.

What, if anything, could loosen her up? He'd seen glimpses of what lay underneath all that cool professionalism, but only glimpses. What would it take for her to let him see more?

Couldn't think about that right now, though. He had to get his head right. He couldn't be in here thinking about Blair. He shoved open the door and stepped out into the bright lights of the hallway. He could continue his prayer just as easily in the choir room, couldn't he?

Given his new job and new location, a new preconcert ritual suddenly seemed quite appropriate.

Despite everything, Blair had been looking forward to the concert. She always anticipated them, though her enthusiasm had dimmed with each passing year. Each new director. Each time she and the students had to start over with someone new.

Callum, to his credit, had done more with the kids than most of his predecessors, but despite the intense work they'd put in this week, the music was still short of where it needed to be. So after Freshman Choir filed onstage, blue robes gleaming in bright lights, and she strode out to take her place at the piano, she was uncharacteristically on edge. Her hands were shaky. So were Callum's.

And he started the first piece faster than they'd ever rehearsed it.

She should've been prepared for that, of course. A collaborative pianist should be prepared for anything. Be able to adapt to anything. Be able to adjust to anything. But all those years of adapting and adjusting had taken its toll. And tonight, at the downbeat of the first concert of the year, her adaptive skills ran out. She was rattled. And she completely flubbed the introduction.

She had to move on. Forget about it. Keep pressing forward. And as a professional, she did. But the kids were shaken. For the rest of the concert, it showed. The freshmen sang so quietly Blair could barely hear them, even from the stage. The treble choir forgot everything they'd ever learned about diction. Mixed Chorus managed the unintentional yet difficult feat of singing in two keys at the same time. And when Madrigals took the stage, they were terrified. Their performance had no glaring errors, but it sounded tight. Insecure. She saw the stress on their faces, and she heard it in their voices.

By the time the concert ended and the audience showered them with uncertain applause, Blair was blazing mad. Half an hour of hobnobbing with parents did nothing to take the edge off.

Especially not when she saw Makayla backstage in tears.

Once Blair had comforted and sent Makayla on her way, Blair was practically in tears of her own. She hauled the heavy quilted cover to the grand piano and wrestled it onto the instrument's ebony surface. What would she even say to Callum? He'd probably already left, and he hadn't even bothered to turn the lights off, so that was yet another thing she had to do before she went home, and—

The stage door opened, and there stood the man himself. He'd shed his jacket, and his tie hung loose around his neck. Despite everything, he was still devastatingly handsome, and that just made her madder.

"That could've gone better," he said as he approached.

She yanked the cover over the back of the piano. "Understatement of the century."

"What *happened*?"

"I don't know, Callum. Maybe you'd like to explain why you started the first piece so fast." *Arrrggh.* She'd put the piano cover on backward. Again.

"We'd taken it almost that fast in rehearsal." He took a spot on the opposite side of the piano and picked up the edge of the cover, helping her rotate it clockwise. "What's another notch or two on the metronome? Given preconcert adrenaline, they were going to take it faster anyway."

"Directing a high school choir is like steering a cruise ship, Callum. Maybe you're used to driving a speedboat, but we are not that. You can't just change the tempo on us."

"Well, you're a professional, at least."

"A professional who does not appreciate surprises."

"Noted."

Blair yanked the cover into place and stepped back. "Wait, are you blaming me for how things turned out tonight?"

"The piano is the foundation of the entire performance. If that's not secure, then it can affect things."

"And why in the world do you think it wasn't secure? You're the one who charged in here and acted like you knew what you were doing when it turns out you definitely did not."

He flung an arm skyward. "Okay, Blair. You're right and I'm wrong. You know everything and I know nothing. I should just let you make all the decisions from here on out."

"That's not what I said."

"It's what you implied."

Oh, what a ridiculous, frustrating human being. "So sue me, Callum. Sue me for loving these kids. For caring about them and wanting what's best for them."

"Did it ever occur to you, in all your self-righteous pontificating, that you aren't the only one who cares about them?" His eyes shot sparks.

"Well, given that you've set them up to fail from day one, you've sure got a funny way of showing it."

"Why? Because I choose quality music instead of the middle-level drivel they're used to? Because I demand the absolute best they're able to give instead of halfhearted effort? Because I want them to learn as much as they can here since high school choir is about so much more than music? Because I want them to be equipped for success in life, not just in choir?" He stopped, both hands resting on the newly covered grand, a muscle in his jaw twitching.

"We've been over this. Equipping them for success means giving them confidence, Callum. And *nobody* has confidence after a performance like that." She turned her back on him and walked toward the wings.

"I do," he said quietly.

She spun to face him. "*How?*"

"Because even though this performance wasn't anywhere near where we wanted it to be, we made progress. They're better than they were in August. They're working. They're trying."

"But if you don't give them music they can succeed with, then they'll get frustrated and give up."

He stepped toward her. "They'll get frustrated and give up? Or *you* will?"

"Do you think for one single minute that I would ever give up on these kids? I'm the only consistency they've had for the last seven years, and that's not going to change anytime soon. One of us has to be loyal to them. One of us has to love them. And it's been clear from the moment you took this job that it isn't going to be you."

"So I should just phone it in. Keep them locked up in their comfort zone. Give them music they could sing in their sleep, just so they'll be *successful*?" He framed the last word with air quotes. "What does that even mean, Blair? What is it that you want from me? You're annoyed with all the previous directors because they apparently didn't try hard enough. And I'm working my butt off for these kids, and you don't like that either."

She blinked at him, stunned speechless. At least for the moment.

He ran a hand through his hair. "You're an incredibly difficult woman to please, Blair Emerson. So would you just tell me, once and for all, so we can get through the rest of this year without killing each other . . . what do you *want*?"

He stood there, not ten feet from her, cheeks flushed and breathing fast. He looked rumpled and disheveled and exhausted, and he was the most infuriating person she'd ever met . . . but he had never been more handsome. His methods could use some refining, but his motives were pure. He truly did want the best for her beloved kids. For this school. For the community.

And what did she want?

She wanted this to not be their only year together.

And more than that, she didn't want him to just be her coworker.

She wanted . . .

She wanted . . .

Oh, *crap.*

She wanted to kiss him.

To her shock, it seemed he wanted the same thing. Dark brows furrowed a fraction. Disbelief etched his face.

Then disbelief changed to something else entirely. And maybe he walked toward her, or maybe she walked toward him, or maybe they moved at the same time, but then they collided and he was kissing her and she was kissing him and nothing else in the world mattered.

His hand tangled in her hair. Her hip bumped into the piano. His kiss deepened, filled with the same unbridled passion she'd seen at the podium. With the kids. He was wild and free and unrestrained in a way she'd never been.

Not until now, anyway. His kiss made her come alive. Awakened something in her heart she'd thought long dead. Or maybe that had never even been there at all.

Comfort zone? Ha. She was so far beyond her comfort zone that she couldn't even see it anymore.

And maybe that was okay. Maybe this was exactly where she needed to be.

Maybe this was where God had been leading her all along.

CHAPTER TWENTY-FOUR

December 3, 1969

*T*HE GRANDFATHER clock played the familiar Westminster chime tune, then bonged once.

One. It was one in the morning.

I was back downstairs in the living room. The Stuarts were long gone, and thanks to perfect Flora's tireless efforts, the house wouldn't betray that they had ever even been here. The Christmas tree and the piano lamp were the only lights, bathing the room in a cozy calmness and blessed, blissful quiet.

I, however, was anything but calm. After paging through my music notebook and finding nothing worthy of Whitehall, I now sat at the piano, my left foot clamped down on the una corda pedal, dampening the sound so I wouldn't wake anybody. A pile of manuscript paper stood on the music rack, and I was trying my hardest to recapture the magic of "I Am My Beloved's."

Of course, that was the very definition of magic or inspiration or whatever had struck me and enabled me to write that piece—there was no channeling it or changing it or controlling it. Like the wind, it came from wherever it wanted and went wherever it pleased at whatever speed it liked, and no one could do anything about it. And normally that was fine.

But normally I wasn't staring down the barrel of a deadline.

I was determined to do this, though. It would be my way out of the puppeted life Mother wanted for me. They wouldn't pay for my schooling if I pursued music? Fine. They'd always controlled me through money, and unless something changed, they always would. If I could turn my back on that, if I could prove to them that I was capable of making music a career, then I would win.

In this way, despite our differences in financial status, Victor and I weren't so different. Both of us needed freedom from our family legacies. And neither of us had the monetary means to escape on our own. We needed the Whitehall Conservatory of Music to help us. And I wrote a quality piece once. Surely I could do it again.

But that night—possibly due to exhaustion or desperation or both—writing a quality piece was suddenly a tall order. "I Am My Beloved's" was the best thing I'd ever written, hands down. It had come from the truest, deepest part of me. My soul-level love for Victor, a kind of love I hadn't even known existed. That was what had inspired the music, and that was also what had inspired me to give it to him. Even if he and I were physically intimate—which we hadn't been, not yet—nothing I could give him would mean more to me than that piece.

I didn't think he truly understood the depth of the gift I'd given him, though. Oh sure, he thanked me for it. But now, alone in the cozy light of the Christmas tree, I had to admit that his gratitude seemed . . . hollow. Like he was grateful on the first few levels of himself. But my gift to him came from the deepest possible level of me. And that was what I wanted from Victor. What I hoped he would someday give me. The deepest possible level of *him*.

Oh, I was being silly. Victor had called me an angel. He'd said he loved me. What more could he possibly have done? What more did I truly need from him? Was I so addicted to him that no matter how much he gave me, I'd never be satisfied and would always crave more?

I'd called him earlier, after my fight with Mother. I wasn't supposed to make phone calls after eight, but that had been the advantage of my parents being downstairs with the Stuarts, making up some excuse about my having suddenly taken ill. No one could police me. So I'd sneaked into the upstairs hallway and called Victor, practically bursting to tell him all about Robert and the seventh Brandenburg Concerto and how I was going to audition for Whitehall after all. I couldn't wait for Victor to encourage me, to tell me that of course I could write something brilliant overnight. *You can do anything you set your mind to, Iris Wallingford.* He always used my first and last name together when he wanted to make a point. It was one of the most adorable things about him.

But it hadn't happened anywhere close to that. Victor had sounded distracted. Preoccupied. Finally, after a couple of minutes, he'd said he didn't have the capacity to handle my problems just then. His parents had gotten into yet another fight about him being drafted and possibly going to Vietnam, and that had just reminded him how critically important this audition was and how desperate his situation was, and anything else piled on him right now . . . *"Well, it'd just be too much, Iris. Don't you see?"*

"Oh. I'm sorry, Victor. I didn't think."

Then I said good night and hung up, feeling chastened and humiliated. I'd seen his parents. Even that small bit of a fight I'd witnessed Monday night after the draft lottery had been awful. What must it be like to live in that environment day after day? To have that be all you knew? My problems were nothing compared to his.

Maybe that was why my love for him couldn't get the ideas to flow this time. Maybe a love song wasn't what my muse wanted me to write.

I took the piece of manuscript paper on which I'd sketched a few bare-bones ideas and tossed it aside in favor of a fresh one, then leaned back and surveyed the room. The nativity set my parents had purchased in Italy last summer adorned the mantel. Maybe I could write something about Christmas. There were so many good texts to choose from. "Gloria in excelsis Deo," maybe. Or "Ave Maria."

I walked over to the mantel and stared at Joseph in his purple robes, Mary with her clasped hands and blue head covering, and the little infant Jesus, chubby and blond on his bed of ceramic straw. I mulled over both the "Gloria" and the "Ave Maria" texts. Repeated them, emphasizing different syllables, trying to get something to spark.

But nothing did.

Okay, fine. Maybe I'd just start with a melody and hope I could find or create words to fit it. Or maybe I could abandon the idea of a choral piece and just write something for piano. Piano wasn't my strength, but it'd be *something*.

I walked to the window, my steps in time with the ticking of the grandfather clock. A few snowflakes drifted down from the sky. The ticking clock and the snowflakes reminded me of an hourglass. They reminded me of time and how it was running out.

Time *was* running out. Time for writing the audition piece, yes, but this felt deeper than that. Almost like I was nearing the end of something. More than high school. More than this deadline. Time was running out on everything I knew and everything that seemed real. And I didn't entirely understand these thoughts, these feelings, but when they crystallized into a melody, it didn't matter . . .

Oh, there you are, Melody. I've been wondering when you'd show up.

This gift from Melody was quite different from anything she'd given me before. The tune was a desperate one, filled with soaring leaps and an undulating rhythm. A tune striving to go somewhere but not quite able to make it. It was stuck. Not because I couldn't take it there. No, this melody simply existed. Trapped in a world from which it had no escape.

But at least it existed, and the clock had just chimed two, and I had to get something on paper. Despite what my mother told the Stuarts, there was no way she'd believe I really was sick and let me stay home from school. And I couldn't skip class once I got there, because they'd call her and she'd be home and I'd be in even more trouble. No, this had to get done tonight so I could drop it in the mailbox on the way to school.

So I went with it. Maybe this desperate, striving melody would turn into something amazing.

Dull-gray dawn had just peeked through the window when I finally drew the double bar line at the end of the last bar and sat back. Exhilarated and exhausted in equal measure.

I did it. I wrote something for Whitehall.

It wasn't my best work, or even my usual work. I had no idea if it was good enough to get me into Whitehall. But I'd gotten it done, and I was proud of myself for finishing.

I brushed the eraser crumbs off the piano keys—Flora had an eagle eye for any kind of mess—then dug the application out of my school bag and filled it out. Next stop was my father's study for an envelope and a stamp. I scrawled the address across the envelope, folded everything up, stuffed it inside, and licked the envelope closed. With a wish and a prayer, I tucked it back into my school bag and headed upstairs to my room to pretend I'd been in bed all night.

Maybe this wasn't my best. But it was the best I could do under the circumstances.

That was all anyone could ever ask of me.

CHAPTER TWENTY-FIVE

*H*ow did the concert go?"

The slam of Blair's car door perfectly punctuated Joy's question as the two prepared to walk into school together the next morning.

Blair answered with an indecipherable noise.

Joy chuckled. "That good, huh?"

"Well, it wasn't a total disaster." Blair clicked the button on her remote to lock her car. "But I wouldn't call it a success. I screwed up the introduction of the first piece—seriously, I have never missed that before, ever. The whole thing went downhill from there."

Joy patted Blair's shoulder. "So you screwed up a measure or two. So what? The rest of the mistakes aren't your fault."

"Oh, I'm not blaming myself. Not entirely."

Joy gave Blair a sidelong glance. "It's not Callum's fault either."

The very mention of the name jolted Blair. It had bounced around her skull most of the night, accompanied by memories of that catastrophe of a concert and that catastrophe of an entirely different sort on the same stage moments later.

She'd kissed him. She'd actually kissed him.

What on earth had she been thinking?

"Everything was under-rehearsed and underprepared because, bottom line, Callum's repertoire selections were too hard for the kids—which I told him on the first day. And he chose to ignore my advice. So, yes, it is his fault."

"Maybe he's stretching them," Joy said mildly, lifting her tumbler to her lips.

"You're on his side now?"

Joy gave a flick of her pierced eyebrow. "I'm your best friend, but that doesn't mean I always have to be on your side. Especially when you're being closed-minded, stubborn, and unreasonable."

"I am not being unreasonable," Blair shot back. "Those kids were terrified onstage. That's not how concerts are supposed to be."

"Only if you've been singing boring Disney medleys and bad pop mash-ups for the last five years. Which is basically what they've been doing."

Blair whirled to face her friend. "Did Callum get to you before I did this morning?"

"Seriously, Blair, what is up with you? I know you don't like the guy, but . . ." Joy stopped, then her eyes sparkled with mischief. "Except you totally do."

Yes. She did. Thanks to her uncharacteristic display of throwing caution to the wind last night, Callum knew it too. And now Joy knew. Which meant pretty soon all of Peterson would know, and—

Joy squealed and clapped her hands. "Yay! You finally figured it out!"

"Do not make that noise. And do not smile that smile. Yes, I figured it out, but nothing's going to happen."

"Oh, really? Then why are you blushing?"

"Because it's cold out."

"It's not that cold." Joy's eyes narrowed, and Blair's stomach plunged to the sidewalk. "Blair Marie Emerson. Did something already happen with him?"

Blair sighed. "We got in a fight after the concert. And then we wound up kissing."

"*Kissing!*" Joy's cheeks dimpled and turned pink. "So how was it?"

"Awful."

"Nope. Not buying it. There is no way a man who looks like that is a bad kisser."

"I never said he was a bad kisser." Bad kisser was the furthest thing from it. He was a great kisser. An amazing kisser. His kissing talent rivaled his talent in everything else, and in a split second she was right back there onstage, with his hands in her hair and his mouth on hers and her body pinned between him and the piano, and that one kiss wasn't enough, and she wanted more, except she couldn't allow that, because he was leaving at the end of the year and she'd be right back where she was after Derek.

Joy's laughter burst into Blair's thoughts, and she arched a brow. "What?"

"Oh, wow. You are gone. I just asked you a question."

"Sorry. What did you ask?" She raised an index finger. "I do reserve the right not to answer."

Joy made a face. "It's not that kind of question. Ew." She shuddered. "There are things I don't need to know. I just asked what happens now?"

Blair pressed her badge to the sensor, and the door beeped and clicked open. "That is an excellent question." She held the door open for Joy. "And I have no idea."

Joy glanced around the empty hallway, then leaned in. "Are you open to further kissing with him?"

Yet again she replayed the kiss from last night. The fire in his eyes. The pressure of his hands on her back. The way she felt pulled under in the best possible way.

"Okay, you don't need to answer that question." Keys jangled as Joy pulled them from her bag and sorted through them. "It's written all over your face."

Blair's cheeks flamed. "Crap." Thank goodness there weren't many students here yet.

"So you're open to more kissing," Joy said as she unlocked the door to her classroom. "And it seems he is too. So I'm not sure why there's a problem. Unless there's some kind of rule against interpersonal relationships among staff."

"There isn't."

"You've already researched that?" Joy's eyes gleamed. "Interesting."

"It's the opposite of interesting." The classroom door swung shut with its typical loud bang. "He's leaving after this year. He's made that clear from day one."

Joy shouldered open the door to her office. "That's still seven months away. A lot can happen in seven months."

"That's not that long." Blair followed Joy into her office. "And long distance didn't exactly work out so great last time."

"So you get seven months of incredible kissing, and then you go your separate ways."

"And how is that not like last time?"

Joy set her coffee down on her desk. "Well, I'd assume Callum hasn't proposed to you. And moving back to Boston is not the same as cheating on you with some opera singer."

"No, this time I know it's doomed going in. That's supposed to make it better how?"

Joy gave a slight, exasperated sigh. "Like I said, seven months is a long time. Maybe he'll decide he wants to stay. Maybe you'll decide you want to move to Boston with him. Maybe a pair of jobs will pop open for you both someplace random."

"Oh, but I can't leave here."

"Can't?" Joy peered into Blair's eyes. "Or won't?"

"Both." Blair flung her arms wide. "My life is here, my job is here, you're here."

"And as much as we all adore you, we could survive without you if we needed to. If you discover Callum is someone you can't survive without, then you're going to have to be willing to bend a little. Because it is entirely possible that God has a bigger, better, more amazing life for you than anything you could come up with on your own. And maybe that's here . . . but it might be somewhere else too."

Blair folded her arms across her chest. "I thought Derek was his plan for me. We saw how well that turned out." Her current maturity level was on par with the students', but she couldn't seem to stop herself.

"So you feel like God screwed up and you got hurt, and now you don't trust him to drive the car anymore, so you're yanking the steering wheel away and relegating him to the backseat?" Joy stared for a second, then pulled a couple of things out of her bag. "Yeah, let me know how that works out."

Blair opened her mouth to argue but couldn't. Joy was absolutely correct.

Her friend flashed a grin. "I always know I've won an argument with you when you can't think of anything to say."

Blair harrumphed and headed toward the door. "I suppose I can't avoid Callum forever."

"No, you cannot," Joy replied cheerfully. "Have a wonderful day, dahling. Be open to possibilities. Lean not on your own understanding. All that jazz."

"Mmph," Blair said again.

"I expect a full report at the end of the day" came Joy's cheerful farewell.

Good thing Joy could be cheerful. Blair's stomach knotted. Did she want Callum to bring it up? Did she want him to ignore things like he had after homecoming? Was he still angry? Was she?

She sighed and slipped through the door into the hallway that led to the choir room.

Some days there just wasn't enough coffee in the whole entire world.

The chair creaked beneath Callum's weight as he polished off the last of his emails and leaned back. Three hours. That was how long it had taken to get through everything he'd been ignoring. At least he'd found a silver lining to not having been able to sleep, finally giving up, and coming into the office at four in the morning.

It was his own fault, of course. He shouldn't have kissed Blair. He shouldn't have done a lot of things he did last night.

But their fight wasn't entirely his fault. She had been . . . unreasonable. Yes, that was it. Unreasonable. The perfect way to describe her. And she'd been that way since the moment he'd met her, when she'd looked him up and down and decided, in a single glance, that he didn't measure up. Doubtless all his predecessors since Vic had received the same look. Maybe it wasn't a coincidence that nobody lasted long at Peterson.

No, that was unfair. Their reasons for departure—childbirth, a job in their hometown, a messy divorce, et cetera—had been legitimate. Blair likely had nothing to do with them. All the same, he had never met someone so stuck in their ways, so resistant to change. Since August she'd ranted and raved about how they needed someone who cared about the kids. And he did. Far more than he'd ever planned on or wanted to admit.

He thought she'd have been happy about that. But no, she wasn't, because he was pushing them, and God forbid anyone get pushed out of their comfort zone *ever*. He'd reached his wit's end with her.

Or so he'd thought.

But then he'd asked what she wanted, and she turned those big brown eyes and those full pink lips toward him, and that single moment of helplessness, of vulnerability, made it clear she had locked far more inside her than he knew.

Had he wondered what lay beneath that icy exterior? Well, now he knew. Pure fire. A volcano had erupted between them, and in a split second there were hands and lips and he was melting . . .

And then Blair had pulled back and stared at him like a frightened wild animal. A second later she'd slipped backstage and out the door, vanished as though she'd never been there at all.

Last time he checked, when someone was happy about being kissed, they didn't flee the scene without a word. They didn't turn their phone off and ignore their texts and send all their calls straight to voicemail.

So regardless of who'd started their latest argument, he needed to apologize. With any luck at all, they would put it behind them and go back to life as usual—their tentative truce, their unpredictable partnership.

Yeah. And maybe unicorns would fly into the choir room and deposit rainbows and lollipops and tenors who sang in tune.

God, I've made a mess of things. Again. And once more, I find myself desperately in need of your help. If you could send some my way, anything at all, I'd—

The door cut his prayer short, and there stood Blair. She wore a white wool coat he'd never seen before, one that made her hair shine like fire.

"Morning." She swept past him without making eye contact.

"Morning." He watched her enter the office, hang her coat on the hook inside the door, and turn toward her desk. Any second now she'd find the cardboard cup from Teddy's, because a few minutes ago he'd celebrated being almost through his emails with a coffee-and-breakfast run and had grabbed a cup for her.

Apologies always went better with coffee.

Sure enough, she emerged from the office, coffee in hand. "You brought coffee?"

"Think of it as a caffeinated apology." He offered a hopeful smile. "I'm sorry about last night."

She lifted the coffee halfway to her lips, her expression maddeningly unreadable. "Are you sorry for the concert? Or the . . . after-concert part?"

Both. And yet . . . neither. The first piece had needed a faster tempo, and he hadn't realized it until just before the concert. *I'm sorry for taking a calculated risk? I'm sorry for thinking these kids were better singers than they are? I'm sorry for caring about them in a way you disagree with?* No, he couldn't say that.

I'm sorry for kissing you? Couldn't say that either. Not without lying through his teeth.

"I'm sorry I hurt you."

She tilted her head to the side. "I wasn't hurt. I was angry."

"As was I. And I'm apologizing for expressing that anger in a less-than-professional way."

Blair's eyebrows shot up. "So you kissed me because you were angry with me?"

"No, I kissed you because I wanted to kiss you. And at the time, I thought you felt the same way. But if I misread the situation, or if something changed during, then . . . I'm truly, deeply sorry it happened, and I hope you can forgive me enough to maintain a truce for the rest of the school year."

She studied him over the rim of her coffee cup. "I didn't . . . *not* want that kiss."

"Wow. A double negative. What a ringing endorsement."

"*Callum.*"

"Sorry," he mumbled. "I didn't sleep well."

"Neither did I."

He grinned. "I figured there was at least a chance of that. Hence the coffee."

"Thank you, Callum."

He ran a hand through his hair. "I . . . didn't have any idea kissing was something you wanted."

"Neither did I," she admitted.

"If I'm honest, I've never . . . that kiss was . . ." Why did words have to be so hard? Music was the only thing that could describe a kiss like that.

Her cheeks turned pink, and she fiddled with one of her earrings. "Yeah."

Now he wanted to kiss her again. "I wouldn't be entirely opposed to another one. If you felt the same."

Last night's fire lit in her eyes. Her lips parted. She started to say something but then looked away. Stared at her coffee cup as if it contained ancient secrets.

"Blair . . . please stop hiding from me." A desperate, unplanned plea.

She met his eyes again. "What do you mean by that?"

He stood and took a cautious step toward her. "You are a gorgeous, passionate, amazing woman. You're an incredible musician. You care about those kids more than I've ever seen anyone care about kids. You have this big, huge, beautiful heart, and they get to see it, but it feels like you're walling it off from me, and . . . and . . . and it hurts, if I'm honest. I'm starting to take it personally."

She pushed a lock of hair behind her delicate ear. His heart pounded. A distant intercom announcement in the hallway summoned some kid to the front office.

"I've been hurt before." The words came out so fast he could barely make them out. "Badly. By someone who I thought loved me, but who in fact just used me as a stepping stone to further his career."

"I'm sorry that happened to you. I'm sorry that guy didn't see what a treasure you are. But that's not what I'm doing here."

"I believe you," she said slowly. "At least . . . I want to believe you. But what happens if you and I get involved and then you up and leave? How is that not using this place—using me—in the same way Derek did?"

Ouch. She had a point. How would he not just be using her as a stepping stone? Especially now that his heart was involved. And hers.

And how could he think rationally when she watched him with those luscious brown eyes and teased every cell in his body with the warmth from hers?

"Can't we cross that bridge when we come to it?" he asked.

"Not when you've made it abundantly clear that you're only here for this year. If you and I start something, and then you leave, I . . . I'm not sure how I recover from that. It takes a lot for me to trust someone."

His heart sank. "So . . . you're saying you don't trust me."

"Not entirely, no."

"Fair enough." He sought her gaze. "How can I earn that trust?"

"Don't make promises you don't intend to keep."

"Done." He hadn't made any promises to her, and he sure wouldn't start now.

She stepped toward him. "And don't take advantage of the fact that I am ridiculously, dangerously, terrifyingly attracted to you."

"If it helps at all, I am ridiculously, dangerously, terrifyingly attracted to you too."

Her eyes widened. "You are?"

"I'm afraid so, Blair."

She offered a tentative smile. "This is . . . this is a big deal for me, Callum. Opening my heart to someone. Trusting. Especially when I can't see the outcome."

He took her hand. Pale and graceful, those skilled fingers resting in his suddenly shaky ones. "I'm sorry your ex betrayed your trust. I'm sorry for the pain he caused you. Your heart may be scarred, but it is still beautiful. And the last thing I ever want to do is give it any more wounds."

She looked up at him, her eyes large and golden brown and honest and vulnerable, and he was drowning.

"Does this mean we need a moratorium on kissing?" he asked, heart in his throat.

She paused for what felt like an eternity and then shook her head no.

"So . . . this means I *can* kiss you?"

She grinned. "Well, not in front of the kids."

"Oh, heavens no. Never."

"Can you imagine?" Her grin widened. "We'd be fodder for the rumor mill for the rest of the year. Might even make the yearbook."

That smile would be his undoing. "Blair, could we not talk about the kids for a moment? Please?"

Her smile bloomed across her face, and she nodded.

Relief coursing through his veins, he bent his head and kissed her.

Their kiss wasn't a volcano this time. No, this time it was music. A sweet melody, winding and unraveling and reverent and tender. With this kiss, he hoped to salve her wounded heart, to fill in the cracks her ex had left, to show her that he'd never violate the precious trust she'd just given him.

He had no idea what the future held beyond May, but with each passing moment, each movement of her lips on his, it was becoming frighteningly clear that all the plans he'd made to be alone for the rest of his life, to move back to Boston and leave Peterson in his rearview mirror, might need some substantial revision. Because the idea of being without Blair suddenly seemed unbearable.

She pulled away, her breath tickling his lips. "Callum." His name was a song when she said it.

Unable to speak, he brushed his thumb against her cheekbone, then leaned his jaw against her temple. He was still shaking.

"Callum . . . the bell's about to ring."

Who could think about the bell at a time like this? But in reply, it rang, and he pulled back with great reluctance. "I suppose we should adult, then, shouldn't we?"

She gave him a smile, slow and languid, that nearly undid his resolve. "We're kind of adulting now, if you think about it."

With a groan, he stepped back. Blair retreated to the office, and he turned toward the board, picked up the dry-erase marker, and tried to remember what in the world his rehearsal plans were for the day. Out of the corner of his eye, he could see her at her desk, brushing out that long, silky red hair.

Had he truly promised to maintain professionalism? Because that was a stupid, stupid promise. He clearly hadn't thought it through. Professionalism meant he couldn't touch her again until lunch at the very earliest.

Right now that felt so far away, it might as well be next year.

CHAPTER TWENTY-SIX

Late February 1970

*I*T WAS just past four on a chilly, sunny afternoon as Victor and I walked from school to his house. That had become our new afternoon routine. As soon as the bell rang, we'd either go to the library and hang out there for a while, or grab a Coke at Sammy's before walking home.

Our delay was because the postman came around four every day, and we had two mailboxes to check. We went to Victor's house first because it was closest to school. Sometimes, since his father was between jobs again, Victor borrowed the car and drove me home.

We walked hand in hand, our shoes in rhythmic counterpoint, the winter sun casting shadows of branches on the sidewalk. Holding hands was such a simple thing, but it brought so much joy. It meant we were a couple. An *us*. We were in this together. At this point, holding Victor's hand felt like a comfortable habit. Like something we'd do for the rest of our lives.

Except this must've been one of Victor's distant days. His moods had become less and less predictable the last few weeks. Sometimes he was the sweetest guy in the world. The bouquet of roses he gave me for Valentine's Day was stunning. And he always told me I was beautiful on days when I needed to hear it most.

But other times he seemed distracted, as though his mind was on the moon. I could be feeling my most beautiful, and he seemed to not even see me. And sometimes he could be a little acidic. Last Wednesday, I wore a new skirt that made me feel like a million bucks. I couldn't wait to see his reaction, but instead of telling me I was gorgeous, he'd just eyed me over the rims of his glasses and said, "Iris, don't you think that skirt is a bit short?"

I'd laughed it off. "Victor! You sound like my father."

"I mean it," he'd replied. "I don't want other guys ogling my girl."

Part of me was thrilled he called me his girl. But another part of me was embarrassed. Later at home, I hung the skirt in the back of my closet. I was pretty sure I'd never wear it again.

Victor was just stressed. I had to keep reminding myself of that. Every day that passed brought us one day closer to getting the letters that would decide our future.

Inspiration struck. Maybe if I made him laugh, he'd relax a little bit.

"Remember today in choir when Johnny Lenn got the restroom pass stuck on top of the rafters in the cafeteria?" I giggled just thinking about it. Mr. Gilbert's restroom pass was a broken, old choir folder, and Johnny had a habit of tossing things to himself while he walked. He'd thrown the folder so high it got stuck, and we'd all gone out to have a look.

"We lost six minutes of rehearsal time," Victor pointed out. "That part wasn't so amusing."

My cheeks burned, and I stopped giggling. Sometimes I felt like such a child compared to him. He was more than a year and a half older, so that was part of it. But sometimes I couldn't shake the feeling that I annoyed him. That my laughter irritated him. Some days it even seemed as though he couldn't stand me.

That just must be part of being in a relationship with someone. You're constantly thinking of the other person. You want to please them, you want them to love you, so you second-guess everything you do. But if that's the case, then why do love songs only focus on the part that feels amazing?

We stopped on the sidewalk in front of Victor's mailbox. The postman was halfway down the block, so the day's mail had already come.

Victor glanced at me with a nervous smile and opened the box. My heart pounded as he pulled out a handful of envelopes and sorted through them. One or two were bills—I saw the big red OVERDUE stamp—but then . . . could it be . . .

"It's here." Victor held up an envelope with Whitehall's crimson logo. I smiled, and my heartbeat accelerated. *It's here. This is it.*

"Aren't you going to open it?" He was taking forever. I couldn't stand the suspense.

His eyes turned cold. "I need a minute, Iris."

"Of course. I'm sorry. Wait until you're ready."

He stared at the envelope as though willing it to contain the news he needed to hear. He blew out a breath that puffed up in the chilly air around us. Then he tore the envelope open.

He turned away from me, and I tried to peek over his shoulder, but his height meant I couldn't. So I gave up and just prayed. *Please let it be good news. Please let him have gotten in. Please don't make him go to Vietnam. Please, please, please . . .*

"I got in."

He spoke so softly I could barely hear him. "What did you say?"

He turned to me, all smiles, and showed me the letter. "I got in, Iris! I got in!"

I took the letter from his hand and read it out loud. "'Dear Mr. Nelson, I am delighted to inform you that our Committee on Admissions has accepted you to the class of 1974 as a member of our Music Theory and Composition Program. Please accept my personal congratulations on your outstanding achievement . . .'" Happy tears blurred my eyes, and I couldn't read any more, so I just beamed up at Victor and handed the letter back. "You got in!"

"I got in." The paper shook in his hand. "Oh, Iris, I can't tell you how relieved I am. How thrilled. There's just . . . there aren't words for it. I don't have to worry about 'Nam anymore. I don't have to worry about my parents anymore. I get to start over. I get to learn from . . ." He trailed off and squeezed his eyes shut. Twin tears dove down his cheeks.

"Victor." Moved at his outpouring of emotion, I pulled him close and just held him. He wasn't the only one crying.

"I'm so happy, Iris." His voice was ragged. "I'm just so happy."

And that was it. That was all he said.

He didn't thank me for writing the piece that changed his destiny.

Did he even remember that? Did he remember that even though his name was on that acceptance letter, his work hadn't been in that envelope?

He did. Of course he did. How could he not? He'd thank me. I knew he would.

Wait a minute. If his letter had arrived, then mine likely had too. It sat in my mailbox. Waiting for me.

Unless my parents already got the mail. Unless they already knew . . .

"Let's go to my house next." I grabbed his hand and tugged him toward the car. "Want to drive me so we'll get there faster?"

Victor pulled back. "But I have to go tell my parents the good news."

It was so strange. When I cried, my face turned red and blotchy, and my eyes stayed swollen for a good ten minutes. But Victor's face looked totally normal. Hadn't he just sobbed on my shoulder a second ago? One would never know. How did he *do* that?

I blinked up at him. "But don't you want to come see if we both have good news?"

"Well yes, of course, Iris, but I have to tell Mom that she doesn't have to worry about me going to 'Nam anymore. I have to go tell Pop that he can stuff it, because I'm better than he thinks I am. I have a way out now."

A way out that I gave you. And I need to go see if I managed to find a way out for both of us, not just you.

As though he'd read my mind, he put a hand on my shoulder. "I don't know what you're so worried about, Iris. If I got in, there's no way you didn't."

"I'd still like to know, though. Preferably before my parents do." Would they hide an acceptance letter from me? My father wouldn't. But Mother . . .

"Just let me tell my parents," Victor said. "Let me tell them, and we'll—"

"You know what?" I fought to keep my irritation out of my voice. "Go. Be with your family. I'll walk home. It's not that far." I'd done it before, after all.

"Iris Wallingford, you are an absolute gem. What would I ever do without you?" He kissed my cheek, then started up the walk toward his house. "You'll call me tonight, right? Let me know the good news?"

"Of course." Did he really not want to be with me to find out? Was he really going to make me do this alone?

"Mom," he called as he opened the door, and then he shut it without even looking back.

Okay. That was that.

I started home—that white-columned world I'd be trapped in if I didn't get into Whitehall—fueled by adrenaline and anger, my heels tapping against the sidewalk in a rapid staccato. It wasn't that cold out, thankfully, but I didn't think I'd have felt it if it had been.

Victor was probably right. One of my pieces had been good enough to earn an admission. Surely the other one would be too. Right?

I bit my lip as I opened the mailbox. Sure enough, there sat a crisp white envelope with the same bold crimson seal.

I tore it open, my heart hammering in my throat.

Dear Miss Wallingford,

On behalf of the Admissions Committee, I want to thank you for submitting your application. We have carefully reviewed your materials, and while you were a competitive candidate, we regret to inform you that we cannot offer you admission. We wish you the best . . .

The letter fell to the ground, and my heart sank right with it, shattering into a million pieces along with my hopes and dreams and ambitions.

I didn't get in.

I didn't get in.

CHAPTER TWENTY-SEVEN

*B*LAIR WAS downing the last few bites of her lightning-fast lunch when the door to the choir room opened and Callum walked in with their special guest: a slender brunette in a pencil skirt.

"You must be Blair." She extended a hand. "I'm Keira McLane, with Channel Six."

"The face behind the emails." Blair shook her hand. "It's wonderful to meet you in person."

"Thank you again for all the work you guys did for my grandma." Keira set her bag down next to the piano, and the heavyset older man behind her put down his camera equipment. "She can't stop raving about how sweet and helpful your kids are."

Warmth bloomed at the compliment. "They're great kids. I'm just the one who's lucky enough to get to work with them."

Keira indicated her cameraman. "This is Seth, my partner in crime."

"Just pretend I'm not here." Seth gave a friendly wave and started setting up his tripod. He and Callum talked quietly, Seth gesturing toward chairs and Callum moving them to set up a little conversation area in the crook of the piano.

"Wow, this room hasn't changed as much as I thought it would have." Keira strolled around the choir room. "It's like traveling back in time."

"I think all the directors since Vic left have been afraid to make too many changes." Blair pulled out her phone to check her makeup.

"I can't tell you how excited I am about this story," Keira said. "I love local history. I'll cover the city council meetings and the gourd festival and whatever else the station has for me, but my real passion is uncovering hidden stories of the past."

Callum gestured toward the chairs he'd set up. "This okay, Keira?"

"Perfect." Keira settled into the chair across from Blair and Callum. "We'll talk for half an hour or so, but most of this will wind up on the proverbial cutting floor. Final story is only going to be about three minutes. You know how it goes."

Blair glanced toward Callum to find him grinning back at her. Had he ever been interviewed on television? Doubtless he had. That must be why he seemed so comfortable.

After handing out microphones and making sure all the technology was in working order, Keira crossed her legs at the ankles and glanced down at her notes. "Okay, Callum, I think most of your biographical information is on your website. Anything to update?"

"Nothing professional, no. But I did lose a loved one to suicide five years ago. I think that's part of why Iris Wallingford's story is so compelling to me." His jaw flexed.

Blair's heart squeezed. She reached over and placed her hand on top of his. He covered it with his own and flicked an appreciative glance her way.

"I'm so sorry for your loss, Callum." Keira's brown eyes shimmered with compassion. "But thank you for answering my first question without me even having to ask it. I wondered what drew the two of you to find out more about Iris."

"It all started with a piece of music we found." Blair withdrew her hand and glanced toward Callum. "Did you think to pull that out? I sure didn't."

Callum grinned. "Put it on the piano before I went to meet Keira."

"Excellent." Blair turned back toward Keira, trying to ignore the huge camera behind the reporter. "Anyway, we found a handwritten, unfinished piece of music in the choral library. It was tucked into a box for another piece."

"The piece is brilliant," Callum put in. "We immediately became obsessed with it."

"You more than me," Blair said around a laugh. "But I remembered hearing rumors that Iris Wallingford wrote music, so when we found this, we got curious."

Keira leaned forward. "Could we hear it?"

"The whole world should hear it." Callum walked to the piano.

Blair followed. When she was settled at the bench, Callum cued her with a glance. The music was just as moving as before, but it tugged at Blair's heart in a way it hadn't when they played it the first time. Iris was no longer a stranger, and through the music Blair heard the heart of a talented teenage girl.

Next to her, Callum sang the text in that beautiful rich baritone of his. When she'd played through this piece before, they'd barely known each other and didn't like much of what they did know. Now they'd kissed. More than once. Something shimmered between them now.

"That's beautiful," Keira said when they reached the end of what Iris had written. "I'm not anywhere near the musician you two are, but it's gorgeous. I can see why you were inspired to try to find out more about who wrote it." She scrolled through her phone. "Oh, I wanted to be sure to ask this. Grandma said Iris was dating Mr. Nelson back in high school. Did the two of you know about that?"

"That's one of the more interesting things we discovered. We found a picture of the two of them together in the yearbook." Blair scooted to the choir office, grabbed the yearbook off her desk, and brought it in. She laid the book open on top of the piano. "See? Right there."

"Huh." Keira studied the photo. "Mr. Nelson never mentioned dating the girl who died, at least not that I remember." Her phone buzzed as they sat back down, and she glanced at it. "Okay, wow. Jeff just sent me an article from 1970 about Victor Nelson being accepted to the White-hall Conservatory of Music in Chicago."

Callum's eyebrows shot up. "Vic went to Whitehall?"

"That's . . . no, that's not right." Blair frowned. "The diplomas on his wall were from UI-Chicago and UIUC, I think."

Keira tapped her phone. "Yeah, his bio says he graduated with a double major in composition and choral music education from the University of Illinois at Chicago, and he has a master's in choral conducting from UIUC. No mention of Whitehall."

"If I'd gone to Whitehall, I'd sure mention it in my bio," Blair said. "It's like the Juilliard of the Midwest."

"Does it say anything about his composition teachers?" Callum asked. "I can't remember off the top of my head who he studied with."

Keira rattled off a couple of names, neither of which meant anything to Blair.

Callum perked up. "The second one sounds familiar."

Keira once again consulted her phone. "Okay, I googled the name, and that professor was at Whitehall. So it's possible Mr. Nelson attended there but never graduated. Any ideas why that might be?"

The door to the choir room opened, and Dad poked his head in. "Blair? Are you— Oh, I'm sorry." He glanced at the reporters and cameraman. "Didn't realize I was interrupting. I needed to drop something off. Is this a bad time?"

"Kinda." Blair grinned an apology. "We're just being interviewed about the piece we found in the choir library. Turns out Iris Wallingford did write it, if Peggy Sue Weldon's memory serves."

"Funny you mention Iris, because Bob Porter from the alumni association had some information for me. Nothing that needs to be on camera, probably, but it might help."

"Well, pull up a chair." Keira stood and shook Dad's hand. "Mike, nice to see you again."

"How's that new Journey treating you?" he asked with a grin.

"Runs like a dream," Keira replied.

Dad turned toward Callum. "And you must be the new choral director."

Callum stood and extended a hand. "Yes, sir. Callum Knight. Pleased to meet you."

"Likewise. I've heard a lot about you."

Callum's eyes flicked toward Blair. "Uh-oh. That could go any number of directions."

Blair made a face. "It's all good things. Well. Okay. Mostly good things."

Dad strolled over to the far end of the risers. "Just pick up where you left off."

"We just discovered Vic Nelson was accepted to the Whitehall Conservatory in Chicago and apparently studied under one of their composition teachers, but none of his degrees are from there," Keira said. "We're trying to figure out what happened."

Dad took off his glasses and polished them on his navy-blue Emerson Dodge polo shirt. "Well, Bob said he and Vic Nelson were both drafted that year. Bob's birthday was called second, and he told me Vic's birthday was also drawn pretty early in the draft. But I don't think Vic ever served—he certainly never said anything if he did—so he'd have to have had some type of deferment or exemption. A physical ailment, conscientious objector status . . ."

"Or college." Keira's lips curved.

Blair frowned. "But deferment wouldn't have been dependent on where he went to college, right? So that still wouldn't explain him not going to Whitehall."

"Money, maybe?" Keira asked.

Callum leaned forward. "You'd think that might be the case, but with Whitehall it's the opposite. There are a couple of very exclusive music schools—Curtis in Philadelphia being the main one—that are tuition-free. At least, Whitehall was tuition-free when I applied there. Maybe it was different back in the seventies."

Blair glanced toward Callum. "You applied to Whitehall?"

He shrugged. "Yeah, but I didn't get in. Just like a lot of people."

"Like me." She waved a hand with a self-deprecating grin. "I didn't expect to, though. It was a total lark. Went to UIUC instead."

Callum grinned. "And I went to Michigan."

She studied him, the green in his eyes catching the light. What would it have been like if they'd both wound up in Chicago? If there were no Derek for her, no Rayne for him. Would they have escaped some of the scars they carried with them all these years later? Or would they have simply received different ones? Perhaps even at the hands of each other?

God knew. His best for both of them hadn't been Whitehall. And for whatever reason, he'd allowed the pain of Derek and Rayne to penetrate their lives and bruise their hearts.

But maybe he was working some good out of it after all.

Dad turned. "Blair, didn't you ask Mr. Nelson for a recommendation letter when you applied to Whitehall?"

"You're right. I did." Memories rose up within, painful and confusing. "Of course I did. I told him my piano teacher thought I should apply there, and he never said a word about having gone there himself. Y'know, come to think of it, he didn't even write my recommendation. Both my piano teachers did, and I asked him as well, but he said he was on a composition deadline and didn't have a moment to spare."

"I remember how upset you were when you came home." Dad patted Blair's hand. "You'd been counting on a recommendation from him."

"It never occurred to me that he'd say no." Blair tucked a strand of hair behind her ear. "I wondered if I'd done something to upset him."

"But if Vic got accepted and didn't go, or went but didn't graduate . . ." Callum leaned forward.

Keira nodded. "Then he might have had a very good reason for not telling you he had connections there."

Dad tilted his head. "Maybe the best thing Vic could've done for you in that moment was not associating his name with yours."

Wow. She'd never thought about it as possible protection. What would have happened if she'd gone to Whitehall? Maybe she didn't truly want to know.

But what had happened with Vic and Whitehall? Why wouldn't he have mentioned being accepted there?

Callum cleared his throat. "This isn't the first time we've caught Vic in—well, maybe not a lie, but definitely an omission of truth."

Keira perked up. "Oh?"

"He told me he didn't know Iris at all," Callum continued. "But the yearbook showed them together. When I asked him about it later, he said they'd dated briefly."

"And my grandmother caught them kissing in the library." Keira pursed her lips, then turned to Seth. "Are we rolling right now?"

"We don't have to be," Seth replied. "Want me to shut it off?"

"Would you, please?" Keira smiled her thanks, then turned back to the group. "Okay, here's the deal. My reporter instinct is going crazy right now. Vic Nelson knows more about Iris than he's letting on, and I think the two of you especially should be on your guard."

Blair glanced toward Callum in alarm. "Are we in danger?"

"I don't know," Keira replied. "They ruled Iris's death a suicide. The police officer who responded to the call passed away in 1992, and his report is pretty bare-bones. Iris's parents said she'd always been a little odd, and she was being treated for 'anxiety,' which was what they called depression back in the 1960s. But while having depression raises one's risk of dying by suicide, it's obviously no guarantee."

"Iris's work doesn't seem like that of a suicidal person." Callum leaned forward, hands on his knees. "From a compositional perspective, it seems hopeful. Like it's striving for something. Heading toward something."

"Maybe there's a chance it wasn't suicide," Keira said.

"Wait, do you think Iris was murdered?" Callum asked.

Blair's head spun. "And that Vic did it?"

Keira held up her hands. "Let's not get ahead of ourselves. It's just a theory. But I am a little suspicious."

"Do you think we need to call the police?" Dad asked.

"Unless someone does or says something threatening, there's nothing they can do," Keira replied. "But just to be on the safe side, until we know for sure what's going on, I'm not going to air this story yet."

"What are you gonna tell the boss?" Seth asked.

Keira waved a hand. "That if Iris was murdered, then this is a much bigger story than anyone thought." She reached into her bag, pulled out two of her business cards, and handed them to Callum and Blair. "If you find anything else, or think of anything else, call me."

Blair rose along with her. "I'll walk you out. It'll give Callum time to get ready for class."

As soon as they were through the choir room door, Keira turned a conspiratorial glance toward Blair. "So . . . you and Callum, huh?"

"What about me and Callum?"

"Are you two just coworkers? Off the record, of course."

"Off the record . . . I'm not quite sure what we are. We're still figuring that out."

Keira smiled. "I get that. But just between you and me, it looks like you're really good together. Like you genuinely care about each other. Whether it ever develops into more or not, I think you've got a great thing going."

"I'll help with the chairs." Blair's father was already in motion.

"Thank you, sir," Callum replied.

"Call me Mike," he insisted. "And congratulations on the new job. I'm sure everyone has filled you in on what a great program this is and how happy we are to have you, so I'll skip all that and just tell you I hope things are going well for you."

A pleasant change, not to be reminded of the pressure that came with filling Vic Nelson's shoes. "Thank you. I appreciate it. It's . . . going."

"The standard Midwest cry for help." Mike grinned. "I'm sure my daughter isn't making things much easier for you."

What on earth could he say to that? "Well, she's very talented, hard-working, cares about the kids . . ."

"And more than a little standoffish," Mike finished. "It's okay. You can say it. She's been hurt, and she keeps people at arm's length as a result. But I've got a good feeling about the two of you. I know she likes you, so you've got that going for you."

Wait, how much did Mike know? Some girls were super close with their fathers. Was Blair one of them? She didn't seem the gossipy type—at least, not when Joy wasn't involved. But then again, Callum was discovering a side to Blair he hadn't seen before. A side most people probably didn't see.

"I planned to give these to her, but since she's not here . . ." Mike retrieved his wallet from his pocket and fished out what looked like a ticket. "Any interest in going to a concert at the U of I tomorrow night?"

Callum glanced at the ticket, recognizing the name of a professional chorus from St. Paul, Minnesota. "Possibly . . ."

"With Blair, I mean. Not with me." Mike winked. "That might sweeten the deal for you. Blair and I were supposed to go together, but I had a meeting rescheduled, and it's one I can't miss, unfortunately. Any chance you might like to go with her?"

Callum chuckled. "The question is, would she like to go with me?"

Mike leveled a no-nonsense gaze at Callum. "Callum, I've been praying she'll move on, that she'll find someone who'll help her get over that scuzzbag, but she seems buried in her work. Like she's stuck. Frozen. But ever since you arrived, and especially the last couple weeks, she's got her old zip back. There's a light in her eyes that hasn't been there for years, and I'd bet every dollar to my name that you're the reason why. I think there's every chance in the world she'd like to go with you."

The door opened, and Blair walked in. "Who'd like to go with who to what?"

"That concert tomorrow night," Mike said. "I had something come up. Can't make it. But I think Callum here would love to take my place. If that's okay with you, of course."

Blair gave her father one of those inscrutable expressions Callum had come to know well. At least it wasn't just him who got those. That was oddly comforting.

"Is everything all right?" she asked.

"Perfect," Mike replied. "Just a meeting that's already been rescheduled twice, and it really needs to happen, and tomorrow night was the only time everyone else could be there."

Blair's gaze slid toward Callum. "You don't mind the time away from composing? I know you just got your muse back."

"I could always use a break to get some more inspiration." He couldn't keep the smile off his face, and he was glad to see Blair return one of her own.

"Okay then." The bell rang, and Blair immediately jerked back into business mode. "We'll figure it out after school."

"You kids have fun." Mike gave Blair a kiss on the cheek, then slipped through the choir room door just as the first students trickled in.

Callum strode back into his office, set down the concert ticket, picked up his iPad, and tried to get his brain back in gear. It had been a heck of a lunch break. Vic Nelson was untrustworthy at best and dangerous at worst. There might indeed be a solid reason Iris's music didn't communicate suicidality to Callum. And perhaps most earth-shattering of all, he held in his hand a ticket to his first real date with Blair.

CHAPTER TWENTY-EIGHT

Early March 1970

*I*T WAS light out when I opened my eyes.

Light.

I guess that meant another day had arrived.

Time to start thinking up more reasons why I needed to stay home from school and in bed like I had every day for the past week.

Had it even been a week? I wasn't sure. Time meant nothing anymore. All that had meaning were my pillow and my blankets and the nauseating pink floral patterns everywhere in my room.

Lying here, surrounded by all those pink flowers, made me feel like I was at my own funeral.

Or at the very least, the funeral for my dreams.

Every time I closed my eyes, the crisp white paper loomed large.

Competitive candidate . . .

Regret to inform you . . .

Wish you the best . . .

It was supposed to be another acceptance letter. Victor and I were supposed to be celebrating together. Planning our future as composers together. Victor Nelson and Iris Nelson. That was supposed to be the marquee.

My not getting in? That wasn't part of the plan.

I grieved it for a while, but grief had faded to numbness. It was like all the life force had bled out of me. I had no energy. No enthusiasm. No will to face the endless march of monotonous days.

As promised, I'd called Victor with the news, about an hour after I'd received the letter.

"I didn't get in, Victor."

"What's that, Iris? I can't hear you. My parents are fighting again. Mom thinks Whitehall is great news, but the old man is drunk again. I can't wait to get out of here. I guess I can start counting the days now, can't I?"

"You can. But I can't. Victor . . . I didn't get in."

"You didn't?"

"Nope."

"Oh. I'm sorry to hear that."

"Me too."

"Hey, listen, Iris, I gotta go. The fighting just got louder. I don't know how much more of this I can take . . ."

I'd walked away from the phone. I wasn't even sure I'd hung it up. I'd just gone upstairs to bed, and that was the last time I'd been downstairs.

I spent the whole next day in bed. Told Mother I didn't feel well. She was a germaphobe, especially when she had some important social function coming up, which was pretty much always. As expected, she'd barely even come into the room.

Flora had taken care of me. Brought me soup. Set it on a tray next to my bed, and then did that mom thing where she felt my forehead. I could tell by her skeptical expression and gentle clicking of her tongue that she didn't buy I was sick.

"Please don't tell anyone. I can't face the world. Not yet."

"I get it, Miss Iris. I know the darkness. This too shall pass. Soon you'll be free from all this."

But it hadn't passed. And I wasn't free. The cloud had descended. Spinning and dark and whirling until I wanted to scream. But screaming wouldn't help. It'd just make it worse, and it'd worry my parents. If they were even capable of worrying about me as a person and not just something to prop them up and make them look good.

The second day, I begged off school for cramps. Not a lie—I did have them. But they weren't as debilitating as I'd made them seem. Mother had just sighed and walked away. She apparently didn't have the time or energy to deal with me.

I lost track after that. There was a weekend in there somewhere, I think, but without the anchor of church, Sunday came and went unnoticed. I had no idea what time or day it was. My life was just an endless, infinite loop of bad. That was all it had ever been. Bad and bad and nothing but bad, and on the rare occasion something good happened, it was only a matter of time until it too turned bad.

Victor hadn't come to see me. Not that I really wanted to see him. I didn't want to look him in the face, to know that his dreams were coming true and mine had crumbled to dust. He might have called a couple of times, but Mother wouldn't let me talk to him. *"If you're too sick to go to school, then you're too sick to talk to your friends on the phone."* Which was fine. What on earth would I have said to him?

But I wished he'd fight to see me. I wished he'd come over and demand to come in and help me feel better.

I wished I knew he felt as sad for me as I felt happy for him.

I wish I felt like he missed me.

Does he?

Does anyone?

If I just disappeared, would anyone care? Would anyone even notice?

Through the fog came a knock at the door.

"Iris?" My mother. "Are you awake?"

Was I? I honestly had no idea.

"I'm coming in, Iris. Dr. Richards is here."

Wonderful. Dr. Richards was the ancient physician my parents had been dragging me to forever. Guess he was so ancient he still made house calls. Either that or my parents had flung enough money at him to get him to come over.

There he stood, all snow-white hair and thick glasses. "Hello, Iris. Well, my goodness, you've grown. You're a beautiful young woman now." He pulled out the chair from my desk and sat down beside the bed. "Not even a smile, huh?" he said. "Well, let's see what the trouble is."

I struggled to sit up. My whole body seemed made of lead.

Dr. Richards went through all the standard stuff. He checked my temperature, listened to my heart and lungs, had me open wide and say *aaahhhhh*.

"Do you have a boyfriend, Iris?" He felt the sides of my neck while he said this. His fingertips were cold and smelled like soap.

Why did he need to know?

When I didn't answer, he turned toward Mother. "Does she have a boyfriend?"

"She's been seeing a boy, yes. Victor . . . something." She waved a hand, as though he was nobody important. A thought that should be dismissed as soon as possible.

Dr. Richards cleared his throat. "Well, ma'am, a lot of girls these days are doing things with boys, and sometimes that explains these mysterious ailments."

Mother gasped. "Are you and Victor . . . are you having *sex*, Iris?" She hissed the word in an exaggerated stage whisper, like it was something dirty and awful.

"No," I managed. "We're not." No lie there either. I wasn't ready for something like that.

"Are you sure?" Mother eyeballed me, like she wasn't even sure I knew what sex was. Based on what she'd taught me about it, that would have been an accurate assumption. Everything I knew about it I'd learned from books.

Dr. Richards studied me. "You're not nauseated or anything, are you?"

I shook my head.

"When's the last time Aunt Flo came to visit you, Iris?" Mother asked.

If I'd had the energy, I'd have rolled my eyes. "Last week. I had cramps, remember?"

"How do I know you're not lying to me?"

"Ask Flora. She emptied my trash. She can tell you."

Dr. Richards glanced from Mother to me and back again. "If she had a visit from Flo last week, Mrs. Wallingford, then pregnancy is out of the question."

Mother folded her arms across her chest and studied me far longer than necessary. "I suppose. If you're sure."

Dr. Richards tucked his stethoscope into his pocket. "I think she's got anxiety."

"Anxiety?" Mother drew back. "So she's just worried? What on earth do you have to worry about, Iris?"

"It's more serious than that, I'm afraid," Dr. Richards said. "It's a mental disorder. Iris's brain doesn't work the way most people's brains do. But there are treatments for it."

They kept talking, but I was half asleep again. Their voices drifted in and out, Mother's high-pitched one and Dr. Richards's low-pitched one. It sounded almost like a song, the way they were talking. Maybe I could write it later. When I had the energy.

"So this medication?" Mother said. "It will help?"

"Many people do see improvement, yes."

"Well, by all means, put her on it, then. And don't tell anyone." She turned to me. "Iris, don't tell anyone."

That would have required my talking to people. She had nothing to worry about.

"I assume she'd be fine to go to school tomorrow?" Mother asked.

"Well, she's not contagious, so—"

"All right, Iris." Mother yanked open the pink-flowered curtains, and I squeezed my eyes shut against the onslaught of bright daylight. "You get the rest of the day to loll about in bed, and then you're going back to school tomorrow."

Dr. Richards patted me on the shoulder. "Feel better, Iris."

They left, mercifully shutting the door on their way out.

So that was it. I had a mental disorder.

Maybe the medication would make me feel better. Maybe not. It still wouldn't fix anything.

My composition notebook was on my nightstand, and I struggled to sit up again. I wanted to jot down those pitches I'd heard when Mother and Dr. Richards were talking. Not that it mattered. I probably wouldn't ever have the connections to get any of my work out there.

But music still swirled inside me. It still demanded to come out.

Why had God put it inside me, then, if he didn't have any plan for me to use it?

I wished I could ask him. I wished I were face-to-face with him.

I wished I could just skip the rest of this miserable existence and go straight to be with him.

Oh. My notebook wasn't on the nightstand after all. I'd left it on my desk.

All the way across the room.

Too far.

Okay. Music could wait.

Two books sat on my nightstand. My Bible and a book of poetry by Langston Hughes. *The Weary Blues*. We were supposed to read a bunch of the poems for English. Probably best to start catching up, then, since I had to go back to school tomorrow. Even better, maybe I'd find a text.

The book fell open to the spot I'd bookmarked. "Suicide's Note," the poem was called.

> The calm,
> Cool face of the river
> Asked me for a kiss.

River . . . water . . .

Wait. There was a psalm that talked about water.

I grabbed my Bible. Yes. There. Psalm 69. A couple of phrases leaped out at me.

> The waters are come in unto my soul . . .
> I am come into deep waters, where the floods
> overflow me.

Maybe I could combine these somehow. Maybe I could . . .

Yes. The sopranos and altos could sing the Hughes text. The tenors and basses could sing the psalm. They could alternate back and forth, just like Mother and Dr. Richards's voices. The perfect way to capture how I felt.

The way I was sinking.

I had to get up and get my notebook, though. My body didn't have the energy, but the music within compelled me. It proved stronger than my leaden limbs.

So I tossed back the covers.

I got out of bed.

And I started writing once more in my notebook.

I didn't know why I was composing. Not anymore.

I just knew that I couldn't *not* do it.

CHAPTER TWENTY-NINE

$\mathcal{C}$ALLUM HAD never been to Champaign–Urbana before. Growing up in the northern suburbs of Chicago, attending college in Ann Arbor, and relocating to Boston shortly thereafter, he'd never had a reason to visit central Illinois. To his surprise, he found it charming. Maybe it was the gorgeous autumn drive up from Peterson, with crisp blue skies and trees painted crimson and gold. Maybe it was the fact that instead of being at home in an empty apartment, he was here with Blair on an unexpected mini road trip.

Or maybe it was seeing the place through Blair's eyes. When they'd arrived at the University of Illinois Urbana–Champaign, she'd given him a tour of the areas she'd frequented as a student, pointing out the Music Building and Smith Memorial Hall. She peppered him with stories and anecdotes and musical memories. For an entire afternoon, Blair graced him with her softer side. Warm, open, and relaxed. Just like she always was with the students.

After dining on cheese fondue at a little café across the street from the concert hall, Blair escorted him up what seemed like a million stairs to the entrance of Krannert Center for the Performing Arts, the School of Music's crown jewel. His breath caught when they entered Foellinger Great Hall, all gleaming, golden wood and gorgeous acoustics. The same acoustician who'd renovated the famous Avery Fisher Hall at Lincoln Center had also designed Foellinger, Blair had told him.

Callum stared open-mouthed and settled into his seat, frissons of excitement pulsing through his body. What would it be like to direct a choir in this space? To hear one of his pieces performed in a place like this?

A quiet gasp from Blair pulled him back to the present, and he glanced her way. "Everything okay?"

"Yeah. Fine." She stared straight at the stage, her concert program closed on her lap. Her face looked like it had been carved from marble, and her eyes had grown cold.

Callum resisted the urge to sigh. Clearly she wasn't fine. He just hoped that, unlike at work, he wasn't at fault this time.

"Blair." He lightly rested his hand on her forearm. "Come on. What is it? What did I do?"

"It's not you." She opened the program again, and her slender finger pointed to a name. "That's Derek."

"*The* Derek?"

"Yup. *The* Derek. I'm not the kind to stalk my exes on Facebook, so I had no idea what had happened to him or where he ended up. I had no clue he sang in this chorus, or I never would've come."

So what did that mean for tonight? Did she want to leave? Was she still hung up on this guy? Was he . . . competition?

"Do you want to get out of here?" he asked.

Blair paused, working her lip in thought, then shook her head. "We're here. And I've heard really good things about this choir. Let's stay."

"Okay. Only if you're sure."

"I'm sure."

He sought her gaze. "Do you want to talk about it?"

Blair glanced at her watch and shrugged. "Well, we've still got a few minutes before the concert starts, so . . . sure. I guess."

"Only if you want to."

Blair bit her lip. "I don't. Not really. But if we're going to be"—she gestured between them—"then I need to get it out there."

"Okay." He reached for her hand. Maybe the slight touch would ground her. Keep her in the present. Keep her focused on him.

"He's a tenor."

Of course he was a tenor.

"We met on an elevator in the Music Building my first day on campus. We started talking and had this instant connection. We ended up skipping our next classes and going out for coffee instead." Bittersweet nostalgia carved a slight crease in her cheek. Crinkled the pale skin next to her eyes. "He needed a pianist for his junior recital, and I already knew some of his rep, so we decided to work together. I was his pianist for everything for two years. And right after his senior recital—onstage, no less—he proposed."

"Onstage? Wow." Blair didn't seem the public-proposal type.

"Yeah, he made it quite the production. But that's Derek for you."

"Must have been fairly confident in your answer."

"I gave him no reason not to be," she said. "I fawned over that guy. Rearranged my entire life for him. Gave him my absolute best, both personally and professionally, because he promised we'd have a future together. We planned to get married after we'd both finished school. He went to Wisconsin for grad school, so we knew there'd be some long distance involved. But . . . while I was finishing my undergrad degree and planning our wedding, he was meeting Marguerite."

A soprano. Had to have been.

"One night, about a month before the wedding, I decided to surprise him." She gave a shuddery sigh. "I drove up to Madison after I finished a concert. Didn't tell him I was coming. But the surprise was on me. Because Marguerite was with him. And it was exceptionally clear what they'd been doing just before he answered the door."

Callum's heart ached, and he put his arm around her. "I'm sorry, Blair."

She rested her head on his shoulder for a second. "Thank you."

Suddenly her prickliness made sense. People were always leaving her, both professionally and personally. Sounded like Derek's abandonment had been the most painful. Blair wasn't icy. She was hurt. And she protected herself the only way she knew how.

Well, maybe she didn't have to do all the work herself anymore. He wanted nothing more than to protect her. To care for her. To never do to her what that dirtbag Derek had done. To never promise something he couldn't follow through with.

And there was the sticking point. Because he couldn't promise he'd stay. His plan was to move back to Boston. That had always been the plan, because that would get him his real life back.

But now that ambition rang hollow. How would following through with his plan not be doing what Derek had done? How would she not view that as him just using her? He knew his motives, but that didn't matter, because his actions would speak loud and clear. Not just to her, but to the kids. And as much as she loved them, that might be the deepest cut of all, because he'd just be using them too. No matter what he accomplished with them, no matter what kind of success they had together, none of it would matter to the kids if he left them after this year and forced them to adjust to yet another new director next year.

And what did he have waiting for him back in Boston, exactly? A choir that had gone under financially and no longer existed. Memories of Rayne around every corner. The environment that had stripped him of inspiration and rendered him unable to compose.

He had a choir here. Granted, they were teenagers and not professionals, but in an odd way that made it more meaningful. The adults in his Boston choir, though amazing singers, came fully formed. Any wisdom he imparted just frosted the cake. Teaching his Peterson choirs let him bake the cake, which, to his surprise, satisfied him all the more.

He was composing again too.

Wait. Was going back to Boston still what he wanted?

For the first time, his answer to that question leaned toward a no.

Maybe his mother had been right. Maybe God did indeed have a plan. Peterson was part of it. He'd accepted that a while ago.

But maybe it wasn't the stepping stone he'd thought it to be. Maybe it was his intended destination all along.

Blair and Callum joined the throngs streaming from the Great Hall into the lobby after what had been, overall, a wonderful concert. She'd enjoyed it.

She would have enjoyed it more had she not spent the last two hours watching Derek.

With his blond hair, surfer tan, and cocksure stage presence, he hadn't changed at all. If it weren't for the fact that she sat in the audience with

Callum instead of onstage at the piano, she'd have thought herself right back in school.

She picked up her pace, her heels clicking against the parquet floor, and hoped Callum would follow her. Because as much fun as this trip down memory lane had been, she was ready for it to be over. Enough of the past. She wanted to hop back into the car with Callum and go grab dessert somewhere and be in the present. Get Callum's thoughts on the music. Not the performers, but the actual music, from a compositional standpoint. She'd never been close to a composer before, and the opportunity to get that perspective on things fascinated her.

Okay, Callum himself fascinated her. More so every minute. Especially when she'd trauma-dumped about Derek, and Callum put his arm around her and told her he was sorry.

Everyone in her life kept pushing her to get over it, move past it, stop clinging to it. And they were right, of course. She needed to. But Callum, who frankly had the most reason to urge her to get past her pain, hadn't done that. He hadn't tried to yank her onto dry ground but had instead paused for a moment in the muck with her.

Maybe because he'd been through the muck himself. Rayne's death. Derek's infidelity. Both had resulted in deep wounds and the stark realization that a promised, cherished, hoped-for future had vanished like mist.

Whatever the reason for his compassion, it meant the world to her. Most likely it had also started to heal some of the broken places in her heart. She'd have to tell him that. And she would, as soon as they got out of this crowded lobby and someplace quiet. As soon as—

"Blair?"

Oh, crap. She knew that voice.

Part of her wanted to pretend she hadn't heard it, grab Callum's hand, and sprint for the exit.

But the other part forced her to stop walking and turn around to face the past she longed to forget.

"Hello, Derek."

And there he stood. In the flesh. The person who'd ripped her heart from her chest and stomped on it. The reason she'd become so defensive and closed off. He was standing right there. The ten or so feet between them shimmered with all their moments. The ecstasy. The heartbreak.

"I knew it was you." Too-white teeth flashed in an easy smile. "I'd know that red hair a mile away."

Then he was in front of her, leaning in for a hug. Like they were college pals who'd lost touch for a few years rather than people who'd planned a life together before he torpedoed it.

On sheer instinct, she stepped into his arms. Returned his embrace. And she felt nothing.

He brushed his lips against her cheek, a ghostly echo of the past. Still she felt nothing.

She felt *nothing*.

Callum appeared to her right and extended a hand to Derek. "Callum Knight. Wonderful concert."

Derek's eyes widened. "Wait a minute. *The* Callum Knight? Oh, man. I've loved your work for a long time. The Cambridge Chamber Chorale . . . they were an incredible choir. And your compositions are genius. I'm honored to be in such elite company right now."

Wait, was Derek sucking up to Callum?

He totally was. And Callum picked up on it. The glimmers of amusement in the glances he shot her way confirmed that they'd be laughing about it later.

Yet again she was Derek's stepping stone. That was all she'd ever been. Just a rung on the ladder to his finding something better. In this case it was a professional connection. He hadn't wanted to reconnect with her at all. He must have recognized Callum and wanted to use her to meet him.

In the past that would have hurt. But now she just wanted to laugh. Because now she didn't care.

Derek Fogarty in the flesh, and she didn't care. She felt nothing for him whatsoever. She could walk away without giving him another thought.

Quietly, when she hadn't been paying attention, she'd been set free.

When had God healed her heart? When had he set her free? How long had she been acting like she was still in a cage while in reality the door had been open and she could've walked out anytime she wanted?

All this time she'd been angry with God for taking Derek away from her. But God hadn't been holding out on her. He'd been protecting her. She'd dodged a bullet by not marrying Derek, and at last she could let their relationship go. She wasn't grateful he'd cheated, but she was grateful his true nature had come to light before she'd tied herself to him for life.

She felt like falling to her knees in gratitude right there in the lobby, right there in the middle of Derek and Callum and two thousand other people. Instead she slipped her hand in Callum's. Twined her fingers with his.

Callum glanced at her with some surprise, then turned back to Derek. "Nice meeting you."

"Oh, the pleasure's all mine," Derek replied. "Could I get your contact info?"

"Google my name. My info is right there on my website." Without waiting for another word, Callum turned away, hand in hand with Blair, and steered her toward the exit.

"Are you okay?" he asked.

"I am." She stepped out of the lobby and breathed deep of the clean, crisp autumn air. "Better than I have been in a long time."

This. Right here. This was where her hand belonged. This was why it hadn't worked out with Derek. This was why she'd stayed so long in Peterson.

God had just been moving pieces into place.

Callum stood there beneath a streetlamp, people streaming past, the lights from a passing bus illuminating his jacket. He had never been more handsome. Things had never felt so right.

"What?" A slight frown creased dark brows.

She took both his hands in hers. "All these years I've wondered what would happen if I saw Derek again. I wondered what I'd feel, what he'd say, what I'd say . . . but never in my wildest dreams did I think I'd feel absolutely nothing."

Callum nodded slowly. "Nothing, huh?"

"Nope. Not a thing in the world."

Cautious hope flickered in his eyes. "What do you think that means?"

She stroked the back of his hand with her thumb. "I think it means I'm truly over it and maybe, just maybe, ready to let someone else into my heart."

A grin tugged at the corners of his lips. "Oh? Did you have someone in mind?"

In response, she stretched up on her tiptoes and kissed him.

Unlike their first kiss, this one wasn't the result of Sturm und Drang. This one was a welcome. A pair of gates opening wide to the exploration of what could be, what might be, what—God willing—would be.

When they parted, their mingled breaths puffed up in the chilly air around them. No need for words. Only music could fully capture this moment. Doubtless he had ideas swirling around his head and might need a quiet place where he could write them down.

"Want to go grab a slice of pie somewhere?" she said. "I know a place."

"Lead the way."

They made their way back to Callum's car, and as he started the engine, Blair checked her phone for messages.

"Huh," she said. "I've got a text from Vic."

Callum glanced her way as he pulled away from the curb. "Vic?"

"Uh-huh." Suspicion threaded through her as she opened the message.

> Tell that reporter she can call off the dogs, Blair. I didn't kill Iris.

> She left a suicide note.

CHAPTER THIRTY

March 1970

*F*OR THE first time in as long as I could remember, my brain was silent.

Not just quiet. *Silent.*

I'd never thought about living in a mind without constant music. I hadn't known it was even possible. But thanks to those pills I'd started taking this month, the music had faded to nothing. Melody and Harmony had gone on an extended vacation.

I wasn't sure how I felt about that.

I wasn't sure how I felt about anything anymore, because I didn't feel very much at all. The medicine had muted my entire being. I didn't feel sad anymore. But I also didn't feel happy anymore. Or angry. I didn't feel *anything* anymore.

I didn't struggle to get out of bed now. I didn't take time to think about whether or not I wanted to do it or could do it. I just did it. I got up. I went to school. I sat in class. I did my homework. I spent time with Victor. I shuffled through the motions of life.

But now that my brain had gone silent, I didn't feel like I was actually alive.

Was this what I needed to treat my "anxiety," as Dr. Richards called it? Did I even truly have anxiety? Apart from that time when I'd had pneumonia as a kid, I'd never spent a whole week in bed before. But I'd heard of people being so sad they couldn't get out of bed. Was that what had happened to me? Or was the doctor right and there really was something wrong with me?

I'd figured out the text to my next composition, the combination of Psalm 69 and the Langston Hughes poem. I'd sketched a few ideas in my notebook. That treble-bass back-and-forth I'd come up with while Mother and Dr. Richards were talking. But that was all the progress I'd made. I'd started taking those pills the next day. And after following up a week in bed with a full day of school, I'd been too exhausted to even think about writing music that night.

Or the next night.

Or the next.

By the time I could make it through a day without my body begging for a nap, the music had fallen silent.

I probably should've felt pretty devastated that the thing that would cure me was taking away the thing that made me feel alive.

And I would've felt that way . . . if I could've felt anything.

I had the song text next to my bed for whenever Melody and Harmony returned from wherever they were traveling. I'd clipped another copy into my music notebook in case inspiration struck during the day.

It was probably part of the adjustment process. My body getting used to the medicine. Dr. Richards had said there might be one. Just had to wait it out.

In the meantime I'd kept going through the motions.

My first day back at school, Victor had kissed me right there in front of my locker and told me he'd missed me. He'd tried to come see me, he'd said, but his father had been angrier and more drunk than ever, and Victor hadn't felt safe leaving his mother alone with the man.

So what's going to happen with your mom when you move to Chicago in six months? I'd wanted to ask but hadn't. Victor would just have to figure that out when the time came.

Victor also said he'd tried to call me every night but that my mother wouldn't let him talk to me.

They were all valid reasons, believable reasons, probably true reasons, but it still hurt that I hadn't heard from him during one of the lowest weeks of my entire life.

Since I'd been back, though, things between us had gone back to normal. We went to Sammy's after school most days, and this day was no exception. Mrs. Standridge, our math teacher, had given us a speech last week about how she knew we were almost done with high school and all our minds were on things like senior prom and graduation but that we still had work to do. "You're not done yet. Graduation is not a guarantee," she'd said. "You actually have to finish the work if you want to walk across that stage in June."

I had no idea what I'd do after high school, but I knew I wanted to graduate and didn't want to be stuck here in Peterson forever and ever. So I took her words to heart, and now Victor and I were working our way through both our math homework and a basket of fries.

Victor polished off the last of his Coke, the squawk of the empty straw cutting into the music from the jukebox, then stood. He said something about needing to use the men's room, but I wasn't really listening. I was trying to finish off the last equation: x equals . . . 46?

Was that right? It didn't seem right.

Had Victor finished this problem? He was really good at math. Maybe I could check to see if he came up with the same answer.

I wiped my fingers on a napkin, then reached for his homework. Question fifteen . . . question fifteen . . . oh. Yes, there it was: x equals 46. So we were both right or both wrong. Either way, good enough. On to the next problem.

I pushed his notebook back to where I found it, but I pushed a little too hard, and the entire stack of his things fell off the table and onto the floor. In the past I'd have been mortified, but in my new numb state, I just stared at the papers and books scattered all over Victor's chair and sliding onto the floor.

Were people staring at me? Did I even care if they were?

No. I didn't. I just needed to pick up the papers and put them back where they'd been. That was the right thing to do.

Victor was one of the messiest people I'd ever known. A true feat, since I was pretty messy too. But he had papers shoved in *everywhere*, in the most random places. A history assignment in his science book. An English assignment in his history folder.

And a crisp piece of paper with the Whitehall Conservatory seal jammed into his math textbook.

His acceptance letter. He'd been carrying it around with him. Not that I blamed him. I would've been too, had I gotten one.

But the handwriting on the back of the letter . . . I hadn't noticed that before.

I squinted to read the scribbly, scrawly handwriting.

> Mr. Nelson—I wanted to take a moment to personally congratulate you on writing such a fine piece for our consideration. In my twenty-two years at Whitehall, I have never come across an audition piece written at such a high level. To be quite frank, "I Am My Beloved's" exhibits a brilliance we rarely see even from our graduate-level students, and to find it in a high school student with no formal training is quite extraordinary. I am excited to help nurture and develop such a remarkably gifted individual, and I look forward to meeting you this fall. Congratulations on your acceptance. Wonderful things are ahead of you.
>
> Cordially,
> R. M. Hochsteiner, Professor of Theory and
> Composition

I stared at the letter. I stared and stared and stared.

That was *my* piece this professor was talking about. "I Am My Beloved's."

I wrote that.

A brilliance we rarely see . . .

Quite extraordinary . . .

A remarkably gifted individual . . .

Wonderful things are ahead . . .

Professor R. M. Hochsteiner thought he'd written those things about Victor Nelson.

But he hadn't.

He'd written them about me.

That piece with Victor's name . . . should have had *my* name.

That spot at Whitehall that belonged to Victor . . . should have belonged to me.

The audition piece I'd sent under my own name hadn't been my best work. But this was.

And not only was it my best, it was brilliant.

The restroom door squeaked open. I shoved the letter back in place, and by the time Victor's shoes appeared on the black-and-white tile floor, I'd nearly finished the last of my clean-up job.

"What are you doing, Iris?" he asked.

"I knocked everything on the floor by accident. I'm sorry, Victor."

He had a blank, dead-fish look in his eyes, but the second they met mine, they brightened. "No need to apologize. Accidents happen."

"I was just checking one of my math answers against yours, since you're so brilliant at math." I probably didn't need to flatter him, but I'd learned to err on the safe side.

Sure enough, it worked, and his dimple deepened. "Did you get it right?"

"I did." I waved an imaginary cheerleader's pom-pom.

"Good job, Iris." He slid into the booth and returned to his homework like nothing in the world had happened.

And for him, nothing had.

But for me, a nuclear bomb had exploded, and I was now dealing with the fallout.

Victor had never showed me that note on the back of his acceptance letter. Never even told me about it.

He probably hadn't seen it at first. We'd both been pretty focused on reading the main text, after all. But at some point, between the excitement, the telling his parents, the whole week I'd spent in bed, the time I'd been back at school . . . sometime in the last few weeks he had to have seen it. He had to know what it said.

He had to know it was about me.

And maybe that was exactly why he didn't tell me.

He didn't want me to know what Whitehall said about me.

I'd let him have my best work, but he needed everyone to believe that it was his work. Maybe he needed to believe it himself too, because that was the level of work they'd expect from him.

He'd absorbed the best thing I could give him into himself and claimed it as his own. Next fall, everyone would think he was some genius. He had a wonderful future ahead of him.

A future that should've been mine. A future I'd handed him on a silver platter. A future he might not have had at all thanks to his birthday being drawn in the lottery.

And he'd never even said thank you.

Wait a minute. Did he even love me? Or did he just love my talent, the fact that I'd give him my best and ask for nothing in return?

Did I mean anything at all to him? Or was I just someone he had to step on—step *over*—to get where he wanted to go?

The room spun. My stomach churned. I couldn't be here anymore. Not now. Not with him. I needed space for my drug-dulled brain to make sense of this. Because it was *Victor*. The man I loved. He couldn't be this person.

Could he?

Maybe he wasn't. He probably wasn't. It was probably the new medicine making me paranoid and anxious and seeing ghosts where none existed.

But it sure didn't feel like nothing.

It felt like . . . the truth.

Maybe I wasn't crazy. Or maybe I was. Maybe the drugs helped me think clearly. Or maybe they made me see monsters.

I needed fresh air. I needed to walk home. I needed to be by myself in my pink-flowered prison and go back over my relationship with Victor and hope and pray that something—anything—from the past few months would convince me he really did love me.

"I'm sorry, Victor." I gathered my books. "I just remembered my mother needed me home by five tonight."

"I can't walk you." He didn't even glance up. "I have to get these finished here. You know I can't concentrate at home."

For the first time, his excuses didn't disappoint me.

Would they, if I were capable of feeling disappointed?

I didn't know.

I didn't care.

All I knew was that I could leave right then and Victor wasn't even asking why. I should take the win and skedaddle.

So I did. I walked out of the café and turned left down the broad, tree-lined street toward home.

This all had to be a dream. Any minute now I'd wake up and look at the clock and realize I'd overslept. That's how this had to go. It couldn't be real. None of it could.

Because if it was real?

Then I'd been completely and totally fooled.

And I'd made the biggest mistake of my entire life.

CHAPTER THIRTY-ONE

$\mathcal{C}$ALLUM'S CONDUCTING and performing career had taken him to many unusual places. But a police station had never been one of them. Until today, anyway.

He sat next to Blair in a conference room at the Peterson police department, where they were due to meet with two detectives Keira had called who'd agreed to take a peek at Iris's file. Apparently Blair's father had pulled a few strings with his golfing buddy the police chief.

Callum and Blair had arrived a few minutes early, so he sipped on a Styrofoam cup of terrible coffee while she scrolled on her phone, nibbling absently on her lower lip, the way she always did when stressed.

The door opened and in strode two plainclothes officers: an intense-looking dark-haired man carrying a white cardboard box, followed by a willowy blond woman with a bag from a local sandwich shop draped over her arm.

The woman extended her free hand to Callum. "You must be Callum. I'm Detective Kate Stanton, and this is my partner, Detective Dan Valentine."

Detective Valentine plopped the box on the table. "We haven't got much time." He popped the lid off the box. "We're kinda on our lunch break."

"That's okay." Callum glanced at his watch. "So are we."

"Teachers and cops, always behind and eating lunch on the run." Stanton passed a sandwich to her partner, then put the other one on the table a healthy distance from the box and unwrapped it. "I glanced through the case a minute ago, and it seems the original investigators didn't spend a lot of time on it."

"Probably 'cause they didn't need to," Valentine piped up around a bite of sandwich. "Seems pretty open-and-shut. Suicide note, bottle of pills spilled on the desk, a history of anxiety."

"Keira McLane mentioned Iris suffering from anxiety." Stanton pulled a sheaf of paperwork from the box.

"That was a catch-all term for a wide variety of mental illnesses back then. It also encompassed depression," Blair said.

Valentine peered over his partner's shoulder. "Says here Iris was prescribed diazepam for her 'anxiety' after spending a week in bed. Parents just thought she was being dramatic. Guess they weren't much help."

Callum's heart twinged for Iris. At least Rayne had been surrounded by people who'd believed her and supported her. How devastatingly lonely Iris must have been.

"I think this is our suicide note." Stanton pulled out a plastic bag containing a piece of paper, and they all crowded around. Callum's heart sank as he recognized the handwriting. Blair read the words aloud. "The waters are come into my soul / The calm, cool face of the river / I am come into deep waters / The river asked me for a kiss / The floods overflow me."

Wait a minute. Why did those words sound so familiar?

"Original report confirms it's her handwriting." Stanton pulled another plastic-covered piece of scrawled-upon notebook paper from the box. "Her parents provided a sample. You gotta admit, the suicide note sounds pretty dark."

"But I don't think that's what this is." Callum studied the words. Where had he heard those before? Iris was quoting something. "My former fiancée died by suicide, and her note was more rambling and apologizing. This is almost like . . ."

"A song text." Blair pulled out her phone. "The 'calm, cool face of the river' part is a poem by Langston Hughes. And the other parts, I think those are from Psalms." Her thumbs danced across the screen. "Yes.

Psalm 69. Iris quoted verses one and two. And while those verses are dark, the psalm itself ends with hope."

"But the Hughes poem is called 'Suicide's Note.'" Valentine held up his own phone, the original title and text of the poem onscreen.

A melody wafted through Callum's head. Not one of his, though. One he'd heard somewhere else. And the text Iris had written fit perfectly. It *was* from a song. But which one?

"Vic said in that text I sent you guys that Iris left a suicide note," Blair pointed out.

"This had to have been what he was talking about," Stanton's voice sounded far away.

"Kind of a dark pun if it was," Valentine commented.

"Unless this was just a song text and nothing more," Blair said.

That melody. Callum knew that melody. Had he performed it? Conducted it? Was it—

The truth slammed into Callum with all the subtlety of a two-by-four.

"It's one of Vic's earlier songs." Callum had sung it. College, maybe? He couldn't remember. Over the years all but the most special of concerts had run together. But he knew the melody now. And he knew its source.

Blair jerked her attention to Callum, her eyes wide. "Are you sure? I'm not familiar with that one. We never performed it."

"We did."

Callum jerked his head up to see Keira McLane enter the room. "Thanks for including me, Detectives. Sorry I'm running late." She took a seat at the head of the conference table, to Callum's left, and dug into a bag from a taco place he'd driven by but never tried. Guess everyone was taking a working lunch today.

"Of course." Stanton smiled at the reporter.

"You performed a piece with this text?" Callum indicated the sheet from the evidence box as he dug for his phone. He searched his favorite choral music website. "It's definitely one of Vic's. Here's the sheet music." There it was. Right in plain sight.

"The phrases are in the same order as in Iris's note." Blair studied the tiny screen, then met Callum's eyes.

"Vic didn't write these lyrics." Callum's chest grew tight. "Iris did."

"Did he credit her?" Blair asked.

Callum glanced down at the screen. "Nope. Nowhere. Vic's is the only name on here." His head spun. Did Vic . . . Was this . . .

"Do you two think Vic Nelson stole Iris's work?" Stanton asked.

Callum had almost forgotten the detectives were even in there.

"Funny you should mention that." Keira unwrapped her taco. "Because I've been in contact with the Whitehall Conservatory. The person I talked to confirmed that Victor Nelson received an acceptance letter in 1970, but his acceptance was revoked a few months later due to some 'uncertainty with the origin of his audition piece.' That was all the information they had."

"Uncertainty . . . because maybe he's not the one who wrote it," Blair said softly.

Leaden truth landed in Callum's gut. "Because maybe Iris is."

"Detectives?" Keira piped up. "What's the statute of limitations on murder?"

"There isn't one," Stanton replied.

"Wait." Blair stared at the detective. "So if Vic killed Iris, he could still be charged, even after all this time?"

"Yep." Valentine tapped the table with his fingertips. "That's why a lot of bigger-city police departments have a couple dedicated cold-case detectives. They specifically work on old murders."

"In a small city like Peterson, we're not so lucky," Stanton finished.

Callum leaned forward. "If Vic stole Iris's work and she found out about it, threatened to rat him out . . ."

"That would be motive." Valentine's mouth was set in a grim line.

Stanton raised her hands. "Look, I love a good murder mystery as much as anyone else, but without solid evidence or a confession, all this is circumstantial at best. It wouldn't even be enough for a warrant, let alone a conviction."

Keira's chair creaked as she shifted. "Okay, Grandma said Iris always carried around a spiral notebook of staff paper. And that piece you guys found in the choir library was torn out of a spiral notebook."

Callum glanced over the edge of the box. "Any chance we're lucky enough to have a spiral manuscript notebook in there?"

Stanton pulled out the rest of the items. "Nope. Just the clothes Iris was wearing, a necklace, and a little cash. These would've been offered to her parents when the case was closed, but I guess they never came to claim them."

"Or maybe they only cared about the notebook and not the clothes." Valentine wadded up his sandwich wrapper and tossed it into a trash can in the corner. "Can we check with them?"

"Unfortunately, no." Stanton flipped a page in the file. "It says here that they moved to North Carolina a few months after Iris died and then they died in a boating accident three years later."

Blair gasped. "Maybe Vic has it."

"He may have had it fifty-plus years ago," Stanton pointed out. "But what are the odds he hung on to it all this time?"

"For your sake," Valentine said to Blair and Callum, "I hope they're pretty good."

Blair couldn't believe it. She'd spent the whole car ride back to school trying to wrap her mind around it, and she still couldn't.

Vic Nelson—her teacher, her mentor, her friend—had at the very least stolen an idea from Iris. And at the very worst, he may have been responsible for her death. Despite that text he'd sent insisting he wasn't.

It was unbelievable . . . but it explained a few things that hadn't added up. Why Vic had never mentioned his connection to Whitehall to her. Why he'd always been in such a dark mood while composing.

"This just confirms it for me." Callum broke into her thoughts as he put his car in park in the school lot. "I believed all along that Iris didn't die by suicide."

Blair unbuckled her seat belt. "From someone who doesn't know as much about this topic as you do, how did you know?"

"She was still writing music," Callum said as they climbed from the car. "Regardless of the text, the fact that she was still composing meant she was still living. Still fighting against whatever demons she had. She hadn't lost that battle yet."

Pain flashed across his face, and Blair slipped her hand into his as they walked into the building. "Do you want to talk about Rayne? You don't have to, but if you want to, I'm here."

"Not too much to tell." The door gave its familiar beep-click as Callum unlocked it with his badge. "Just your fairly typical tragic love story, I guess."

Blair gave him a compassionate smile as he held the door for her. "I'd love to hear it anyway."

A muscle in his jaw twitched. "I don't talk about her much because it's still painful. And I'm hesitant to tell you because I don't want you to think I'm still hung up on her. I loved her very much, and that will never stop being true, but that doesn't mean my heart still belongs to her."

Blair squeezed his hand. "I know a person isn't limited to just one love in life, but selfishly, I'm glad you said that."

"Good." Callum squeezed back as they turned the corner toward the choir room. "We met in Boston at a gig. She was the featured soloist in a performance I conducted." His lips curved in a bittersweet smile. "I always thought love at first sight was total crap until I met her."

Blair unlocked the choir room door. "I'll take your word for it."

"She was a beautiful woman with a beautiful voice, and by some miracle she fell for me as fast as I fell for her," he said. "But she had bipolar disorder, so there were a lot of ups and downs. And when she felt better, she always went off her medication."

They entered the choir office, where he settled into his chair and she perched on the edge of his desk. "I always used to watch her take it, just to make sure she did." He pinched the bridge of his nose, his face awash in painful memories. "But then the pandemic hit. We were locked down. And one of Rayne's roommates had received a kidney transplant, so she had to be super careful. And that meant we didn't see each other in person for months."

His eyes shone, and Blair gripped his hand. "That sounds so hard."

"She insisted she was still taking her meds, and maybe she was. I don't know. But without singing, without me, without exploring the city and trying new restaurants, without going to Sox and Celtics games, without any of the other things that brought her life, she went downhill." He breathed a shuddery sigh. "The number of cases would go down, and that'd give us some hope that maybe we could get back together, but then they'd spike again and we'd lock down . . ."

"It was an awful time to be a musician." Blair squeezed his hand. "To be a *human*."

A tear snaked from the corner of his eye, and he gave his face a rough swipe. "To make a long story short, everything fell apart. The choir disbanded, Rayne and I started fighting . . . We called off the wedding because of COVID restrictions, and with no hope and no end in sight, it was the perfect storm for her. Rayne's disease prevented her from seeing that the storm, bad as it was, would eventually end."

"I'm sorry, Callum." Her heart broke for him, and she pulled him into her arms, longing to take even a fraction of his pain away. "I'm so sorry."

"Yeah." He wrapped his arms around her, his voice tight. "Me too."

The door to the choir room opened, and they jumped apart. Blair glanced through the office window, but to her relief, it wasn't a student. It wasn't even another teacher.

It was Vic Nelson's wife.

"Marilee." Blair hurried into the choir room and wrapped the older woman in an embrace. "Oh my goodness. Feels like it's been ages."

"It's good to see you, Blair." Marilee's sweater still held the distinctive floral smell of her perfume. Even after all these years, at least one thing had remained the same.

"Have you met Callum?" Blair asked as they parted.

Marilee shook her graying head. "Not formally, no."

Callum emerged from the office, and Blair made the introductions, then turned another smile on Marilee. "What brings you here?"

The older woman's hands trembled, and her gaze darted around the choir room like a nervous bird. In fact, her whole demeanor seemed off. Uneasy. Guarded.

"Marilee?" Blair sought her gaze. "Are you okay?"

"Can I get you some water?" Callum asked.

Marilee shook her head with a sheepish smile. "No, thank you just the same. I'm fine. I'm just . . ." She balled her hand into a fist. "Vic has been acting strange the last few weeks. Ever since people started buzzing about Iris Wallingford again. He's been holed up in his study. He's like a ghost."

"Is he composing?" Callum asked.

"I don't know what he's doing." Marilee shook her head again, then muttered to herself. "No. No. I have to do this. I have to. It's the right thing. Regardless of where it leads, God's made it clear."

Blair eased closer to Marilee and put her arm around the older woman's shoulders. "Would you like to sit down?"

"No, I'm not staying. I just need to do one thing, and then I'm taking an Uber to the airport. I'm going to stay with my sister, at least for a while." Marilee opened a large handbag and peered inside. "I found this on a shelf in Vic's study while I was dusting last week. I must've seen it a thousand times, but I'd never really looked at it. This time I did, and I think you need to see it."

The world shifted into slow motion, and Blair knew what Marilee had brought even before the falling-apart spiral notebook came into view.

Marilee lifted her chin, squared her shoulders, and handed Blair the notebook. "This belonged to Iris Wallingford."

CHAPTER THIRTY-TWO

March 19, 1970

*A*NOTHER DAY, another afternoon of homework. Victor's father had landed another job and would be gone for hours, so on this day we were studying at Victor's house. The days were all running together. Graduation was in sight, and I just wanted to be done. To get away from here somehow. Away from Peterson. Away from my parents.

And yes, even away from Victor.

I saw him in a completely different light now. Ever since I started wondering if he was using me, all the things he'd done that had never made sense clicked into place. My suspicions explained absolutely everything about him. How fast we fell for each other. How he always made me come around to seeing things his way.

How I'd been so thoroughly enraptured with him that I gave him my best work and let him submit it as his own.

I'd stopped taking my anxiety pills a few days ago. I wanted to see whether they were making me paranoid. And since then I'd felt . . . I don't know, better. Clearer. Less sleepy. More like myself.

Did I really have anxiety, like the doctor said? Maybe. Probably. But anxiety wasn't why I'd spent a week in bed. That wasn't a mental disorder—that was disappointment. Dramatic disappointment, yes. But disappointment nonetheless.

Victor lay sprawled on his bed, history textbook open and propped up on his pillow. His mostly empty bottle of Coke stood on the desk beside him, and he'd taken his glasses off to rub his eyes. I sat at the desk working on math homework.

Victor reached over and patted my knee. Nothing he hadn't done before and nothing that used to make me uncomfortable. But now, rather than being drawn to Victor's nearness, I was almost repelled by it. The whole left side of my body, the side closest to him, seemed to shrivel and shrink back. The muscles tensed.

Why was this happening? This was Victor. The man I loved.

But this was Victor. The man who might have been pretending to love me.

My brain may not have figured out yet whether I trusted him entirely or not, but my body seemed to have decided.

Nature called, and I stood. "I'm going to the powder room. Need anything? Another Coke? Some water?" Why was I being so nice to him? Must have been like a reflex. Like I'd been programmed somehow.

He put his glasses back on and smiled up at me, but it didn't reach his eyes. "Another Coke would be great. Thanks."

He handed me his empty bottle, and I took it to the kitchen and tossed it in the trash, then visited the powder room just off the kitchen. When I finished, I washed my hands, grabbed a fresh bottle of Coke, and returned to his bedroom.

Victor wasn't on the bed anymore. He'd moved to the desk.

What was he doing? Looking at my math homework? Checking it over to make sure I didn't have too many wrong answers?

No. It wasn't my math he was holding.

It was my music notebook.

My blood chilled. "Victor? Wha . . . what are you doing?"

He glanced up, the expression in his eyes stony and cold. "Turnabout is fair play, Iris. I'm doing to you what you did to me last week at Sammy's when I went to the little boys' room and came back to find you going through my stuff."

I set the Coke down with a little more force than necessary, and it thunked loudly onto the desk. "I told you. I knocked your books on the floor by accident. I was checking a math problem."

He plopped the notebook on the desk and folded his arms across his chest. "The back of my Whitehall acceptance letter is a funny place to look for that."

I *knew* it. He knew what Professor Hochsteiner had written on the back of his letter—about *my* piece. And he hadn't told me. On purpose. He hadn't forgotten. He chose not to tell me, for reasons only he knew.

Something in me snapped. All the frustration of the last few weeks—months, maybe my whole life—balled up inside me, fierce and hot. Maybe anger, maybe God, maybe a combination of both. But something gave me the courage to meet Victor Nelson's eyes and ask the question that had been on my heart since last week.

"When were you going to tell me what Professor Hochsteiner wrote?"

Victor regarded me like I was a fly buzzing around his head. "It was on my acceptance letter. With my name on it. Addressed to me. It wasn't any of your business, Iris." He lifted his chin. "Going through someone's mail is a crime, you know."

"Only if it's unopened." I didn't actually know that, but I'd bet he didn't either. "And that piece you sent for your audition was *my* piece."

"Which you gave to *me*, at which point it became *my* piece. As far as Whitehall is concerned, *I* wrote it. Professor Hochsteiner thinks that's *my* work. That's what got me in."

"But you and I both know you're not the one who wrote it." I punctuated my last few words with angry gestures. "'A brilliance we rarely see.' 'Quite extraordinary.' 'Remarkably gifted.' All that was written about *me*, Victor. Not you. No one up there knows the quality of your work, because you didn't send your work. You sent mine."

He stood, cheeks pink. "And you gave it to me. It was your idea. I didn't ask you for your piece. I tried not to take it. The only reason I did was because I was desperate. This whole mess is your fault, Iris, not mine."

I stepped to the side as though to dodge the arrow of blame he'd just shot my way. "What are you going to do when you get to Whitehall and you can't get any good ideas? Huh? Did you think of that?"

"Of course I did," he said through gritted teeth. "And you ruined my plan for that too. We were supposed to go together. Compose *together*. Become Victor Nelson and Iris Nelson. Names in lights, remember?"

Suddenly the plan took a sinister turn. Two names in lights, but would only one have been doing the actual work?

"And if you truly were the genius Hochsteiner thinks you are, then how come you couldn't do it twice? How come one of your pieces was 'a brilliance we rarely see'"—he made air quotes—"and the other one wasn't even good enough to get you in? Honestly, Iris. Your ego is the size of Alaska right now, which is exactly why I didn't show you that note. This is what I thought would happen. Do you ever think about anyone's needs but your own?"

"*I'm* the one who only thinks about myself?" If I weren't furious, I'd have laughed in his face. "What about you? This whole time it's been about you, you, you. Nothing but you. Your family issues. Your draft number getting called. Your future. Whitehall wasn't just about your future, Victor. It was about my future too."

"Oh, please, Iris." His neck and cheeks mottled a deep red. "Your family is loaded. You can afford to do whatever you want, whenever you want. And you're a girl, so you don't ever have to worry about getting drafted either. You get all the lucky breaks. You have no idea how good you have it. You have so much privilege you can't even imagine what it's like to be from the wrong side of the tracks."

"And yet the things I wanted most in the world, money can't buy." My eyes filled with sudden tears. My words were truer than I realized.

I couldn't make my parents accept me as myself.

I couldn't make Whitehall see my talent.

And I couldn't make Victor love me. Not the way I wanted and needed to be loved. I wanted to be loved thoroughly and completely—not for what I could give to someone but for who I was. And nobody in my life loved me like that. Absolutely nobody.

Wait. Someone did.

A gentle rebuke hit my heart, beautiful and bittersweet. Jesus loved me that way. He loved me exactly as I was. So much that he'd given his life for me. And I'd been chasing everything but him. Worshipping the image of what I wanted my future to be.

That was what Victor was. A bronze statue. An idol. Shiny on the outside but hollow on the inside. He didn't love me. And I'd been foolish

AMANDA WEN

enough to love him. To give him my music. Music that had once belonged only to God.

And I'd given Victor my heart too.

Well, I was taking them back. Both my heart and my music. But not
to keep for myself.

To give back to the one who gave me those things in the first place.

"I'm sorry, Iris." Victor reached for my hand. "Forgive me. I'm just a
little on edge."

I pulled my hand away. "Why? Because you're afraid you won't be
able to handle the high expectations Whitehall has for you?"

Pure rage filled his eyes. His face. It scared me, and I wanted to run,
but as soon as it appeared, he tamped it down.

"I wouldn't be in this mess," he said, his jaw tight, "if it weren't for
your harebrained idea to give me your piece. Now you have no choice.
You owe me."

I got him out of being drafted, and I owed him? "What exactly do I
owe you?"

"Your music notebook."

The words were a knife to my chest. "Absolutely not."

"It's only fair."

"Fair?" My voice sounded shrill. "What, exactly, is fair about me giving you my very best work, the very best of me, and then realizing you
only wanted what I could do for you? You never loved me, Victor. You
never even cared about me."

He looked wounded, but his expression took longer to lock into place
than a genuine one should have. "Iris, where is this coming from? I'm
hurt. I'm genuinely hurt that you'd think that about me."

He wasn't denying it. He was just saying he was hurt.

Once again he'd made it all about him.

"Those pills must be doing a number on you," he scoffed. "The Iris I
know would never be so cruel."

His accusation stung, but I pressed on. "The Iris you know was a
weak little girl who had no idea she had actual talent, and now that she
does know, she's going after what's rightfully hers."

He laughed. "Oh, really? And how do you plan to do that, exactly?"

232

I folded my arms and met his cold-fish eyes. "I'm going to tell White-hall what we did."

He didn't even blink. "No one's going to believe you. Think for just a second about how crazy this sounds. 'Hi, I wrote a piece that got rejected—but this other piece, the one that's so brilliant you had to write a personal note about it? Yeah, I wrote that one too, except it just so happens to have my boyfriend's name on it.'"

When he put it like that, it did sound a little crazy. Couldn't let him know that, though. I put on my bravest face. "I'll never know unless I try."

"And you'll forever be branded as someone nobody can believe. Iris, you're mentally ill. So much so that you need medication."

"I'm not taking it anymore."

"And there's the problem. Right there." Victor's voice was calm. Sooth-ing, almost. "Iris, you need help. And the worst part is that the problem is in your mind." He tapped my forehead. "Your brain doesn't work right. The doctor said so himself. But because your mind doesn't work right, you can't see how crazy you sound right now."

No ... wait ... I went off the medication because I thought it made me paranoid. I felt clearer now that I'd stopped taking it, yet Victor seemed just as conniving. Manipulative. He ... he was probably manipulating me right now.

Or was it my brain that lied to me?

"Go home, Iris." He swept a lock of hair off my forehead, his touch as light and sweet as cotton candy. "Go home and take your medication. You'll feel a lot better once you do. Trust me."

Trust him? I couldn't do that. Not anymore.

But I wasn't sure I could trust myself either.

"This'll all be better in the morning." He brushed his lips against my cheek. "You're lucky I'm the forgiving sort."

"Forgiving?" I stepped back. "But I don't need you to forgive me. Be-cause I'm not apologizing. I've done nothing wrong."

"Sweet little crazy Iris." His expression seemed almost paternal. "Please go home and take your medicine."

I nodded slowly, an idea forming. "You're right, Victor. Of course you're right. I ... I don't know what I was thinking. I'm not in my right mind."

He smiled. "There you go. See? A couple of those pills and it'll all be better in the morning."

"Would you get my jacket?" My voice was honey-sweet. "I think it's on the hook by the front door."

"Of course."

The moment he left the room, I swept my music notebook off the desk and stuffed it into my bag, along with the rest of my homework. Then I headed down the hall to the living room, where he waited for me, my jacket in hand.

"Thank you." I took it from him and walked out the door, cool as a cucumber, then turned back. "Oh, and one more thing, Victor. When I write that letter to Whitehall, I'll tell them I gave my piece to my former boyfriend. Because I deserve someone who loves me. Not just someone who wants to use me to get ahead."

Without waiting for a reply, I took off down the street as fast as I dared. I half expected him to chase after me, but he didn't. Since his father was at work, the car was gone, and Victor would have had to run.

He hated running.

And I was pretty sure he didn't care about me enough to chase me down.

Had he realized I'd taken my music notebook back?

Well, even if he had, I was too far away now for him to catch me. And if he came to my house, I'd have Flora tell him to go away. That I didn't want to see him, now or ever.

Sure. He could have my notebook.

Over my dead body.

CHAPTER THIRTY-THREE

March 19, 1970

*D*EAR PROFESSOR Hochsteiner,

I'm not sure how to start this letter, but since you've probably never received one like it, you might not know how it should start either, so I'm just going to dive in.

"I Am My Beloved's," submitted for your consideration by Mr. Victor Nelson, was actually my piece. I wrote it entirely on my own. I am enclosing another one of my compositions as proof. I think you will see the similarities in style as well as handwriting.

Why would someone voluntarily submit their own work under someone else's name? I've been asking myself the same thing, and the answer that keeps coming to mind is that at the time I thought it the right thing to do. Victor's number was drawn early in the recent draft lottery, and we both were afraid for his future. He was so afraid, in fact, that he could not come up with an idea for his audition piece on his own. Desperate to help him and under the pressure of the approaching deadline, I offered him my work, and he accepted it and submitted it under his name.

Since "I Am My Beloved's" is mine, not Victor Nelson's, I am humbly and respectfully requesting that the spot you awarded him be given to me instead, or that an additional space in the program for next fall could be carved out for me to attend. As I am the one who wrote the piece, I am the one who earned that spot, and thus I believe a spot is rightfully mine.

If our mutual deception is so grievous that you cannot accept either of us, I understand and won't bother you any further. But since in your note to Victor you expressed an eagerness to work with the composer of "I Am My Beloved's," and since you said such things as "a remarkable talent" and "a brilliance rarely seen," I wanted you to know the truth. Whatever decision you make regarding that truth is yours alone, and I will respect it.

But if you find it in your heart to accept me to Whitehall, I am all yours.

Most sincerely, apologetically, and hopefully,
Miss Iris Wallingford

I removed the sheet of paper from my father's typewriter, scribbled my signature at the bottom, then grabbed an envelope and a stamp from the desk drawer. My heart hammered. I still feared Victor pounding on the front door and demanding my notebook. But I'd left his house hours ago and had seen nothing. Heard nothing.

I wondered whether that would still be the case if he knew what I was doing now.

But coming clean was the right thing. Whether Victor agreed with me or not, I needed to do this. I doubted they'd reward me with his spot at Whitehall. But nothing ventured, nothing gained.

Even if Whitehall wasn't part of my future, I'd be fine, because I was free. I'd freed myself of Victor and all his self-centered drama. I still didn't know what real love with a boy felt like. I knew now what it was like to love one. But I didn't know what it was like to be loved by one, because Victor hadn't truly loved me.

Though I was sure I'd feel sad about that at some point, I now felt more relieved than anything else. Two and a half more months of high school and then Victor would be out of my life forever and I'd never have to see him again. I could cut ties and move forward and find someone who loved me for me. Or not. Maybe I'd be happier on my own. Maybe I'd become a famous composer. Maybe a music teacher. For a second it was tempting to dream.

Oh, well. Whatever God decided. He had a wonderful plan for my future.

Plan.

Dream.

Future.

Melody rushed into my heart. Harmony followed close on her heels. A piece entered my head. Just a motive, a few bars. But it was beautiful, and I had to write it down.

Wait. No. I had to mail the letter to Whitehall first.

What was their address? My rejection letter was probably still in my room somewhere. I rounded the corner and went down the hall to my room. Maybe my desk?

I moved a pile of papers, and in the process I knocked over the little bottle of pills.

Right. Those pills.

I needed to start taking them again.

Victor thought I suspected him of lying to me, of using me, because I'd stopped taking the pills. If I went back on them, that would show him it had nothing to do with the pills.

Let's see . . . how many days had it been since I'd taken them? Two . . . three . . . four . . . Four days.

I was supposed to take two a day, so . . . wow. That'd be eight pills.

That seemed like kind of a lot. But I had to get caught up, right? Had to get my brain back in working order.

Maybe if I just took half. I could take the other four tomorrow, and then I'd be all caught up.

I picked up the bottle and squinted to read the little label. *May cause drowsiness.*

Well, it was almost bedtime anyway. Maybe a good night's sleep would be just the thing.

I had a glass of water on my nightstand, so I downed it along with the pills. Thank goodness they were small.

Okay. That was out of the way. Now I needed to find the rejection letter from Whitehall so I could get the address.

Oh. There. In the desk drawer. I carefully printed the address on the envelope I'd retrieved from my father's study, then sealed and stamped it.

The music was getting louder in my heart. More insistent.

I'm sorry, Melody. Apologies, Harmony. I'll pay attention to you soon, I promise. But you represent my new life, and I have to start it on the right foot.

I went downstairs, slipped out the front door, and hurried down the sidewalk. It was cold out, because of course it was. This was the part of the year when it seemed like spring would never come. But the tree in the front yard boasted tiny buds.

Spring would be here soon. We just had to hold on. Be patient.

I whispered a brief prayer and slid the letter into the mailbox. As soon as I did, I felt ten pounds lighter. Whitehall would know the truth now. Whether it made any difference or not, whether it meant Victor didn't get to go anymore, whether it meant neither of us did, I couldn't control. All I could do was the right thing. And telling the truth was the right thing.

Back in the warmth, I hurried upstairs to my room and sat down at the desk.

Thank you for your patience, Melody. Much appreciated, Harmony. And thank you, God, for these new ideas. Let's get to work.

As usual when I composed, I lost track of time. The notes seemed to pour from my heart to the tip of my pencil and onto the page. Notes of worship. Of repentance for placing Victor on the throne that belonged to God. Of gratitude for the second chance he'd given me, of the plans he had for my life. I erased, revised, and rewrote until what was written on the paper matched what I heard in my head.

After writing the soprano line, the main melody, I felt a little dizzy. An annoyance, though. Nothing debilitating. Barely noticeable. I sipped some water and kept going.

The harmonies filled in nicely. The first page was done. As I turned to the second page, though, I noticed my fingernails looked a touch blue.

Blue? That had never happened before.

Must've just been the cold. Or maybe I'd been gripping the pencil too hard. Cutting off circulation. I tried to relax my grip, but my hand wouldn't cooperate.

I didn't know what was going on with me, but I needed to finish this piece before I could pay attention to anything else. Melody and Harmony could be unrelenting taskmasters, but the work was so lovely, so enjoyable, that I didn't mind at all.

And this piece . . . this piece felt important. Something about it was absolutely crucial for me to write down. The notes burned in my heart, dying for an escape onto the page. I wrote and wrote and wrote, and when I'd fully harmonized the first phrase, I wanted to cheer like crowds do when their team scores a touchdown.

This piece was . . . It was *good*.

I rarely thought that about my own work, but this time it was undeniable. This piece was even better than "I Am My Beloved's."

Probably because it wasn't about Victor. He had nothing to do with this piece. In fact, I'd barely even thought about him for however long I'd been . . .

. . . what was the word . . .

Writing. Yes.

What? What was I . . .

Oh. Yes. The piece. I didn't write it for Victor. I wrote it for God, and about God, and about how much he loved me even though I didn't deserve it, and about how even if a human man never loved me the way I needed to be loved, Jesus would.

He already did.

Tears streamed down my face, and my heart felt like it was breaking. I just wanted to go to bed and pull the covers up over my—

No. I did that before. This felt a lot like before, when I didn't get into Whitehall in the first place.

Was the anxiety coming back?

Couldn't let that happen. I had work to do.

The pills were right there. A few of them still lay scattered on the desk. I grabbed two? Three? I didn't count them. Whatever. I swigged them down with the last of the . . .

. . . the water.

Yeah. The water.

Wow. I was exhausted. Composing usually took it out of me, but never like this. I felt like all the life force had just drained from me. Like I'd run a marathon and followed it up by climbing a mountain. My arms and legs weighed a ton. My eyelids . . . it took all my strength to keep them open . . .

No. I had to *finish*.

But the notes on the page, they just swam and blurred, and I couldn't even hold my pencil anymore.

I was so sleepy that I worked hard even to breathe.

I . . . I had to go to bed. I had to sleep. I needed rest. I couldn't force it anymore. *I'm sorry, Melody. Sorry, Harmony. I'll be back soon, I promise. I'm just so very, very sleepy.*

The bed was so plush. So inviting. The roses on the quilt became almost three dimensional. Like a field of flowers welcoming me into their fragrant embrace.

So I fell. I let them hold me.

They really were beautiful flowers.

When my eyes opened, light streamed into my bedroom.

Was it morning already? I hoped not. I still wanted to sleep.

The light was so beautiful. I wanted to go straight toward it, but I thought its brightness would hurt my eyes.

I rolled over, and . . . someone sat next to me. A man.

I should've been scared, but I only felt peace. The deepest peace I'd ever known. The man wore a long robe, and his skin and eyes were brown, his hair was black, and he had a beard . . .

I'd never seen this man before, but I knew his name in an instant. Jesus.

He smiled at me with such love, such kindness . . .

"What . . . what are you doing here?" I asked.

"It's time to come home, Iris." His gentle voice sounded like a cello. A whole orchestra of cellos, rich and sweet.

"Home? But this is my bedroom. I'm already home."

"Not this home. Your real one. With me."

The light brightened, but strangely, it didn't hurt my eyes.

"Wait . . . home? Home? Like . . . *heaven*, home? I'm only seventeen."

That didn't seem important anymore, though. In the light, Jesus was so warm and wonderful and inviting, and I felt so loved. So very perfectly loved.

This was the love I'd longed for my whole life. From my parents. From Victor. From my nonexistent friends. The love was here, in the person of Jesus. It *was* Jesus, and how could I not have gone with him? I'd have followed him anywhere.

At the very edges of the light, in my peripheral vision, Flora hovered. *Flora?*

What was our maid doing in my room? Why was she coming toward me with a pillow in her hands?

"Don't worry about her." Jesus's voice was as gentle as ever. "Just come with me."

So I did. I took his hand, and he helped me up. As heavy as my limbs were earlier, now they were featherlight, almost like I didn't even have them anymore. I floated to him, and he caught me in his arms.

I heard music. Just the faintest strains of music, but they wrapped themselves around my heart anyway. Voices and strings and instruments I'd never heard before, never even imagined, music so gorgeous it brought tears to my eyes.

"There's so much music at home, Iris." That deep, rich voice rumbled against my cheek. "And you'll help create it. You're going to write beautiful music here. You and I. Together. Forever. We've got all the time in the world."

He carried me toward the light. The music built with every step.

And in his arms, in this light, surrounded by this music, was where I'd always wanted to be.

CHAPTER THIRTY-FOUR

$\mathcal{F}$OR CALLUM, the rest of the day couldn't pass fast enough. After the bomb of Marilee Nelson bringing in the lost spiral notebook containing the complete works of Iris Wallingford, the bell had rung, and he'd had to flip the switch back into teacher mode. Part of him wanted to check out for the day and make the kids watch *Wicked* and write bland, predictable observations about it. The rest of him, the responsible conductor part of him, knew there weren't enough rehearsal days before the December concert as it was and he'd better make the most of the ones he did have.

But that notebook, now sitting on Blair's desk, called to him. The siren song of potential answers to questions that had burned in his heart since the day they'd found that worn sheet music in the library.

Finally, *finally*, the bell rang and the students trickled out. As soon as the last of them had left, Blair made a beeline for the office. But instead of starting her usual cinnamon-candle-and-peanut-butter-cup ritual, she grabbed Iris's notebook and met Callum's gaze. Her eyes held the same combination of excitement and trepidation that filled his own heart.

"Do you think she knew?" Callum asked.

"Who?" Blair made her way toward the piano. "Marilee?"

"Yeah. How much did she know and when did she know it?"

"I have no idea. But the important thing is she brought us the notebook now." Blair set Iris's notebook on the piano's music rack and turned toward him. "And she's afraid enough of him that she flew to Florida to stay with her sister."

Callum nodded. He'd be lying if he said he wasn't at least a little bit afraid of Vic Nelson now too. He definitely wasn't the person Callum had believed him to be for all these years. Who was he really? And what was he capable of? Fear of the unknown chilled him and made him cross the room and dead bolt the door to the choir room.

"Vic doesn't still have a key to this place, does he?" Callum jiggled the door handle to double-check.

"No, thankfully. They put new locks on everything two or three years ago."

"That's probably for the best." One more jiggle—still locked—and then he sat down on the piano bench next to Blair.

She turned toward him, her fingertips on the upper-right corner of the spiral notebook. "Shall we?"

He nodded, and she opened the front cover.

Everything was ivory with age, and some of the pencil markings were blurred. Iris had scrawled her name in ballpoint pen inside the front cover, and the handwriting looked every inch like that of a teenage girl. No inkling of her musical genius.

That came on the second page. The first page of written music. A choral piece, four-part, a cappella. "Song in the Night" was the title, though there was no text beneath the notes. Some bars were scratched out, a few arrows indicated possible revisions . . . but there was the music. The music of Iris Wallingford. Right there. Before his very eyes.

What he wouldn't give to have known her. To have her here, alive, now, in his class. To be her teacher.

Oh, who was he kidding? He probably wouldn't be able to teach this girl anything. But he could sure learn from her. Talk with her. Listen to her. Be a safe place and person for her. So just in case the thought ever crossed her mind to take her own life, he could speak to those lies and shower down truth over her.

He couldn't have saved Rayne. But he'd like to believe that maybe, just maybe, he could've helped Iris.

He glanced toward Blair. "Do you mind if I play this one?"

"Not at all." She gave his upper arm a quick squeeze. "I know how much this means to you."

He put his hands to the keyboard and was surprised to find them shaking. Not so much that he couldn't play, though. And while his piano chops weren't the caliber of Blair's, he could find his way around a choral score well enough to bring Iris's music to life.

It was beautiful.

And haunting. His heart ached. What this girl could have been had she lived. What music she could have written.

And wait . . . just like the song text the police had assumed was her suicide note, this melody seemed very familiar.

To his right, Blair frowned. "Does that sound like Vic's 'Voice in the Wilderness' to you?"

Crap. "Unfortunately, yes."

Blair rose from the bench and disappeared into the choir office. A moment later she returned with a file box in her arms, which she set on the lid of the piano. The red-lettered cover of one of Vic's earlier pieces came into view, and Blair set the sheet music next to Iris's notebook.

Callum's heart sank to the basement storage area beneath the choir room. The similarities were uncanny. Eerie.

"It's not an exact replication." Blair sounded like she was grasping at the last few molecules of hope.

"No, but it's close enough." He stopped playing. "Vic stole this idea."

"What's the copyright?" Blair flipped back a page. "It's 1980. Ten years after Iris died."

"And long enough for everyone to forget about her." Feeling sick, Callum returned to Iris's notebook, turned the page, and resumed playing. Another piece. Another beautiful melody. More richly developed harmonies.

"I can't believe this." Blair put a hand to her forehead. "That motive is in 'My Love Is Like a Red, Red Rose.'"

"Iris has a different text to this," he said over the music. "So the rhythm isn't the same. But that's her tune."

Once more he trailed off, his hands still on the keys, and met Blair's eyes.

"I'm almost afraid to look," she said. "But I have to know how much of his other music is copied from Iris's."

"Me too."

He rose from the bench and followed Blair into the storage room, where the two of them pulled down all the file boxes of Vic's music. Then they went into the choir room and sat on the floor in front of the piano, taking one piece from each folder and spreading them in a circle. Blair reached up, grabbed Iris's notebook off the music rack, and put it between herself and Callum, and the two launched into a sordid game of Musical Match. Which piece of Victor's corresponded with which page from Iris's notebook? Ever the detail person, Blair wrote down each instance on a sheet of paper she'd snagged from the recycle bin.

Not all of Victor's works were plagiarized—at least, not from pieces they'd found in Iris's notebook. And not everything Iris had written had found its way into Vic's music.

But enough of her pieces were copied that the last remaining illusions Callum held about Vic Nelson as a person, as an artist, as a mentor, shattered in a storm of shimmering shards.

"I can't believe this." Callum glanced through Blair's lengthy list. "I struggled to come up with ideas for . . . for years, Blair. Literal years. And I never would've stolen an idea from someone else. It never even occurred to me. It's just . . . it's despicable. It undermines the very creative process we seek to honor."

"I know. I'm as disgusted as you are." She took the list back and set it next to the notebook with a weary sigh. "Vic was my teacher. My coworker. He's my . . . *was* my friend. Iris should have had so much more life. She should've had the opportunity to accomplish what Vic did. To surpass Vic. She deserved to have her name on that music, not his."

Blair's voice broke, and she put a hand to her face. "I'm sorry, Callum, I just . . . this is a lot."

"Of course it's a lot." He pulled her close. "You have nothing to apologize for. Vic betrayed you. He betrayed Iris. He betrayed all of us."

"Yeah," she choked. "He did."

The indomitable concrete wall of Blair Emerson had crumbled. He held her as she wept, stroking her hair and pressing kisses to the top of her head.

So what if they were sitting on a cold, hard choir room floor in middle-of-nowhere Illinois? So what if they were in the center of a pile of plagiarized music and demolished illusions? There was no place on earth Callum would rather be than right here. With Blair.

Because he loved her.

The truth rushed in on the wave of a new melody, but he didn't feel immediately compelled to write it down. In fact, he didn't care if he ever did. If God meant it for him, it would come back. And if it didn't, he'd still remember the music of this moment.

This was why Blair had inspired him to write after so many years in the desert. Why he felt alive for the first time since Rayne's death.

He was in love with Blair.

He loved her battle-scarred heart. Her stubborn insistence on getting up and trying again every time life coldcocked her. Her care for the kids. Their verbal sparring, their disagreements, even her prickly, exacting nature and her ridiculous cinnamon candle. All the things that had once irritated him about her now either didn't matter or had become something he loved.

He wanted to spend his life like this. Comforting her when she was upset. Working together, giving their all to achieve a common goal. Making music with her. Feeling her rock-steady, reassuring presence at his right hand—his right hand in the choir room and in life.

Had he truly thought his real life was in Boston? Was it only a couple of weeks ago that he was counting the days until he could go back?

Now he couldn't even fathom it.

His real life was here. In Peterson. Teaching. Composing.

With Blair.

"Callum?"

Her eyes were wide and bright with tears, her face was flushed and blotchy, and a chunk of hair had fallen across her cheek.

"Yes?" Whatever she asked him right now, he would be powerless to resist giving to her. Literally anything at all. His car. His life savings. A kidney. Whatever she needed, if it made her happy, he'd—

"I think we need to call the police."

Oh. Right. That.

They were in something of a mess with Vic, weren't they? His mentor and her former teacher and colleague was a pathological liar and plagiarist at best and a murderer at worst.

Yeah, they should probably do something about that.

"I agree," he said.

She smiled, pure sunshine after a rainstorm. "You agree with me? Well, that's a first."

He laughed and pulled her close once more.

In an afternoon of weighty darkness and world-altering revelations, love was a welcome ray of light.

CHAPTER THIRTY-FIVE

*T*HE FOLLOWING Wednesday, Blair stood in a small observation area outside the interview room at Peterson's police department, Chief Stephens at her right. Through the one-way glass, alone at a table, sat her former teacher. Her former colleague. Her former friend. Waiting for detectives to interview him about Iris's death.

Normally she wouldn't even be allowed to be here, but being Peterson royalty had its perks. Chief Stephens, after consulting with his detectives, had given her the go-ahead to observe.

She didn't really want to be here, but she needed to be. She needed to see firsthand that Vic Nelson, who'd cared for her and nurtured her and been almost like a second father to her, had only been playing a role. She knew his every conducting gesture, every nuance of facial expression . . . she could read his mind. Or so she'd thought.

She only knew the person he'd pretended to be. She didn't know who he truly was.

By being here for this interview, maybe she'd find out.

The door to the interview room opened, and a suit-clad, silver-haired man walked in and sat down next to Vic. His lawyer, most likely. They talked quietly to each other, their heads together, and then Vic nodded and straightened. His hands lay folded on the table, and a cold, fishlike stare deadened his eyes. She'd seen the look before, usually when he was annoyed with the choir, but never to this extent.

A moment later the door opened again, and Detectives Stanton and Valentine walked in. Introductions were made, and then Vic piped up.

"Am I under arrest, Detectives?"

"No." Valentine settled into a chair across from Vic. "By no means. We've just received new information on Iris Wallingford's death, and we need to tie up a couple of loose ends."

Vic's eyebrows raised. "You mean her *suicide*. Did Blair and Callum put you up to this? Or that nosy reporter?"

Vic's attorney rested a hand on his client's forearm and whispered in his ear.

"We're just curious about how you came to have this." Stanton pulled Iris's music notebook from a bag and set it on the table in front of Vic.

He remained expressionless. "An old notebook? Probably one of my own composition notebooks from back in the day."

"Open the front cover," Valentine instructed.

Vic did, and Blair's stomach churned.

"Says Iris Wallingford on it," Valentine said.

"So I'll ask again." Stanton leaned forward. "How did you get this?"

"How did *you* get this?" Vic demanded. "I haven't seen it for years."

"Your wife brought it in," Valentine replied. "She says she found it on a shelf."

"Marilee's lying," Vic burst out. "She's in on this too? Lies. It's all a pack of lies."

Blair froze. She'd never once heard Vic Nelson raise his voice. Not even when the choirs' behavior warranted it. Not even when they were down to the wire and not prepared for a concert. Never, as a student or as a professional, had she heard him shout.

Stanton didn't blink. "She's also filed for an order of protection against you."

An order of protection. Had Vic abused her? Blair's heart ached for what Marilee Nelson must have endured hidden in plain sight.

Vic let out a bark of laughter. "That'll never stick. I've never laid a hand on the woman. What kind of monster do you people think I am?"

"Well, your former girlfriend wound up dead." Valentine leaned forward. "And her music wound up at your house."

"And in at least two dozen of your published compositions," Stanton added.

Vic's lawyer side-eyed his client. "You never told me that."

"Iris was a genius," Vic said.

"That why you submitted a piece she wrote to the Whitehall Conservatory back in 1969?" Valentine asked.

Vic rolled his eyes. "This again. That was all Iris's idea. *All* hers. It never even would have occurred to me if she hadn't brought it up. She insisted."

"She made you an offer you couldn't refuse." Stanton leaned back, arms folded across her chest. "And once you saw her genius, you needed more of it. No way could you write like she could. Whitehall would've seen through your ruse the first day of school. No, you needed her whole notebook."

"We talked to Whitehall," Valentine added. "They said you were never a student there."

"Professor Hochsteiner confirmed it when we spoke with him." Stanton's words were casual, but her gaze was anything but.

"That old coot," Vic scoffed. "What is he, nearly a hundred by now?"

"Still sharp as a tack, though," Valentine replied. "And he told us Whitehall revoked your acceptance."

Vic stiffened. "It was a mutual decision."

Valentine let out a quiet chuckle. "Mutual . . . kind of a funny way of saying they knew you couldn't hack it as a composer because the audition piece wasn't your work to begin with. Iris mailed him a letter confessing to what the two of you had done."

Stanton leaned on the table, locking eyes with Vic. "Postmarked the day she died."

Vic's attorney cleared his throat. "What exactly are you insinuating about my client? We're well past the statute of limitations on intellectual property theft."

"We're not interested in Iris's music," Stanton said evenly. "We're interested in how she died."

"You gotta admit, all this sounds like motive," Valentine pointed out.

Vic exploded, rising out of his chair. "I didn't kill Iris! All I wanted was her notebook. She owed it to me. She *owed* me. She came up with this whole cockamamie scheme, and she got me into a situation I had no way out of. She was supposed to come to Chicago with me, and we were supposed to write music together. Have both our names in lights. That was the plan all along."

"And then she screwed it up by not getting in with the other piece she wrote," Stanton pressed. "You had to go it alone. So you had to make sure your name could still be lit up."

"Iris's music was brilliant," Vic protested. "Even Hochsteiner thought so. It deserved to be brought to life."

"But only under your name," Valentine pointed out. "Her work shows up in a whole lot of your pieces. And your name's the only one on them."

"Which brings us back to how this sounds suspiciously like motive," Stanton said.

Vic sighed and stared at his hands. Was this the moment Blair had dreaded?

"I told you, I didn't kill Iris," Vic said softly. "By the time I saw her, she was already dead."

March 19, 1970

People in Peterson never locked their doors. Even the rich ones. Nobody needed to. Peterson was the safest place around.

So Victor knew, when he crept from his bed just after eleven and walked to Iris's house, that he'd be able to get in. Knowing Iris, that notebook would be on her desk. He could count on that.

People could be so predictable.

Something was off with her, though. She'd been so moldable. So eager to please. She'd been putty in his hands—until she'd seen what that idiot Hochsteiner had written about Victor's audition piece. *His*.

Yes, she'd written the music, but for him. About him. Inspired by him. It might as well have been his. And once he sent that application, it became his. She'd given the piece as a gift. And a gift, once given, became the property of the recipient, to do with whatever they liked.

He'd thought Iris understood that. Apparently she didn't.

Eventually she'd come around to his point of view. She always did. Sometimes she took a little convincing. Sometimes she needed time to think it over and see that he was right. But he always was, and the sooner she realized that, the better.

Probably the pills were making her act strangely. Or maybe the lack of pills. Whatever. He didn't know. Frankly, he didn't care. He just wanted his Iris back. His sweet, malleable Iris. The one who would agree to contribute music when he got stuck, to perpetuate the deception—which she'd started—that he was the compositional genius.

He needed her music. He needed to at least scribble a few copies of some things so, if she never came around to his point of view, he'd be covered.

He'd give her notebook back. Probably. Unless she kept being stubborn and unyielding. Then he just might keep it.

He reached Iris's house, that pile of white-columned wood, and went around to the servants' stairs in the back. Servants' stairs. How pretentious must someone be to build special stairs just for servants—for people who weren't highborn enough, rich enough, or good enough to use the regular ones? No, people like him had to go in the back.

The joke was on them. Going in the back meant he was much less likely to be caught.

The second stair creaked beneath his weight, and he froze. But nothing indicated that anyone had heard.

He slunk along the wall, down a long hallway. He didn't know which room was hers, since he'd never been allowed in the house before, but he'd figure it out.

Not that one. That appeared to be a guest room. It looked sterile. Unused. Like no one had touched it in quite a long time.

Not that one either. It was lived-in but neat as a pin. A place for everything and everything in its place.

And this one was just another empty guest room. How charming. Iris's house had more bedrooms than people. Whole rooms for nothing but extras and trinkets.

This exact level of overindulgence justified his actions. Of course Iris had talent. She also had money. Even if she didn't have talent, or if her talent didn't get her where she wanted, she could buy any future she desired.

He, on the other hand, would be cannon fodder in the jungle. He didn't have her money.

So he needed her talent.

It was only fair.

Ah. There. That had to be her room. The one next to the main staircase. The messy desk, the clothes strewn on the floor . . . this room had life in it. This was Iris's room.

He peeked in the doorway, then immediately flattened himself against the hallway wall, heart pounding. Someone was in there. Flora, heading away from the bed with a pillow in her hand.

He hadn't planned for Flora. He hadn't realized she lived with them. Had she seen him?

He ducked into the guest room and waited until Flora passed by. She didn't even turn in his direction. She just went into another room—the neat one—and closed the door.

He waited in pregnant silence. Counted to a hundred. Two hundred. Flora didn't come back.

Okay. Maybe it was safe now. He'd only be in there a minute or two anyway, and then he'd leave. Crawl out through the window if he had to.

Shoes in hand, he crept silently back to Iris's room. She was in bed, fast asleep. And just as he'd suspected, her notebook lay open on her desk.

Huh. She must be working on something new. No time to ponder that, though. He'd ponder at home. For now, he just needed to take it.

He picked it up and stuffed it between his sweater and his undershirt, then tucked them into his belt.

Mission accomplished.

An orange pill bottle was spilled on its side, with a few pills scattered on the desk. Knocked over, as if someone had taken them in a hurry. Good. She'd done what he'd told her to do and taken her medicine. Maybe now she'd get back to normal and he wouldn't have to resort to risky maneuvers like this one to get what he needed.

This too was all her fault.

Wait. What was that note? He picked it up.

> The waters are come into my soul
> The calm, cool face of the river
> I am come into deep waters
> The river asked me for a kiss
> The floods overflow me.

The spilled pills . . . the note . . .

He whirled around and studied Iris more closely.

She wasn't breathing.

He felt her neck for a pulse and found none.

He jerked his hand away.

Iris was dead.

He was in the room with a dead body.

His stomach whirled and spun, and he feared he might throw up. *No. You can't. Rein it in. You're so close.*

Besides, if Iris was dead, then she wouldn't need the notebook. He wouldn't need to spend the time copying her work. He could just . . . take it with him to Whitehall.

He shoved the note next to her body, where it would surely be discovered.

Wait. Flora had been in here. Did she already know about Iris?

For all he knew, Flora was alerting Iris's parents. Calling the police.

Any minute now someone would burst in and find him in her bedroom standing over her dead body. And then he'd go to jail, and jail would be even worse than the jungle.

That was definitely not part of the plan.

He couldn't go out the window. No way to close it from the outside. Too high up.

But wait a minute. Iris's room was next to the main staircase. Not the servants' stairs he'd come up. The main stairs. Those led straight down and out the front door.

Fitting. He was now worth every bit as much as Iris had been. He had her music. Her talent could become his own. Nobody ever had to know.

If Iris had given up on life, that was her problem. As long as he played his cards right for the next thirty seconds or so, then the world would be his oyster.

One more peek out into the hall. Nothing. No voices. No stirrings. No indication that anyone was awake or anything was amiss.

He tiptoed out of her room. Down the main stairs.

They didn't creak.

Not even a little bit.

Then through the front door and out into the fresh March night and that was it.

Easy as pie.

And limitless possibilities lay ahead.

"Flora?" Blair stared, wide-eyed, at Chief Stephens. "Who's Flora?"

Chief Stephens had the original case notes on a clipboard in front of him. "The Wallingfords' live-in maid. She's mentioned in the initial report, but since all signs pointed to suicide, no one interviewed her."

"But if Flora came from Iris's room, and Victor saw Iris dead . . . could Flora have killed Iris?"

"That's a definite possibility," Chief Stephens replied.

"I was—I am—a good composer," Vic was saying. "I hitchhiked to Canada right after graduation and found a job at a grocery store. Worked for a couple years and saved like crazy. I went to Illinois on my own merit. I may not have been Whitehall good, but I was good enough. My career has proven that."

"Your career that's peppered with stolen work," Valentine scoffed.

Vic's attorney stood and closed his briefcase. "However, as my client has just made clear, he had nothing to do with Iris Wallingford's death. She was either a troubled young woman who took her own life or a troubled young woman whose life was taken by the family maid. In either instance, the only crime you'd have on my client is trespassing and theft, both of which are no longer prosecutable offenses. If there's nothing else?"

"Just one thing." Stanton moved between the attorney and the door. "How did one of Iris's unfinished works end up in the choir library at Peterson High?"

Vic shook his head. "I took it in years ago when I was stumped and up against a deadline, but I got another idea. Didn't end up using Iris's. I must've put it in the library and forgotten about it." A proud grin spread over his face. "That piece I wrote without her won multiple awards, though. Like I said, I guess I didn't need her after all."

The attorney cleared his throat. "My client is obviously innocent of Iris's death, and he will stop talking now." He pinned Vic with a look. "Now if you'll excuse us."

He opened the door for Vic, who marched past the detectives, triumph oozing from every pore. "I told you people I didn't kill Iris."

"Yeah, well, don't leave town just the same," Stanton said as he passed. "We'll be in touch."

Blair's hands were shaking. How thoroughly Vic had duped her. But now he'd taken off the mask and she'd seen what was underneath, and she was utterly repulsed.

Chief Stephens patted her shoulder, then walked into the interview room and addressed his detectives. "Sounds like we need to track down Flora."

CHAPTER THIRTY-SIX

"So Vic Nelson didn't kill Iris?" Joy stared at Blair across the table in the faculty lounge the next afternoon, eyes wide, brows arched over her glasses, a sandwich halfway to her lips.

Blair shrugged. "That's what he says."

"Do we believe him?"

"I don't believe anything that man says anymore." Blair reached for a carrot stick. "But the police are talking to Flora. Apparently she's still alive."

"Huh." Joy took a bite of sandwich. "I thought for sure Nelson did it."

"I thought so too. Part of me—most of me—hoped he hadn't."

Joy met Blair's gaze. "But part of you hoped he had."

"Does that make me an awful person?"

"Absolutely not. He lied to you. Lied to everyone. Pretended to be a decent human when he was anything but. And he stole Iris Wallingford's work." Joy shook her head. "Too bad they can't arrest him for that."

"Afternoon, ladies." Callum's voice was at Blair's back, and she turned to greet him with a smile.

"Hi," she said.

"I just got a call from Detective Valentine." Callum leaned against a vacant chair at their table. "Detective Stanton will be calling you, but I wanted you to hear this from me."

Blair's shoulders tightened. "Okay . . ."

"Flora confessed to Iris's murder." Callum's jaw was tight. "She told the detectives that she saw the note and the pills and thought Iris had tried to take her own life. But when she checked on Iris, she was still alive, so rather than call for help, Flora decided to 'end her suffering and be merciful,' as she put it. She smothered Iris with a pillow."

"In what universe is that merciful?" Joy burst out.

"Flora's misguided one, apparently. But now they're reopening the deaths of Iris's parents. I guess in the original police report someone noticed that the boat looked like it had been tampered with, but the case went cold right away. No leads."

Blair stared at Callum. "Do they think Flora killed the Wallingfords too?"

"Valentine says he and Stanton are in touch with police in North Carolina, who are handling that case since it's their jurisdiction. One way or another, though, she'll be brought here to face charges in Iris's death."

"Will there even be a trial, since she confessed?" Blair asked.

"Probably not," Joy piped up. "Just a prison sentence."

"Why would she wipe out the entire family?"

"Maybe Mr. and Mrs. Wallingford didn't treat her well." Joy shrugged. "Not a justification, of course, but if they were abusing her, she may have felt like she had no choice."

"But why kill Iris?" Blair pressed. "She wouldn't have mistreated Flora."

"According to the North Carolina police, after Iris died, the Wallingfords named Flora their heir," Callum said. "Maybe Flora knew that would happen. She must have been an excellent maid, and they must not have had family members to leave their fortune to. So that could've been her motive for killing Iris too."

"So she killed a whole family and inherited millions?" Joy spat.

"Sounds like it," Callum replied. "Apparently Flora's been living it up in Hawaii the past fifty years."

"Wow." Blair's mind whirled with the onslaught of new information. "*Wow.*"

"Hey, look at you guys!" Joy gave Callum's shoulder a friendly shove. "Solving three murders all because you found an unfinished piece of music in the choir library! That almost sounds like a TV series. *Choral director and collaborative pianist by day, crime-fighting superheroes by night.*" She framed the words with her hands. "I'd watch the *heck* out of that show."

Blair laughed and shook her head. "I think I'm retiring from solving crimes."

"Shame." Callum tossed a teasing grin over his shoulder as he headed for the door. "You'd be cute in a cape."

Blair turned to find Joy leaning back in her chair, arms folded across her chest, with a cat-that-ate-the-canary grin on her face.

She sighed. "Okay, fine, whatever. You told me so. He is, in fact, devastatingly handsome, and I have a thing for him."

"I think it's more than a thing, Blair. You come to life when he enters the room."

Blair groaned.

"What?" Joy leaned forward. "Why is falling for someone who's handsome and talented and good to you such a bad thing?"

"I said after Derek that I'd never give my heart away again. And I certainly didn't intend to, especially to someone planning to leave in a few months. But it happened anyway. Despite all my efforts not to, I've fallen in love with Callum."

Joy squealed.

"He's only here through May, though, and then he goes back to Boston. So where does that leave us?"

"I wouldn't be too sure that's his plan," Joy replied. "I've seen the way he looks at you. I don't think he'll be eager to leave you behind."

"No, but he might ask me to come with him. And I can't leave here."

"Sure you can. It's simple, really. You pack all your stuff, you sell your house, and you move to Boston."

"You know what I mean. The kids. You. My dad. My whole life is here."

Joy smiled. "And that's why God invented FaceTime and airplanes. Don't get me wrong—I would miss you terribly and I'd call you every single day and I would be mad at Callum for taking my best friend halfway across the country. But I've never seen you like this with a guy before. I think you'd be making a mistake if you weren't willing to at least think about leaving your comfort zone."

As usual, Joy was probably right. But could Blair actually leave? For a guy? That went against everything she believed in.

"Just pray about it, okay?" Joy squeezed Blair's hand. "Open your heart to whatever God has for you. Because I guarantee it's better than anything you'd ever dream up for yourself."

Callum's phone buzzed on the desk just as he finished the last of his lunch. Ralph's picture filled the little screen. Callum raised the phone to his ear.

"Just thought I'd touch base, my friend," Ralph said. "You've kinda disappeared on me."

"Yeah. Sorry. I've been solving a murder."

"And I'm Mary Poppins," Ralph replied without missing a beat.

Callum grinned. "Well, Miss Poppins, you better come floating in on an umbrella next time I see you. Because I have literally been solving a murder." He filled Ralph in on the investigation into Iris's death.

"Wow," Ralph said. "So all Vic Nelson's music is plagiarized?"

"Much of it." Callum leaned back in his chair. "I think eventually he did figure out how to come up with his own stuff. But most of his earlier music was stolen from Iris Wallingford."

"What happens to Iris's notebook now?" Ralph asked.

Callum's gaze fell on the office bookshelf, where the notebook was proudly displayed. "The police gave it back to us. It'll live in the choir office forever and always."

"Good," Ralph replied. "Shame you can't put any of her pieces on a concert."

Callum sat up straight. "Ralph, you've just given me a brilliant idea."

"I've been known to do that from time to time." Callum could easily picture Ralph's smirk. "And speaking of brilliant ideas, how's that commission for Illinois going?"

"It's finished." Callum glanced toward his iPad. "I'm just looking it over one last time, and then it's on its way to you."

"Callum Knight, I am literally doing a happy dance right now," Ralph said. "You should see me. Maybe I should switch this call to FaceTime."

Callum chuckled. "Picturing it is terrifying enough. I don't need the visual."

"Fair enough. So you're officially back?"

A smile spread across Callum's face, and he gave a happy sigh. "I'm officially back."

"So we can expect you in Boston . . . maybe sometime in June? When does school let out in the sticks?"

Callum paused. "Well, about that . . ."

"I knew there'd be a catch."

"Ralph, Boston just doesn't feel like home to me anymore. Don't get me wrong—it'll always have a special place in my heart. But I . . . I really love it here. I thought I'd never belong here, but I do. And I love these kids. I love teaching, in a way I never, ever thought I could."

"And you love Blair, but that much is obvious. You're writing music again. You're happy again. Of course you're in love."

"Well, I am in love." That truth resonated in his soul. He was in love with Blair. "But God's the one who's inspiring the music now. And yes, at the moment Blair is the face of that inspiration, but she's not the reason I can write music again. He is. So I think over winter break I'm going to fly to Boston and officially put my condo on the market." He'd been subletting it to a couple of BU graduate students, but the time had come to sell it.

"Funny you should mention that," Ralph said. "I'm in the market for a new place. And I've always loved your condo."

"You wanna buy it? That'd sure make life easier on my end."

"You serious?"

"I am."

"Then let's talk numbers soon," Ralph said. "We can sign papers when you're here."

"What happened with your apartment?" Callum asked.

"It's . . . no longer large enough for my needs."

Callum read between the lines. "Wait, did you meet someone too? You did, didn't you? Who's the sly dog now?"

"Not sly," Ralph replied. "Just lucky."

"Well, however it happened, congratulations."

"Think Blair would come with you over break?" he asked. "I'd love to meet her."

"I'll bet she would," he said. "She needs to see Boston once before it's officially part of my past."

"So you're serious about staying?" Ralph asked.

"I can compose anywhere," Callum replied. "And for the foreseeable future, I've decided to do that here in Peterson."

"Well, congratulations, mazel tov, and all that jazz. I'll let the world know you're back open for business."

"Thank you, Ralph."

"You're welcome."

"No, I mean it." A sudden lump formed in his throat. "Thanks for believing in me, even when—especially when—I didn't believe in myself. You've been a rock for me these last five years. I hope you know that."

"Okay, okay, enough with the sappy speeches. You can thank me by lowering the price of your condo."

When they ended the call, Callum still had mist in his eyes. God had blown him away with just how perfectly everything had worked out. He had restored and renewed everything, and the tiny little flicker of faith left in Callum's soul had been fanned into a full-on fire. Callum was composing again. He was directing choirs again. Worshipping God with his music again.

And he was in love again.

The office door opened, and the object of that love walked in.

"Hi." He stared at her, starry-eyed. He had to tell her how he felt. He had to tell her what he'd just decided. He had to tell her . . .

"Hey. Just found this in our mailbox," she said.

He tore his eyes from hers and found the manila envelope in her left hand. "What is it?"

"I don't know." She slipped her finger beneath the seal. "But I'm very, very intrigued. Because the postmark says Chicago and the return addressee is someone named Hochsteiner."

Okay, that got his attention. He stood and met Blair in the middle of the office. She slid a sheaf of papers from the envelope and read aloud from the page on top.

Dear Mr. Knight and Ms. Emerson,

I was contacted recently by two detectives from the
Peterson police department investigating the death
of Iris Wallingford. While I didn't know Iris, I had
the privilege of examining one of her pieces. In all
my years teaching at Whitehall, this was the most
brilliant audition piece anyone ever submitted. As you
may already know, Iris submitted this piece under the
name of Victor Nelson. She wrote to me a few months
later confessing their deception, and I wrote back to
her explaining that while I could not award her a spot
at Whitehall, she was welcome to move to Chicago
and let me mentor her privately, and then audition
again the following year. However, by the time my
letter reached her, she had already passed on.

I have held on to this piece of hers for over fifty
years, but I believe now the time has come to pass it
on to you. I trust you will care for it in the manner it
deserves.

Yours most sincerely,
R. M. Hochsteiner

And behind it, a handwritten choral score torn from a spiral notebook. "I Am My Beloved's."

"Wow," Blair breathed.

Callum had no words. There it was. The one finished piece Vic Nelson had never touched but the one that bore his name. The one that had
gotten him a spot at Whitehall. The one Iris wrote. The one that should
have been her ticket.

They had it. Blair held it in her hands.

The genius of Iris Wallingford had come home to Peterson at last.

"Shall we?" Blair motioned toward the piano.

It took him a minute to shake from his spellbound state and realize what she'd asked. She wanted them to discover the music. Together. Just like they had that first day of school.

Eagerness to hear the music, to sing it, to study it, overwhelmed him. "Absolutely."

He followed Blair to the piano and stood over her shoulder, watching her fingers fly over the keys. They sang through the piece together—far, far less than perfectly on Callum's part. But that was because he was watching Blair.

He was singing the lyrics of love . . . to Blair.

As the final chord faded away, he leaned over and kissed her. The kiss went on almost as long as the music had, as his lips found new ways to tell her what filled his heart.

When he parted from her at great reluctance, he feathered his fingertips over her cheekbone and peered deep into those bottomless brown eyes. "I love you."

The shine in her eyes was something he'd remember for the rest of his life.

"I love you too, Callum."

"And I love this piece."

Blair nodded. "It's stunning."

"The world needs to hear it. Iris deserves to have her piece heard."

"She does."

The suggestion Ralph had given him earlier sprouted into full bloom, and he grinned. "Blair? I think I have a great idea."

CHAPTER THIRTY-SEVEN

*T*HE FINAL strains of Ivo Antognini's "O Magnum Mysterium" faded to nothingness.

Just as Callum hoped, the choir froze.

Behind him, the audience was completely still. No coughs, no shuffling paper, nothing.

For this one magic, suspended moment, there was nothing but silence. The music was so beautiful, the choir's performance so effective, that they had done the impossible.

They had made time stop.

Finally, Callum lowered his arms and beamed at the choir, and the audience burst into applause. His gaze, inexorably drawn toward the piano, found Blair, and her sunny smile was all the approval he needed.

Turning toward the audience, he acknowledged the choir and bowed. When the applause died down, he approached the microphone, its stand buried in Christmas greenery and softly glowing white lights, all of which extended over the entire front of the stage.

"Thank you. Thank you all." The last smatterings of applause faded, and Callum looked out over the audience, his heart hammering. "We have a last-minute addition to the program this evening. A couple of them, actually."

A barely audible murmur swept the packed, darkened auditorium.

"As many of you may know, earlier this semester Ms. Emerson and I discovered a piece of music in the choral library. Written by hand, unsigned, unfinished . . . and it was brilliant. I'll tell you all more about it after we sing it, but first I'd like for the music to speak for itself."

Without another word, he turned back toward the choir and retook his spot on the podium. Excitement and emotion shimmered in the students' eyes. They were in on the surprise, of course, but no one else was. Callum had sworn them all to secrecy, and to their credit, as far as he knew, they'd all kept their promise.

He raised his arms, his hands trembling slightly with the import of the moment, and cued the downbeat of Iris Wallingford's composition.

He had made absolutely no changes to her score. No editing. No text. The choir just sang the notes on an "ooh."

Because it was unfinished, the music lasted less than a minute. But the final chord—unresolved, appropriately—hung in the auditorium. Once again, the audience stayed silent, save for a couple of sniffles.

Even after he lowered his arms, the audience remained frozen. He turned to face them, and still everyone stayed still. The lights made it challenging to see facial expressions, but the emotional impact of the piece permeated the atmosphere of the auditorium. The audience was so moved they couldn't even applaud.

Callum approached the mic, his eyes stinging. "That piece you just heard was written by Iris Wallingford."

The audience gasped.

"Iris was a senior here at Peterson, set to graduate with the class of 1970, but her life was cut short three months before graduation. Police originally ruled her death a suicide, but as many of you now know, Iris was murdered by her family's maid. She died before she could complete the piece. And unfortunately, Iris's murder was not the only crime perpetrated against her."

A hushed murmur swept through the audience, and Vic Nelson, sitting in the center of the auditorium, shot Callum a look that could've melted lead.

Callum had been prepared for this from the moment he'd hatched his idea last month. Vic never missed a Peterson choral concert, and although he couldn't face legal ramifications for his plagiarism, he could face consequences to his legacy. That was why Detectives Stanton and Valentine were in the audience, directly behind Vic. And why Chief Stephens had also attended, along with several other Peterson officers, all in plain clothes. In the event Vic reacted poorly, Peterson's finest were more than prepared.

"Iris wrote several other pieces," Callum said. "And nearly all of them were published . . . under the name Victor Nelson."

The murmur grew louder.

"Vic Nelson shamelessly pirated Iris's ideas, put them into his own compositions, and passed them off as his. We know him as a wonderful choral composer, but a big reason he has that reputation is because of Iris Wallingford's music."

Nearly every head in the auditorium swiveled toward Vic, who bolted from his seat.

"This is slander!" he shouted. "How dare you try to assassinate my character! And after all I've done for you!"

Detective Valentine put a firm hand on Vic's shoulder and whispered something in his ear. Scowling, Vic sat back down.

Righteous indignation coursing through him, Callum pressed on, forcing calm into his voice. "It's true that Vic has been a friend to me. A mentor. He's part of the reason I have this job in the first place. But Iris Wallingford was one of the most brilliant composers of her generation. She deserved to have the kind of career Vic had. And she deserves to be remembered for what she wrote. She deserves credit for her work."

The audience applauded, as did the choir behind him.

"Fortunately, there is one untouched completed work remaining, and the choir would like to perform it for you now. Iris submitted this piece under Vic's name to the Whitehall Conservatory. It would have gotten her in had she been honest, and would have launched her career had she lived. The composition professor at Whitehall mailed it back to us last month. So without further ado . . . here is the world premiere of 'I Am My Beloved's,' by Iris Wallingford."

In all her years playing piano for choirs, Blair had never cried during a concert. She wasn't much of a crier in general, but particularly not when she had a job to do.

But tonight, in the holy atmosphere of the Christmas concert, after the speech that had put Vic Nelson in his place and had the kids singing their hearts out, giving their all to the memory of someone they'd never met, her eyes stung and the music blurred. Good thing Iris had written a piano part on the simpler side.

Waves of emotion crashed through her. Vindication for Iris. Sadness at what Vic turned out to be. Pride for how wonderful the kids sounded, how they had given this piece the absolute best they had to offer.

And love for Callum.

Oh, how she loved him.

He met her eyes then and mouthed the words of love from Iris's text, taken directly from Song of Songs. His arms still faced the choir, and she knew him well enough to know that the bulk of his attention was there as well, but him singing these lyrics to her . . . it was the most beautiful moment of her life. She poured all the love she felt for him into the piano keys and prayed he could hear it. That he knew she played for him.

She was meant to be with Callum. She wanted that more than anything. Whatever being with him meant for her future, wherever she had to go, if it was with him, she'd go. She would rather be in outer Mongolia with him than in Peterson without him.

She'd always thought Peterson was her home, but that no longer rang true. It was only home as long as he was there. And when he left here, wherever he went, that would be home.

Her home was Callum.

Because the way he watched her, the emotion that turned his eyes a brilliant shade of emerald, the tender passion in his gaze, the intent with which he mouthed the words . . . no one had ever looked at her like that.

When the piece ended, so did the concert. The audience leaped to their feet, and Blair wiped away her tears as she took her bows. At least she wasn't the only one who needed a tissue. Several kids had red, watery eyes, and even Callum surreptitiously dabbed the corners of his eyes with a fingertip.

When the choir had filed off the stage and the crowd had dispersed, she gathered up her music and walked to the wings, where Callum waited for her.

When she reached him, he kissed her. A deep, dramatic, sweep-her-off-her-feet-into-a-dip kiss with an impulsiveness she didn't know he possessed. Her startled laugh was smothered by his lips, and she relaxed into the strength of his arms and melted into his kiss.

"That was magnificent," he murmured against her lips, then raised her back to her feet.

A circle of students surrounded them, mouths agape and eyes enormous.

"Whoa," Makayla said.

"Are you guys . . . together?" Thalia motioned back and forth between them.

And the always-on *Jake and Brayden Comedy Hour* had apparently encountered technical difficulties, because both boys had lapsed into stunned silence.

"Yes, indeed." Callum wrapped his arm around Blair and pulled her close.

"It's true," she said.

A handful of kids cheered, Thalia beamed, and Jake finally peeled his jaw off the floor and elbowed Brayden. "You owe me ten bucks," he said. "I told you they'd end up together."

After a few moments, the jubilant kids headed back toward the choir room, no doubt eager to spread the word, leaving Callum and Blair alone.

She linked her hand with his as they strolled down the backstage hallway. "I hope you felt that I was playing for you. I hope you felt the love in it."

His eyes shone. "I did."

"Because you know I love you." Her voice shimmered. "I love you with every fiber of my being. And whatever that means for the future, I'm down." She gripped his hand and turned to face him. "I know you want to go back to Boston, and . . . and if you do, I'll go with you. Leaving here would hurt, but leaving you would be impossible."

Callum gazed into her eyes and trailed his fingers through her hair. "Blair, I adore you. You've brought me back to life. From the moment we had our first argument, you sparked something in me that has fanned into flame, and I don't expect that flame to ever go out. I love you. And I want to do whatever it takes to prove that love to you."

Any more words like that, and she'd melt into the floor.

Callum glanced around, then turned back toward her. "Hey. So, okay, since this was the Christmas concert, I guess I can give you your present early."

"My present?" Blair's brows arched. "I . . . I didn't know we were doing presents."

"Yeah, well . . . surprise." Grinning, he slid a plain white envelope from his jacket pocket and handed it to her.

"What in the world?" She stared at him, then slipped her finger beneath the seal and pulled out a single white sheet of paper.

When she saw the words on it, she gasped. "Callum, this is a contract. For next year. For *here*."

"Yeah." A smile slid over his face. "I convinced admin to let me sign it early."

The truth finally sank in, and she flung her arms around him. "You're staying. You're staying." She smothered his cheek with kisses. "Oh, Callum. Thank you. Thank you, thank you, thank you." Her wildest dreams—for the kids, for the program, for herself—had come true.

"Of course." His arms tightened around her waist. "I can't guarantee I'll be here forever. But I can guarantee I'll be here for a while. Because I belong here, Blair. I didn't think I would, but I do. You've got a darn good bunch of kids here, and I love them more than I ever thought I could. They're talented, hardworking, just plain good kids, and they deserve a director who will invest in their future." He slid from her embrace, mischief in his eyes. "Plus, I didn't think it'd be fair to rip their pianist away either."

Blair searched his face. "Is this what you want? Truly? You don't want Boston?"

"Boston isn't home for me anymore, Blair. Peterson is." He shook his head and tightened his grip on her waist. "No, that's not quite right. *You* are. Wherever you are . . . that's home."

He lowered his head and kissed her again, a kiss full of passion and promise.

And music.

Because where words failed, music always rushed in.

EPILOGUE

$\mathscr{C}$ALLUM CREPT into the auditorium, flipped on the house lights, and forced himself to pause and pull in a breath. This was it. The last concert of his second year in Peterson. He was exhausted, of course, and couldn't wait for a break. But he was filled with excitement too. His mind already buzzed with plans for next year.

A slightly more immediate plan too.

He paused at the back of the hall as he always did when entering. At the end of his first year, by a unanimous vote from the school board, the auditorium had officially been named the Iris Wallingford Memorial Auditorium. A large photo of her senior portrait hung on the wall, along with an honorary degree from the Whitehall Conservatory and a framed copy of her unfinished composition. As always, seeing this tribute was bittersweet. Iris's potential had never been realized, but at least through his and Blair's efforts, she'd received long-overdue justice. Flora had confessed to the murders of both Iris and her parents and received consecutive life terms. Given her age, Iris's killer wouldn't spend as long in prison as she deserved to, but at least she hadn't gotten away with it entirely.

As for Vic Nelson, he'd left Peterson, and no one in town had heard from him since the December concert. Rumor had it he now lived with his daughter somewhere on the West Coast. His publishers, when informed of his plagiarism, had ceased production of all the works that could be traced back to Iris. Only his original compositions remained in print—not bad in their own right but nowhere near as brilliant as the stolen ones.

As was his custom, Callum ran a fingertip along the frame of Iris's piece, whispered a prayer, and then proceeded toward the stage, where, heart pounding, he took the cover off the piano. He knew Blair would be here soon to warm up. In fact, he was counting on it.

He tossed the cover backstage, then set up the piano's music rack and propped a piece of freshly printed sheet music on it. It was a brand-new piece, one he'd just composed. Not his best work—he'd saved that for a couple of pieces he was writing for the choir, as well as three new commissions—but it would get the point across.

In this rare instance, the words were far more important than the music.

A door creaked open, and Blair walked in from the wings, blue binder in hand.

"Hi." She greeted him with a warm, sunny smile.

The sight of her made his heart relax. "Hello. You're stunning, as always."

"Thanks. So are you." She kissed his cheek, her eyes sparkling in the stage lights, then turned toward the piano and stopped. "What's this?"

He grinned. "Just a little something I wrote. Not for the concert, of course. Just for fun."

Her brows creased. "And you're giving it to me now?"

"Why not?" He feigned a casual shrug. "Figured I'd give you something to warm up with."

She approached the piano and sat down. "I usually just do scales, but okay." Her frown deepened as she reached for the printed sheets and studied them. "'Marry Me?'" She glanced up. "Is this an arrangement of that Bruno Mars song from a while back?"

Callum paused. "I . . . didn't think of that. But no. It has nothing to do with Bruno Mars."

"Okay, then you'll probably want to come up with a new title to avoid confusion."

"Sure. Yeah. Of course." Wow. This was not going the way he'd planned.

Finally she replaced the music on the rack and started playing. "Huh," she said over the rippling piano introduction. "Is this for a commission? It doesn't have your usual harmonic complexity."

"That's because the music isn't the most important part." Okay. Time for plan B. He hadn't expected to need to spell it out for her quite this specifically, but whatever. He could be flexible.

He lowered himself to one knee next to her, but still she focused on the music.

"Blair."

"Yeah?" She turned the page.

"Blair, I need . . ."

"What?" She stopped playing and finally looked at him . . . then froze. Her mouth was open, her hands still on the keys.

"The title is all that matters in this one. Because it's not just a title. It's a question." He pulled in a breath. "Marry me, Blair. Please?"

Her mouth opened further. "Oh, you're . . . this is . . ."

He fished the ring out of the pocket of his tux jacket and popped open the box. "For real? Yes. It is."

She stared for what seemed like forever, then erupted in a joyous shriek and launched herself from the piano bench into his arms. "Yes. Yes, yes, of course, Callum, yes."

Swallowing against a sudden lump in his throat, he smothered her lips in a kiss, then slid the ring onto her finger. "Hope this won't get in the way while you're playing."

"I don't care if it does." She held her left hand out, turning it this way and that. "It's gorgeous."

"The new lights don't hurt anything." He'd pulled all the strings he had—and a couple he didn't—but finally the district had agreed to replace the noisy, outdated auditorium lights. These were much quieter, which had been his main goal, but they had the added benefit of splitting the oval-shaped diamond into brilliant shards of red, green, and blue.

"They don't." She gazed at him and wrapped her arms around his neck again. "What made you do this now? Tonight?"

"Well, I thought about doing it after the concert—not in public, of course, just with the two of us—but I couldn't wait." He leaned his forehead against hers. "Frankly, I wouldn't have been able to focus on the concert. But I just realized we *both* might not be able to focus now."

Blair smiled. "I think we'll be fine. We're professionals, after all." She pressed a kiss against his lips, then pulled back. "Wow. We're getting married."

"We are."

He still could barely believe it. It wasn't the first time he'd given a woman a diamond. And it wasn't the first time Blair had received one. He'd once planned to spend the rest of his life with Rayne, and Blair had made the same plan with Derek.

But God had had a different plan. And through all the brokenness and pain of Rayne's death and Derek's betrayal, God had been working quietly backstage, weaving all the melodies and harmonies of their lives together to create the masterpiece of here and now.

And Callum would spend the rest of his life thanking him for it.

Acknowledgments

$\mathcal{A}$S ALWAYS, writing a book is not a solitary endeavor, and there are lots of people to thank. This book would not exist without the help of the following people.

My agent, Tamela Hancock Murray, and the amazing team at Kregel Publications. It is an honor to partner with all of you again!

My phenomenal developmental editor, Janyre Tromp. This is the fourth book we've worked on together, and once again I'm blown away by how you've identified ways to make this book the best it can be. I am so grateful for both your expertise and your friendship.

My amazing copy editor, Dori Harrell. Thanks for ferreting out all my weasel words and plot inconsistencies—I would never want a book to go out into the world before it had your eagle eyes on it.

Jaime Jo Wright, who not only has helped me manage my social media but also helped me brainstorm, inspired me to take a more suspenseful direction with this book, and has become a dear friend. Thank you for everything, Jaime.

Erin Mifflin Shell, who has helped shoulder the load of launch team things and who has also become a dear friend. Bonus: She doesn't live that far away!

My amazing critique partners, Theresa Romain and Linda Fletcher, for encouraging me, championing me, pointing out plot holes and inconsistencies, and always being eager to read another chapter. Linda, you know Ralph, Stanton, and Valentine are 100 percent for you.

All my readers who eagerly devoured the Sedgwick County Chronicles and have been waiting—sometimes impatiently—for my next offering. Many of you have reached out to me, come to see me at book signings, sent notes of encouragement, and left wonderful reviews. Each and every one of those gestures means the world to me. I love you all, and I hope you enjoy this book as much as you have my other ones.

The Quotidians, my faithful writing pals and prayer partners. Thanks for always being there.

Lori Hoppock, the energetic first-year music teacher at Earhart Environmental Magnet School who, in 1988, took my bored, smart-alecky third-grade self and turned her into an accompanist. Lori was an inspiration, role model, talented musician, wonderful teacher, and dear sister in Christ, who went to be with him in 2019. Her memorial service was the same day I interviewed for the Haven choir job, so Lori never knew the full extent of her impact on my life, but I can't help but think she had something to do with my day job.

Riley King and Scott Logan, the outstanding choral directors I've had the privilege of working with in Haven, and all the wonderful students who have come through our doors over the years. All of you, directors and kiddos alike, have inspired me to bring my absolute best every single day, and you've brought more joy and laughter into my life than I could have ever imagined. You have changed me in countless ways, and every single one of you has made me a better musician and a better person. Students, part of my job is to teach you things, but I guarantee I've learned more from you than you have from me. Thanks for letting me be your choir mom. I love you all.

The community of Haven, Kansas, for welcoming me, loving me, and making me feel like one of your own. I've never lived in a small town, and I still don't, but you all have shown me how wonderful a small, close-knit community can be. Haven kids are polite, respectful, hardworking, others-centered, and an absolute joy to be around, and I know that the parents, church leaders, and other community members are a big part of why that's the case. Thank you for all you do to raise such amazing young humans and for making Haven the truly special place that it is.

My husband, Cheech, and my three Wenlets—Caleb, Jonathan, and Selah. Thank you, as always, for supporting me in this crazy career, for giving me the time I need to spend with my fictional people,

ACKNOWLEDGMENTS

for making me laugh all the time, and for being the phenomenal humans you are.

My mom, Deanna Peterson, who is my biggest fan and most enthusiastic supporter. You are always my ideal reader.

Jesus, it has been fun to write another book with you. Thank you for opening my eyes to truths I've never known, for working in readers' lives through the stories you inspire, and for showing me just how flung wide open your love and grace truly are. I love you, and any glory this book gets is always and only for you.

Author's Note

$\mathscr{I}$T MAY surprise you to know that of all the parts of putting together a book, research is my least favorite part. I love what I learn from the research, of course, and it is always rewarding to work that research into the plots of my novels, but the process itself I find tedious. The idea for this book sprang from my desire to write something that didn't require a ton of research—or at least, research I wasn't already doing by default. Thus, my heroine has my actual day job: high school choir accompanist.

It's a tricky proposition writing a novel that involves so much of my daily life, so I wanted to make a point to say that Blair is not me and Callum is not anyone I have worked with. While elements of my real-life gig have, of course, found their way into these pages, the main characters are their own people, not inspired by or based on any of my real-world friends and colleagues.

I have, however, woven some elements of my own mental health journey into these pages. I was diagnosed over a decade ago with depression and anxiety (far later than I should have been, frankly) and have had my ups and downs with that diagnosis over the years. Part of the struggle for believers, especially believers who grew up in more fundamentalist environments, as I did, is the church's reluctance to acknowledge the biochemical reality of mental illness and to champion necessary treatments.

In case you or someone you know needs to hear this, I will make it very clear: Mental illness is real. It is not a sin. It is not a character flaw. It is not demon possession. It is not a commentary on your relationship with Jesus or an indication of a lack of faith. Scholars believe many biblical heroes—David, Elijah, Jeremiah, Job, and others—experienced bouts of depression, and those experiences in no way limited their ability to be used by God or to fulfill his plans for their lives.

Depression, anxiety, and other mental health conditions are a result of chemical imbalances within the brain. While prayer, Bible reading, and gathering with other believers are essential for anyone seeking to walk with Jesus, they alone are frequently not enough to combat those chemical imbalances. Can God heal any condition instantaneously if he chooses to? Of course. We see this in the pages of Scripture time and time again. But God can also work through medications, health care providers, and mental health professionals, and I have seen the benefits of those treatments as well.

Believers, would we shame someone who's diabetic for using insulin or someone with asthma for using an inhaler? Of course not. Then we cannot, we must not, shame anyone for taking an antidepressant or an anti-anxiety medication either. While I'm pleased to see many churches take a friendlier stance toward the reality of mental illness in recent decades, we still have a lot of catching up to do. If you suffer from a mental health condition, know that you are not alone. God is with you, and he will shine his bright light through all your broken places.

All that said, Satan can and frequently does take advantage of mental health conditions to whisper lies to us, and one of those lies is that taking one's own life can be the answer. Suicide is not the unforgivable sin, as I once feared, but it is never God's plan for his children. If you or someone you love is struggling with suicidal thoughts, a wealth of resources is available for you. Here in the US, our national Suicide & Crisis Hotline is 988; call, text, or chat 24/7/366. Where you are now is not where you will stay. You may feel that it will never get better, but by the grace of God, it always, always does. I am living proof.

In the historical timeline of this story, Iris does deal with mental illness. As alluded to in the text, in Iris's era, many conditions were lumped into the category of "anxiety," including what we know today as depression. Medications then were also not nearly as advanced as they are now, so the side effects Iris deals with are not typical of today's therapies. I

AUTHOR'S NOTE

am encouraged to see the progress we have made in treating these conditions.

Iris is also dealing with a particularly tricky form of emotional and psychological abuse, courtesy of Victor, called *covert narcissism*. While many narcissists fit the classic stereotype of loud, bombastic egomaniacs, there's another, recently defined form that narcissism can take. Covert narcissists tend to be quieter, more introverted, and much less obvious. Though a covert narcissist can sometimes appear to be selfless, sweet, and kind, their motivation (gaining attention and feeling special) is the same as that of an overt narcissist, and their lack of empathy is the same as well.

Covert narcissists, such as Victor, frequently play the victim or talk down about themselves, thus triggering those around them to offer reassurances, compliments, and other forms of supply. Often they are skilled at reading others, figuring out what will make a person like them, and then adopting a persona that has these exact characteristics in order to quickly win someone's confidence and begin the manipulation process. Though lying, gaslighting, blame shifting, and other tactics are often present, just as they are in other abusive relationships, covert narcissists are notoriously difficult to spot. People can sometimes be in a relationship with one of these narcissists for years or even decades before they realize the true nature of the narcissist. Debbie Mirza's *The Covert Passive-Aggressive Narcissist: Recognizing Traits and Finding Healing After Hidden Emotional and Psychological Abuse* was quite helpful in my research process. If you think you may be in a relationship with someone like Victor, I highly recommend this resource.

Finally, those of you who've come to expect my books to be set in Kansas may have been surprised at my change in location. Though I'm a nearly lifelong Kansan, some of the most important years of my life took place in central Illinois. I received my master's degree in cello performance from the University of Illinois (Urbana–Champaign), but more importantly than that, six weeks after I arrived on campus, I went to a watch party for the Boston Red Sox and met a cool guy named Cheech. To make a long story short (and to quote Jane Eyre), reader, I married him. We got married at our church in Champaign in 2005, and our first

AUTHOR'S NOTE

child was born there in 2009. When Caleb was six months old, God called us back to Wichita, and while I'm grateful he did, we do still miss our friends and our church in C–U. I am so very grateful for the six years I spent in Illinois, and some of the places I mention in this story (Smith Hall, Krannert Center, and the adorable fondue place) are real locations that contain some of my most cherished memories. The Whitehall Conservatory in Chicago, though, is entirely fictional.

The town of Peterson is also fictional, although—in keeping with my tradition of incorporating my own family history into my stories—it does have some basis in reality. My father's family, the Petersons, lived in central Illinois in the nineteenth century. One of them, Abner M. Peterson, was a well-known citizen of Coles County, Illinois, serving the area as a physician, an attorney, and a judge. Upon his death in 1890, he donated both his house and some land to the county. The land is now Peterson Park, a recreational hub in Mattoon, Illinois, and his house, the Peterson House, is located within the park.

The Peterson High School Patriots are in honor of the New England Patriots. I grew up with a lifelong loyalty to the Pats, which served me well when I entered graduate school and met Cheech. And since we lived in central Illinois at the time he proposed, we chose to have our engagement photo shoot at . . . wait for it . . . the Peterson House in Mattoon.

About the Author

$\mathcal{A}$MANDA WEN is a multi-award-winning author of inspirational split-time women's fiction. Awards and honors include the ACFW Carol, the Selah, and the *Foreword* INDIES Gold. She is a three-time Christy Award finalist. In addition to writing, Amanda is an accomplished professional cellist and pianist who performs frequently with orchestras, chamber groups, and her church worship team, and serves as a choral accompanist. A lifelong denizen of the flatlands, Amanda lives in Kansas with her patient, loving, and witty husband, their three hilarious Wenlets, and a snuggly Siamese cat. Connect with her online at amandawen.com.

READ THE DEBUT SERIES
by AMANDA WEN

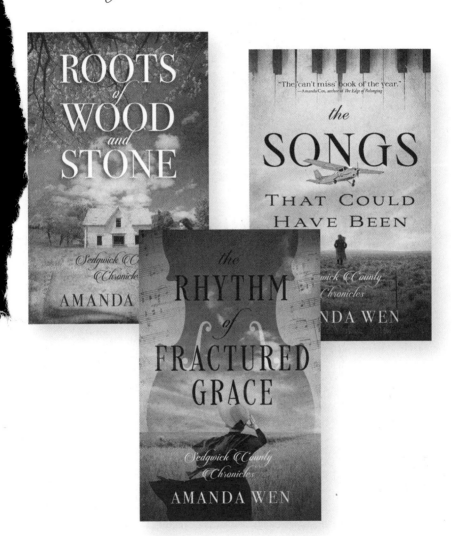

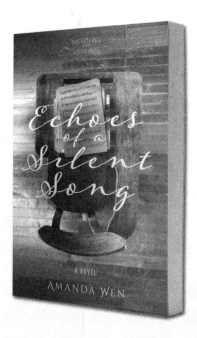

YOU CAN KEEP THIS BOOK MOVING!

Give this book as a gift.

Recommend this book to a friend or group.

Leave a review on Christianbook, Goodreads, Amazon, or your favorite bookseller's website.

Connect with the author on their social media/website.

Share the QR code link on your social media.

KREGEL
PUBLICATIONS

2450 Oak Industrial Dr NE | Grand Rapids, MI 49505 | kregel.com

  Follow @kregelbooks

Our mission as an evangelical Christian publisher is to develop and distribute—with integrity and excellence—trusted, biblically based resources that lead individuals to know and serve Jesus Christ.